HIS HEART OF DARKNESS

*A Frankie Dawson P.I. Mystery Thriller,
Book Two*

Melinda Woodhall

Melinda Woodhall
Visit my website at www.melindawoodhall.com
Printed in the United States of America
First Printing: December 2023
Creative Magnolia

CHAPTER ONE

Evelyn Wright sat forward in the driver's seat of her old blue Toyota and lowered the visor against the harsh glare of the late-afternoon sun, which had already begun its inevitable descent to the west of Barrel Creek Trail. Straining to see through the car's dusty windshield, her anxious brown eyes searched the wooded terrain ahead for the turn-off to Atkins Barrel Works.

She hadn't been out to the old factory for years and was starting to worry she may have already driven past it when she spotted the entrance to the parking lot half-hidden in the shadow of a sprawling Catalpa tree.

Ignoring a wooden *No Trespassing* sign, Evelyn executed a sharp right turn and steered the Toyota across the uneven lot toward a collection of weathered wooden buildings.

As she brought the car to a stop beside the only other vehicle in the lot, she glanced in the rearview mirror and lifted a hand, pushing back a damp tendril that had escaped her messy topknot, cursing the humid heat and its effect on her dark, curly hair.

"Good thing you stay *behind* the camera," she murmured to her reflection. "Otherwise, you'd be in real trouble."

1

Seeing no one in the white Cadillac Escalade parked beside her, Evelyn collected her camera bag from the passenger's seat and climbed out onto the steamy asphalt.

She turned to admire the shiny new SUV, which had been parked at a careless angle with the windows down. A folded copy of the *Memphis Gazette* lay on the dashboard.

Evelyn stopped short as her eyes fell on the headlines.

Human Remains Unearthed at Starbound Casino Building Site.

A voice spoke behind her as she scanned the article.

"Evelyn?"

Spinning around, she saw Ralph McEwan's tall, broad figure walking toward her. He smiled as he approached, and she noted that he'd grown a beard since the last time she'd seen him in person and that a faint network of lines had formed around his eyes.

How many years had it been?

"Good to see you!" he called as if they were old friends.

She nodded awkwardly and looked around at the overgrown lawn and boarded-up buildings, avoiding direct eye contact.

"I was surprised to hear you were in Barrel Creek, and that you'd bought this place," she said. "And more surprised to hear you're already wanting to sell it."

"Well, my father used to take me camping not far from here, and I knew some of the staff years ago, so I guess I acted impulsively," McEwan said with a wry grin. "This is the last barrel factory in the area, you know. The town was named for the industry back in the 1880s, so it's got history. And when I heard the place was for sale, I thought, *why*

2

not?"

He hesitated as he took in Evelyn's politely interested smile, and his own smile faded.

"Well, let's just say I've since learned that the place isn't quite what I'd been led to believe it was."

He cocked an eyebrow.

"I imagine you've heard about the murder of the former owners and the illegal activities that went on here?"

Evelyn nodded uncomfortably.

"I think everybody in the area has heard about that," she said. "The *Gazette* made sure of it."

"Of course," McEwan said. "And you used to work for the *Gazette*, didn't you? I think I read that in your listing in the alumni directory. I bet you still have lots of connections to tell you what really goes on in Barrel Creek."

Swallowing back a bitter reply, Evelyn shrugged.

"Not really," she admitted. "I've...moved on."

Her cheeks reddened under his inquisitive gaze.

She'd been a staff photographer at the newspaper for several decades before she'd been summarily dismissed two years earlier, along with much of the other permanent staff.

The *Memphis Gazette* had closed its downtown office and now ran the operation with remote staff, using freelance reporters while outsourcing printing and delivery services.

In the wake of the shakeup, Evelyn had turned to freelance photography work to make ends meet.

Her dire financial situation forced her to accept even the most mundane projects, such as the commercial real estate photo shoot at Atkins Barrel Works which Ralph McEwan had requested.

A dull ache settled into her stomach at the thought that her photos now appeared on *Property for Sale* ads instead of the front page of a widely circulated newspaper.

"Did you know the couple who owned the property?"

Evelyn realized the real estate developer had asked her a question. He stared at her, waiting for a response.

"No, I didn't," she murmured as McEwan started off toward the nearest building, motioning for her to follow.

Falling into step behind him, she studied his thick head of hair, which was still the rich, coppery brown she remembered admiring in the few classes they had shared during their college days.

She saw no signs of gray, even though she now paid regular visits to a salon to keep her own hair dark. It was the one indulgence to her vanity Evelyn still allowed herself, despite her dwindling bank account.

"Dwight and Cheryl Atkins owned the place before they were murdered," McEwan explained as they approached a long, low building. "A teenage daughter was their only heir, so of course, she couldn't be expected to carry on the family business. Thus the executor of the estate listed the property for sale. That's where I came in."

He stopped outside a metal door and turned to her.

"I contacted Mr. Dawson and made an offer sight unseen."

Evelyn looked at him in surprise.

"Do you mean Henry Dawson? Is he back in town?"

"No, Frankie Dawson," McEwan clarified. "Henry's son. I

believe he was a close friend of the Atkins family. He was the estate's executor and he handled the sale of the property."

As if sensing Evelyn's disappointment, he cocked his head.

"Do you know the Dawson family then?"

"Not really," she admitted. "But I had a good friend who knew Henry. Her name was Maisie Guinn. She was a reporter for the *Gazette*."

McEwan scratched at his beard.

"Maisie Guinn? Her name sounds familiar," he said. "Where'd she go after she left the *Gazette*?"

"I don't know," Evelyn admitted. "One day she was researching an article, and the next day she was...gone. I haven't heard from her in years. I always wondered..."

A loud caw nearby caused Evelyn to jump. She looked up to see a sleek black crow perched on the roof.

The bird's shiny black eyes seemed to be watching her with interest, and Evelyn had the unsettling realization that she and McEwan were all alone on the deserted property.

No one but that crow even knows I'm here. If I were to just disappear like Maisie did...

Clearing her throat, Evelyn gestured to the camera bag that hung over her shoulder.

"I should really take the photos now," she said abruptly. "It's getting late."

McEwan hesitated, then nodded.

"Okay then, let me show you inside."

He dug a hand in his pocket.

"I know I have the keys here somewhere."

Stepping toward the door, he cursed under his breath.

"Someone broke the damn lock," he muttered, shaking his head as he surveyed the twisted metal around the keyhole.

With a strong push on the heavy door, he managed to shove it open, then flipped the light switch on the wall.

"Electricity must have been turned off," he said when nothing happened. "Guess you'll have to make do with the light coming through the windows."

Stepping in behind him, Evelyn looked around the dim interior in dismay, holding her breath against a musty, pungent odor coming from the oak barrels stacked three-high on long wooden racks throughout the cavernous space.

As she moved further into the room, she noticed that some of the barrels appeared to be cracked or rotting.

It wouldn't be easy to make the grimy walls and dusty racks of old barrels look appealing.

"I'll do what I can in here, but I think the best photos will need to be taken outside," she said, wanting desperately to escape the suffocating room. "I'd better get to work. The golden hour won't last."

When she turned around, she saw that McEwan was still standing at the entrance, staring into the shadows with an unhappy expression.

"Right, I'll leave you to it," he said after an uneasy pause. "Just let me know if you run into any trouble."

"I will," Evelyn replied. "I should be able to send you the edited images by the end of the week."

McEwan nodded and turned on his heel, leaving Evelyn alone as the door swung shut behind him.

Taking her camera out of the bag, she got to work quickly, first adjusting the settings and flash, and then deftly moving around the room, sticking close to the windows, doing her best to make use of the dim natural light while it lasted.

Sounds of furtive scratching and scuffling in the rafters overhead kept her on edge and on the lookout for mice or other unwelcome intruders as she worked.

When she slipped back outside twenty minutes later, she gratefully exhaled a sigh of relief before inhaling a deep lungful of fresh air.

Surveying the building's faded wooden exterior, she wondered how she was going to capture photos that would entice potential buyers.

Who in their right mind would want to buy this creepy old place?

As she lifted her camera, Evelyn peered through the viewfinder and focused the lens on the crow, which was still perched on the roof as if it had been waiting for her return.

Pressing the smooth black shutter button, she took a series of photos. But her mind wasn't on her work.

Instead, she was thinking about Maisie Guinn.

Her own words echoed in her ears.

"One day she was researching an article, and the next day she was...gone. I haven't heard from her in years."

The thought that followed prompted a pang of guilt.

And I've done nothing to try to find Maisie in all that time.

How many years had it been since Maisie had simply disappeared without a word of goodbye?

Fifteen? No, more like twenty.

Questions churned through her mind as she moved around the property, taking photos of the long, low buildings and wide expanse of overgrown land surrounding the factory.

Did Maisie really want to start over somewhere else as the police always insisted? Or had something bad happened to her?

She had never been able to shake the suspicion that Maisie's attempt to get a front-page scoop had played a role in her friend's disappearance.

But when the Barrel Creek Police Department told her they had no reason to suspect foul play and no cause to investigate, Evelyn hadn't been able to pull together enough evidence to convince them otherwise.

I wasn't the investigative reporter. That was Maisie's calling.

Evelyn had been, and still was, just a photographer. And she hadn't been able to get law enforcement to accept her theory that something bad had happened to Maisie.

Berating herself for giving up so easily, she finished the shoot with a troubled mind, taking the last photo just as dusk started to fall.

The deepening shadows chased her back to her old Toyota, and as she left the barrel works behind and headed home, she turned on the radio, eager to drown out the questions and self-recrimination that filled her head.

She was nearing her neighborhood when a smooth female voice interrupted with a breaking news bulletin.

"We have new information coming in from the Starbound Casino construction site in Mississippi where human remains were discovered last week."

Evelyn's hands tightened on the steering wheel as the announcer continued.

"The Buford County Sheriff's office has issued a statement confirming that the remains have been identified and that a murder investigation has been opened. However, identity of the victim is being withheld pending notification of next of kin."

Turning onto Overlook Road, she switched off the radio and pulled into the driveway of her modest house, which she knew she was at risk of losing if she didn't get more freelance jobs such as the one Ralph McEwan had hired her to perform.

Full darkness had fallen as she scurried up the walkway, approaching the front door with an uneasy feeling, half-expecting the lock to be tampered with, just as the lock at the barrel works had been. But all appeared to be in order.

Fingers fumbling with the key, she slipped inside, then turned to hang her camera bag on a hook by the door. Instead of moving into the living room, she found herself turning to the hall closet.

Opening the narrow door, she pulled an old photo album off the top shelf, carried it into the living room, and opened it on the coffee table, flipping to a photo that showed two young women standing beside a brightly lit Christmas tree.

Both women were smiling at the camera.

The photo had been taken at the *Memphis Gazette*'s Christmas party, and Evelyn remembered how happy she'd been that day, grateful to have secured a real job and believing her career as a photographer was finally taking off.

She stared down at her younger self with wistful eyes before turning her gaze to Maisie, whose straight, strawberry-blonde hair contrasted with Evelyn's dark curls.

The reporter's laughing green eyes and spray of freckles across her nose gave her the look of a mischievous child.

"Where are you Maisie? And what happened to you?"

With a heavy sigh, she closed the photo album and moved down the hall, making her way into the little kitchen.

Crossing to the pantry, she opened the door and knelt in front of the old-fashioned safe that had been bolted to the floor, hidden under the bottom shelf.

She turned the big black dial to the left, then the right, then the left, before spinning it to a stop and pulling the thick metal door open.

She'd rarely used the safe, which had been in the house when she moved in. It now contained only a single item.

Maisie's notebook, which her friend had left at her house the last time she'd come over. The last time Evelyn had seen her. She'd been saving the book ever since, just in case Maisie came back.

Pulling out the notebook, she opened the cover to reveal a page of handwritten notes that had been taken during one of Maisie's last investigations.

A quick skim of the page brought her back to when the *Memphis Gazette's* newsroom had been a thriving, stressful environment where reporters had vied for the front-page placement of their stories and the biggest headlines.

Evelyn closed her eyes, picturing Maisie grabbing her coat, calling out as she ran for the door, headed to some big scoop.

"Come on, Evie, I need pictures if I'm gonna get Nielson to give me the front page. Let's go!"

But that had been before the advent of multimedia journalists and videographers who could do it all in the field. Before investigating, interviewing, taking photos, shooting video, and editing the final copy was a one-person job.

Back before Evelyn had been made redundant.

There was no longer a viable role at the newspaper for an introverted photographer who hated being in front of the camera, and who had no talent for writing quick, catchy copy.

And now the *Gazette*'s old building on Arcadia Street was deserted, its empty rooms filled only with dust motes and memories. Looking down at the notebook, Evelyn wondered if Maisie Guinn was one of the ghosts wandering its halls.

She bit her lip thoughtfully, then picked up her phone.

Tapping out a number dredged up from the depths of her memory, she braced herself at the sound of a man's voice, then realized she was listening to a recorded greeting.

She exhaled as she waited for the beep, then left a message in a soft, hesitant voice.

"Hi, it's Evelyn Wright. I know it's been a while, but I was working on a shoot at the old barrel works and the man who hired me was asking about Henry Dawson. That got me thinking about Maisie. I was just wondering, have you ever heard anything more from her?"

Clearing her throat, she continued.

"What about those bones in the river? Could they be connected somehow? I was just thinking maybe we should look for her again. Things are different now with social media and...well, call me when you get this message."

After she ended the call, Evelyn poured herself a cold glass of iced tea and flipped through the rest of the notebook. When she was done, she gently set it back in the safe.

Before she could reset the lock, a soft knock sounded on the front door.

"Hello?" a man's voice called out.

Evelyn frowned as she stood and walked to the door.

Leaning forward, she peered through the peephole but it was too dark outside to see the face of the figure standing on the front step.

"Yes? Who is it?"

A long beat of silence followed, and then the man spoke again.

"I'm sorry to just show up like this, Evelyn, but I have information about Maisie. I thought you'd want to know."

The voice was familiar, and Evelyn's heart began to thud in her chest as she slowly opened the door.

"What are you-"

Her words ended in a startled scream as the dark figure stepped forward into the light and grabbed her by the throat.

"Shut up," the man growled. "And stay still."

He tightened his grip and stared into Evelyn's wide eyes.

"Now, you're going to come with me. And you won't give me any trouble unless you want to end up like Maisie."

"You...killed...Maisie?" she managed to gasp.

"No more talking," he warned her. "No more questions."

But she could see the terrible truth shining in his eyes.

As anger surged through her, Evelyn jerked up her knee, connecting solidly with the man's groin.

His hand fell away and Evelyn opened her mouth, sucking in air, preparing to scream.

If he takes me, I'll never come back. My only chance is to-

A slash of metal ended the thought as the man deftly sliced the steel edge of a switchblade across her throat.

Hot blood spurted onto the wall beside Evelyn.

Staggering backward, she fell to the floor.

"Now look what you've done."

The man's words sounded far away.

"You've made a hell of a mess for me to clean up."

With her strength quickly draining away, along with her blood, Evelyn allowed her eyes to close.

There was no way she could survive this, that was clear.

But at least now I know what happened to Maisie.

The question that had haunted her for years had finally been answered. She'd been right. Her friend hadn't left town.

The bastard killed her...and now he's killed me, too.

CHAPTER TWO

Frankie Dawson stood on the sidewalk and stared up at the new sign hanging over the front door, pleased with the effect. In less than a week his private investigation agency would be open for business. All he needed to do in the meantime was find a few clients with deep pockets to help him pay the rent.

The little office on Winchester Way had been the cheapest option Frankie could find during his search in and around the Memphis area. Of course, it hadn't hurt that the building was close to his Uncle Rowdy's bar, which was located just around the corner on Flintlock.

Forgoing traditional marketing and advertising, he was hoping all the free publicity he'd gotten in the last few months for tracking down the Wolf River Killer and exposing corruption at the highest level of the Barrel Creek Police Department would translate into new business.

He figured the shiny new sign above the door ensured that anyone needing his services would be able to find him.

Feeling a trickle of sweat work its way down his back, Frankie remembered the weather forecast he'd heard that morning, which had predicted record-high temperatures all across the state, and headed inside.

Back in the office, he found Sherlock settled into a prime spot beneath the air conditioning vent.

Cool air ruffled the Labrador's thick black coat as he looked up with sleepy eyes, revealing the faint scar that ran down the side of his soft, furry face.

"The sign looks great, Sherlock," Frankie said as he sank into his desk chair. "*Dawson & Bell Private Investigations.* Peyton's gonna love it, isn't that right, boy?"

The dog stared up at him with dark, unreadable eyes and then looked away as if embarrassed by Frankie's unfounded optimism and obvious need for reassurance.

But Sherlock's reaction couldn't dampen Frankie's good mood as he studied the framed wedding photo on his desk.

He and Peyton had been so happy that day.

And we will be again.

Digging in the desk's top drawer, he withdrew a velvet box and opened it, studying the eighteen-carat gold infinity bracelet nestled inside.

"This time it's forever," he said in a quiet voice as if rehearsing the moment he would present the gift to his wife.

While Peyton hadn't come right out and agreed to give their marriage another try, she hadn't mentioned the unsigned divorce papers for over three months, either.

And she had finally come to her senses and agreed to move up to Memphis. In fact, she would be arriving Saturday.

As soon as her last class of trainee officers at the Willow

Bay Police Department had graduated, Peyton would be moving up to help Frankie get his fledgling private investigation agency off the ground.

He'd planned the new sign outside to be a surprise.

It was his way of telling her he wanted them to be full partners both in their personal lives and in their careers.

Her previous experience as a Major Crimes detective with the Memphis PD and the Willow Bay Police Department down in Florida assured him she'd be the perfect partner for his new private investigation enterprise, just as she had always been the perfect wife.

Of course, Frankie knew it would take time to heal the heartache they'd both endured over the last nine months.

Peyton's despair at the loss of her pregnancy and the news that she'd never be able to conceive again had almost broken her, along with their marriage.

But now that they would be living in the same city and working together on a daily basis, they had a real shot at a second chance, and he was determined to win her back for good, no matter what it might take.

Sitting back in his chair, Frankie had just kicked his size thirteen shoes onto the desk when the door to the office swung open and Dusty Fontaine stepped inside.

"You taking a nap or are you running a business here?"

The *Memphis Gazette*'s entertainment reporter wore a sardonic grin on his thin face. He also wore a plaid button-down shirt and faded jeans tucked into brown cowboy boots which sported his signature two-inch heels.

A straw cowboy hat covered his thinning blonde hair.

He and Frankie had first met earlier in the year when Dusty had been investigating a number of missing women in the entertainment industry.

The information he'd provided Frankie had played a vital role in taking down the Wolf River Killer, and they had stayed in touch ever since, getting together every now and then to trade barbs and light-hearted insults.

It was the kind of prickly camaraderie Frankie missed having with his old partner, Pete Barker, who was currently enjoying retirement down in Florida.

Sliding his feet off the desk, Frankie jumped up and gestured around the room with pride.

"This isn't just a business," he said. "You happen to be standing in the best P.I. agency in Barrel Creek."

"I'm pretty sure this is the *only* P.I. agency in Barrel Creek," Dusty countered. "Why didn't you set up shop in downtown Memphis? There's plenty of empty real estate on Arcadia Street for rent."

He surveyed the office, then pointed to the empty desk.

"And where's your partner?" he asked with a frown. "I thought the sign out there said *Dawson & Bell*. The better half of the team appears to be missing."

The comment earned an agreeable grin.

"I can't argue with that," Frankie admitted. "Although I'm not sure I like your sudden interest in my wife."

"I'm just looking out for you," Dusty replied. "After all, we both know you wouldn't be standing here today if Peyton hadn't saved your hide out by the Wolf River."

A memory flashed through Frankie's mind.

Peyton stepping out of the shadows the night they took down the man who'd been terrorizing Barrel Creek. She had arrived just in time to save his life.

"Don't worry, the better half of this agency is driving up from Florida on Saturday," Frankie assured him. "Now, what do you want? You hoping for a quote from the local hero for the evening edition?"

Squaring his thin shoulders, he smoothed back his shaggy hair and adjusted the limp collar of his wrinkled shirt.

Dusty snorted.

"Actually, I'm not here on *Gazette* business," he said. "It's a personal matter. I'm here to retain your services."

The expression on his face grew serious.

"I want you to find someone. It's a missing person case."

His somber tone stopped the sarcastic response that sprang to Frankie's lips.

Dropping back into his chair, he motioned for the reporter to take a seat across from him.

"Who's missing?"

"A woman named Maisie Guinn," Dusty said. "Twenty years ago she was fresh out of college. An up-and-coming reporter on the *Gazette*'s news beat. I guess she'd be in her early forties by now."

He took off his cowboy hat and placed it on his lap.

"Just before she left the *Gazette*, Maisie confided she was researching a story on Enrico Sombra. She told me she had an inside source. Someone who knew the guy was pushing drugs at his casino," Dusty said. "I warned her Sombra was dangerous and told her to let someone else handle it, but she said it was too late for that. She said it was *personal*."

Dusty's voice was grim.

"Not long after that, she just...stopped coming to work. A few of us at the *Gazette* reported her as missing but the police refused to open an official investigation. They claimed there were no signs of foul play."

He sighed.

"They were convinced Maisie left town looking for greener pastures, but I didn't buy it. At least, not at first. But then a few weeks later her editor received a resignation letter. I figured I'd been wrong."

Frankie opened his mouth to ask a question, but Dusty wasn't finished with his story.

"After that, I never heard from Maisie again," he continued. "And I never heard *of* her, either."

Fidgeting with the brim of his hat, he shook his head.

"She didn't publish any articles, didn't make any posts on social media. I would search for her name every so often, thinking she must have found a new job, thinking maybe she was writing for another paper, but nothing came of it."

He lifted his eyes to meet Frankie's.

"That girl was talented and ambitious. She wouldn't just give up on a juicy story and walk away, would she? And why disappear without a word of goodbye to anyone?"

Frustration tinged his words.

"So, when Evelyn Wright called me last night and..."

Frankie held up a hand.

"Who's Evelyn Wright?"

"She's a photographer who worked with me at the *Gazette*. She was laid off a few years ago, and we haven't spoken in a while. When she called last night out of the blue and left a message asking about Maisie it got me thinking."

He shrugged his shoulders.

"So, I decided that I want *you* to find Maisie."

Looking down at the scribbled notes he'd taken so far, Frankie scratched at the stubble on his chin.

Cold cases were never easy, and taking on an investigation that may involve a well-connected criminal like Enrico Sombra would be dangerous, to say the least.

Frankie's only previous visit to Sombra's Gambling Hall & Casino was one he'd rather not remember, much less repeat.

"I don't know. We're not officially opening until next week. I'm still setting up my operation," Frankie protested. "And I bet there are plenty of P.I.s in Memphis who already have contacts over at the Mississippi casinos, so-"

"Those guys won't give me mate's rates," Dusty interrupted. "Besides, none of their fathers were listed in Maisie's notes as a source for the hit piece she was planning to write on Sombra."

Frankie felt the last of his good mood slip away.

"Maisie Guinn knew my father?"

"That's what her notes say," Dusty confirmed. "I took a box of Maisie's things from her desk after she'd sent in her resignation. I was worried her desk would be reassigned. Some of her journal entries were very enlightening."

Jumping to his feet, Frankie began to pace the room.

"But why look for her now, after all these years?"

"I told you, I got a call from a friend of hers," Dusty said.

He pulled a phone from the back pocket of his jeans and tapped a few times on the display, then held it up as a woman's voice filled the room.

"Hi, it's Evelyn Wright. I know it's been a while, but I was working on a shoot at the old barrel works and the man who hired me was asking about Henry Dawson. That got me thinking about Maisie. I was just wondering, have you ever heard anything more from her?"

Frankie thought the message was over, but the caller cleared her throat and continued.

"What about those bones in the river? Could they be connected somehow? I was just thinking maybe we should look for her again. Things are different now with social media and...well, call me when you get this message."

The room fell silent as Frankie digested what he'd heard.

"What did she say when you called her back?"

"I didn't see that I had a message until late last night," Dusty admitted. "When I called her back, she didn't answer. I tried again this morning, but still no luck."

He looked at his watch.

"And I was supposed to hit the road to Nashville an hour ago," he said. "I'm gonna be late if I don't get moving."

A sense of unease settled in Frankie's chest as he replayed Evelyn Wright's voicemail in his head. She had mentioned the barrel works and the man who'd hired her.

Is she talking about Ralph McEwan? Why would he be talking about my father? And what does he know about Maisie Guinn?

The thought of his father prompted a sudden, intense craving for a cigarette.

A long drink of whiskey would do the trick, as well.

Frankie dug in his pocket for a stick of gum.

"You're a reporter," he said irritably. "And you didn't do too bad looking into the Wolf River killings. So, what do you need me for? Why don't you go ask around?"

Dusty shook his head.

"Oh no," he said with a wary laugh. "The people Maisie was investigating back then were dangerous. I'm thinking they still are."

He motioned toward Peyton's empty desk.

"And I don't have a sexy shooter watching my back like you do. Besides, I'm expected in Nashville. Nielson will have my head on a platter if I don't get my story in by deadline."

"Nielson?"

"My editor-in-chief...and a major pain in my ass," Dusty said, watching Frankie stick the gum in his mouth and begin to chew. "He says an entertainment reporter shouldn't be working the crime beat, and this time he sounds like he means it. So, you want a paying client, or not?"

Thinking of the upcoming rent, Frankie hesitated.

Right now he was still just a one-man show. But he needed to start bringing money in.

The proceeds of the sale of Atkins Barrel Works had allowed Frankie to pay off the mortgage for the house Dwight and Cheryl Atkins had left their daughter in their will.

The remaining balance should just about get Josie Atkins through college without debt.

He was hoping the new P.I. agency would provide him with the income to support her in the meantime.

"Yeah, okay," he said, already dreading Peyton's likely reaction to the news. "Tell me more about Maisie Guinn."

Dusty reached into his shirt pocket and pulled out an old snapshot showing a young woman with strawberry-blonde hair and cat-eye glasses.

"Maisie was young and ambitious and eager to see her byline on the front page," he said as he handed the photo to Frankie. "She also had it in for Enrico Sombra. She knew your father did some work at his casino and persuaded him to talk. She wouldn't let go once she got her teeth into something."

Frankie's heart now sat in his stomach.

"I know what my old man was doing out at Sombra's Casino," Frankie said. "And it wasn't working."

Deciding he didn't want to share his family's dirty laundry with the reporter, he shrugged.

"In any case, I haven't seen my old man since I was...what, seventeen?"

He shook his head, unable to believe it had actually been twenty years since he'd last heard from his father.

His alcoholic, cheating, excuse for a father had been out of his life ever since, not even coming back for Franny's funeral.

Henry Dawson probably didn't even know his daughter had been murdered.

The cheating bastard probably doesn't even care.

The thought still hurt, even after all this time.

Memories of the day he'd buried his younger sister intensified his craving for a tall shot of whiskey.

Chewing hard on his gum, Frankie imagined himself going into Rowdy's Music Bar & Grill and asking Jasper Gantry for a shot of Johnny Walker neat.

Make it a double. Or better yet, leave the whole damn bottle.

His mouth watered at the remembered taste of whiskey on his tongue and the delicious sting at the back of his throat.

But you'd wake up with a pounding headache and poor Franny and your good-for-nothing old man would still be just as gone.

Frankie nodded at the little voice in his head, trying to convince himself that Henry no longer mattered.

As usual, his heart refused to play along.

"Right, well, it sounds as if Maisie went AWOL around the same time your dad skipped town," Dusty was saying as Frankie dragged his mind back to the subject at hand. "It's been about twenty years. That's long enough."

Looking down at his phone, the reporter tapped several times on the screen, then dropped it back into his pocket.

"I texted you Evelyn Wright's phone number and forwarded that voicemail she left me. She and Maisie were close so I'm hoping she'll have more information to get you started than I do."

Dusty stood and headed toward the door, then stopped and turned back with a frown.

"I almost forgot. I've got that box of Maisie's things in

24

my car. I thought you might want to go through it."

Following the reporter out to the tiny parking lot beside the building, Frankie waited as Dusty opened the trunk of his baby-blue Thunderbird and pulled out a cardboard box.

He handed the box to Frankie, pointing to a small black leather case that lay on top.

"Back-up discs," Dusty explained. "I knew they'd wipe Maisie's desktop computer eventually, so I copied the files in case she came back for them. But I don't have a CD reader anymore, and no way to access them."

"You go on to Nashville," Frankie said, already sweating again. "I'll deal with accessing those old discs if it comes to that. But first, I think I'll talk to Evelyn Wright and find out what she knows."

* * *

Frankie pulled the Mustang onto the driveway of Evelyn Wright's modest house on Overland Road and shut off the engine. He turned around, planning to tell Sherlock to stay in the car but the Labrador had already jumped through the open window and was standing in the front yard.

"Fine, but you stay right there," he told the dog as he climbed out and surveyed the house. "I'll find out if anybody's home."

Walking up to the front porch, Frankie spotted a folded copy of the *Memphis Gazette* still lying where it had been thrown that morning by the delivery driver.

The newspaper lay in its plastic wrapper beside a potted

rose bush, resting among a scattering of faded red petals.

The front door was slightly ajar, and as he lifted his hand to knock on the doorframe, Frankie saw a streak of what appeared to be dried blood.

His hand dropped back to his side as a sickening sense of déjà vu swept over him.

"This can't be happening again, can it?" he murmured to Sherlock, who had ignored his order to stay and who was now standing beside him on the porch.

The last time he'd entered a house uninvited he'd found Cheryl Atkins' dead body lying on the floor in a pool of blood and her husband Dwight lying dead in a room down the hall.

Willing away the images of that terrible night, Frankie reached forward and slowly pushed open the door, bracing himself for whatever might be waiting on the other side.

He frowned down at the empty foyer floor, confused by what he was seeing. There was no body sprawled out for him to find. No thick pool of blood for him to traipse through.

"Hello?" he called out, suddenly wondering if he had overreacted. "Evelyn Wright? I'm sorry to..."

His words died away as the door swung fully open and a patch of sunshine fell onto the floor. Something wasn't right.

Crouching down, he ran a tentative finger along the smooth brown surface, leaving a trail in the dark, sticky residue that coated the vinyl flooring.

Sherlock let out a loud bark as Frankie's eyes fell on the

pale green wall and white baseboard beside him.

Dark stains, the color of deep red wine, ran down the wall and along the crevices of the baseboard.

"What the hell happened here?"

Tripping over Sherlock, he took a stumbling step back, wiping his hand on his jeans, suddenly aware of an unpleasant coppery scent coming from the house.

"I don't think that's wine, Sherlock," he said as if the dog had made the suggestion. "I think it's blood."

Had Evelyn Wright had some sort of accident? Had she attempted to clean it up herself and...

Suddenly, Sherlock was running down the hall, heading toward the kitchen.

"Stop, Sherlock!" he called. "Stay!"

But the Labrador had disappeared beyond the doorway.

Following after him with a muttered curse, Frankie hurried through the living room, determining in a single glance that it was empty and undisturbed.

"Come out of there, right now, Sherlock," he called as he stepped into the little room and flipped on the lights.

He stopped short when he saw that the kitchen was also empty and that the back door was wide open.

Striding across the room, he'd almost made it to the door when his foot slipped out from under him and he went down on one knee beside the pantry.

As he pushed himself back to his feet, Frankie looked over to see an open safe under one of the pantry shelves. He also saw several large splats of blood on the white porcelain tiles.

They formed a trail to the back door.

Frankie followed the trail outside, catching sight of Sherlock halfway down a sandy gravel footpath that cut through a small garden and ended at the back gate.

The dog was sniffing a patch of grass that appeared to have been trampled by something heavy.

As he approached, Frankie made out a set of footprints along the path as well as two deep furrows, which he decided could be drag marks left behind by somebody's heels as they'd been dragged toward the back gate.

Had someone been attacked and taken out to the retention pond behind the neighborhood?

Could that someone have been Evelyn Wright?

Pushing through the gate, Frankie looked around, half expecting to see a body lying by the pond.

But the expanse of dry, dying grass was empty.

"That's weird," he said as Sherlock joined him outside the gate. "The tracks just stop and–"

His eyes fell on a deep gouge in the dirt.

"Those are tire tracks aren't they?" he murmured, glancing at the Labrador. "Guess we'd better call this in."

Taking out his phone, he considered calling 911, then thought better of it. With a sigh, he clicked on a contact he hadn't called since the Wolf River Killer had been captured.

As the phone began to ring, he sighed.

Here we go again.

CHAPTER THREE

Detective Nell Kinsey quickly moved past Barry Pagano's office, hoping to avoid the eagle-eyed gaze of Barrel Creek's new chief of police. As she rounded the corner, she exhaled in relief and allowed her shoulders to relax. Slipping into the small office she shared with her partner, Detective Sheldon Ranger, she felt the phone in her pocket begin to vibrate.

Her eyes widened as she saw Frankie Dawson's number on the display. She hadn't spoken to the private investigator in several months. Not since they'd worked together to close the case on the Wolf River killings. But after receiving a last-minute request from the Buford County Sheriff's Office that morning, she owed him a call.

"Frankie? This is strange timing. I was just about to call you," she said. "Sheriff Crockett over in Buford County, Mississippi contacted me this morning regarding some human remains found over at a new construction site and-"

"Hold on, Kinsey," Frankie said. "I don't know about Buford County, but I think I might have found some human remains right here in Barrel Creek. Only, I can't seem to find the human they belong to."

Kinsey wasn't sure she'd heard him correctly.

"You found *what*?"

Her exclamation caused Ranger to glance up in alarm. He stared at her over the desk with alert blue eyes as she gestured for him to wait.

"Well, it's blood mainly," Frankie was saying. "There's some footprints and drag marks, as well. And tire tracks."

He was starting to sound impatient.

"You can see for yourself when you get here. Just come over to Evelyn Wright's house. It's on Overland Road. And I suggest you bring a CSI team with you."

Twenty minutes later Kinsey's Ford Interceptor pulled into the driveway of a small, white house. Frankie and his black Labrador, Sherlock, were waiting on the front porch.

"You sure took your time," Frankie said as Kinsey stepped out of the vehicle. "Whoever was here...whoever left that blood in there will be miles away by now."

He lifted a bony hand to scratch at his stubbly chin.

"Why don't you just tell us what's going on?" Ranger suggested in a testy voice that reminded Kinsey the two men didn't get along. "Start with why you were here."

Frankie gestured toward the front door.

"I started working a missing person case this morning and came here to interview a woman named Evelyn Wright and saw blood on the door," he said. "There's more in there."

His skinny shoulders lifted in a shiver of distaste.

"The door was open and I could see stains on the wall and along the floorboards, too. When Sherlock ran inside, I called out to see if Evelyn was home but nobody answered, so I went in after him."

He glanced down at the Labrador in disapproval.

"I gotta get him signed up for an obedience class or something, I guess," he said with a shrug. "For some reason, this dog just doesn't want to listen."

At this, Ranger crossed his arms over his broad chest and shifted impatiently from one booted foot to the other.

"Try to stay focused, Frankie. Was anyone in the house?"

"No, but the back door was wide open. I thought maybe someone had just run outside. And there was blood on the floor and in the yard. Come with me and I'll show you."

Frankie turned toward the house but Ranger stuck out a big hand to stop him.

"Oh no, you stay out here with Kinsey," he ordered. "You may have already contaminated the scene. We can't have civilians trooping all over the place."

The big detective rested a hand on his holster.

"I'll go in and secure the house. Then we'll all wait outside for the CSI team to arrive before anyone else goes in."

Kinsey nodded in agreement.

"And while he's in there, you can fill me in on this missing person case you're working on, can't you, Frankie?"

The P.I. nodded reluctantly, but his eyes followed Ranger as the detective slipped into the house with his gun drawn.

"Why don't you start by telling me what your case has to do with the woman who lives here?" Kinsey suggested.

Frankie turned back to face her.

"Her name's Evelyn Wright. She's a photographer who used to work with Dusty Fontaine at the *Memphis Gazette*," Frankie said. "Dusty's my client. He hired me to find a reporter who went missing. A woman named Maisie Guinn."

His shoulders sagged as if the excitement and the heat were weighing him down.

Lowering his long, lanky body, he sank onto the porch's top step with a loud exhale.

"A *Gazette* reporter went missing?" Kinsey asked.

A frown creased the smooth brown skin of her forehead.

"I hadn't heard about that. When was she last seen?"

"About twenty years ago," Frankie replied. "Although an official investigation was never opened. That's why Dusty asked me to look for her."

Kinsey cocked an eyebrow.

"Why'd he decide to start looking for this woman now?" she asked. "If she's been gone for twenty years, maybe she doesn't want to be found."

"Maybe you're right," Frankie agreed. "But Dusty got a voicemail from Evelyn Wright and it put the idea in his head. That's when he hired me to try to find Maisie."

Pulling out his phone, he scrolled through his messages, then tapped a few times on the display.

"I've got the message from Evelyn if you want to hear it."

Kinsey nodded and leaned forward with interest as he opened the recorded voicemail and tapped the *PLAY* icon.

"Hi, it's Evelyn Wright. I know it's been a while, but I was working on a shoot at the old barrel works and the man who hired me was asking about Henry Dawson. That got me thinking about Maisie. I was just wondering, have you ever heard anything more from her?"

The caller cleared her throat and then continued.

"What about those bones in the river? Could they be connected somehow? I was just thinking maybe we should look for her again. Things are different now with social media and...well, call me when you get this message."

"Henry Dawson?"

Ranger spoke from the doorway.

"Is he any relation to you?"

The question hung in the air for a long beat.

"Henry's my old man," Frankie finally said. "Apparently, he was also a source for an article Maisie Guinn was working on. But nobody's seen either Maisie or my father around here for almost twenty years."

He took a stick of gum from his shirt pocket and pulled off the foil wrapper. He'd just inserted the gum into his mouth when the CSI van pulled up and parked along the curb.

"Hold that thought," Kinsey said.

Hurrying down the steps, she waited for the crime scene technicians to unload their equipment.

"We've got blood and signs of a possible assault in there," she said, joining the technicians in pulling on protective coveralls and booties. "We've secured the house and ensured the scene hasn't been disturbed."

She braced herself as she reached the front door, dreading what she might see. She'd been shaken by the scene she'd witnessed at the Atkins' house several months earlier, and residual nightmares still plagued her.

But the foyer appeared to be empty.

"Be careful," Frankie called from his ringside seat on the porch steps. "There's blood on the floor and walls. And some in the kitchen, too."

Stopping in the doorway, Kinsey looked around the small foyer, taking in the sticky, discolored flooring, and the dark, garish stains on the green wall.

"What's in there?" she asked.

She wrinkled her nose against the pungent, coppery odor that filled the air and pointed toward a narrow closet door.

Something dark and sticky had oozed from underneath it.

"I only took a quick look in there," Ranger said. "But I'd say someone tried to clean up the mess they'd made."

He had pulled on coveralls and was standing behind her with his gloved hands on his hips.

"They didn't do a very good job. See for yourself."

Holding her breath, Kinsey grasped the knob and pulled the door open, staring in at a pile of blood-stained towels.

"That's a lot of blood," she said weakly, backing away. "Could someone survive losing that much blood?"

Ranger looked doubtful.

"I'm no medical expert, but I'd say it's unlikely, which is why we're going to treat this scene as a homicide."

Just then the phone in Kinsey's pocket buzzed, offering a perfect excuse to step back outside onto the front porch.

Sucking in a breath of hot, morning air, she glanced at her phone. Sheriff Crockett had left another message.

"You okay?"

She spun around to see that Frankie was still on the porch.

He'd moved from the steps and was leaning against the wooden rail, his arms crossed over his thin chest.

"Yes, I'm fine." She held up her phone. "Just checking my messages. I owe Sheriff Crockett a reply."

"That's right," Frankie said. "You wanted to ask me something about the remains found over in Buford County. Go ahead. I'm free now."

Kinsey threw a guilty look toward the front door.

I should be inside with Ranger working this scene, shouldn't I? Not running errands for Sheriff Crockett.

But then, Frankie was standing right next to her. She might as well ask him what she needed to know so she could get back to Crockett.

Otherwise, the old boy might escalate the request to Barry Pagano, and the last thing I need is to have the chief on my back.

Turning back to Frankie, she cleared her throat.

"The Buford County sheriff called this morning in regard to the human remains that were discovered at the Starbound Casino construction site," she said. "You must have heard about that. It's been in the news, and—"

"Yeah, I saw something about it in the *Gazette* yesterday," Frankie said. "What's that got to do with me?"

His eyes were wary and she couldn't blame him. He'd already been falsely accused, convicted, and subsequently exonerated of a crime once before down in Florida.

Who was she to tell him it couldn't happen again?

"Crockett didn't mention you at all," she assured him. "But he said the remains they found had been hidden in an old barrel and buried in the field they're now digging up."

She thought back to her conversation with the sheriff.

"He also said the barrel had the name Atkins Barrel Works charred on the lid, along with a lot number. He wanted to know if I could help him trace the barrel back to the person or company who purchased it."

"I told him the factory had recently been shut down, but that I'd call the executor of the Atkins' estate and ask what could be done. As executor, I figured you would know if there were existing records stored somewhere."

Frankie's face had gone pale.

"One of the Atkins barrels was used to dispose of a body? You think it could be related to the Wolf River killings?"

The possibility had already crossed Kinsey's mind, but Frankie plowed on without giving her a chance to respond.

"Bill Brewster could have used a different MO over the years, I guess," he muttered as if talking to himself. "He could have dumped some victims into the river and dumped others into barrels and buried them."

A worried frown creased his forehead.

"I guess it's possible, but I don't think it's likely," Kinsey hurried to assure him. "I can't see Brewster going to the trouble of driving an hour away to bury a barrel across the Mississippi state line. Not when he had easy access to the Wolf River all those years."

Glancing back at the front door, she bit her lip.

"But maybe if you check the factory's records, we can find out who purchased the specific barrel that held the remains. I'm assuming there's some sort of database that tracks the lot numbers and buyers?"

Frankie shook his head.

"I guess you didn't hear that the barrel works closed down. The property and buildings have already been sold to Ralph McEwan, a bigshot real estate developer. I'm pretty sure any records or databases have been deleted."

He grimaced.

"Turns out the place wasn't making much money from selling actual barrels. And without the income Dwight had been bringing in from his smuggling operation, there wasn't enough money to keep it afloat."

Kinsey stared at him in disappointment, realizing there was nothing left for her to do but call up Sheriff Crockett and break the bad news.

Leaving Frankie on the porch, she jogged down the steps and crossed over to the Interceptor.

It was too hot to stand out in the sun, so she climbed into the driver's seat, started the engine, and turned on the air before taking out her phone.

Sheriff Crockett answered on the second ring.

"Unfortunately, the barrel works was used by a criminal organization that has since been disbanded," Kinsey explained. "No records exist."

She had expected a negative reaction to the news, perhaps frustration or anger, but the sheriff sounded unperturbed.

"I wouldn't be surprised if we never find out who buried that barrel," he said. "Only thing inside it was bones, teeth, and hair. Although we did manage to lift prints off the wood last week, and even found a match for the prints in AFIS."

Kinsey's pulse quickened at the news.

"So, you know who was in the barrel?"

"We sure do, although that information hasn't been released to the press or public yet. We won't make it public until we notify Valentina Rojas' next of kin, which may not be an easy process.

"We really don't know much about her at this point, other than she had a record for solicitation. That's how we got her prints. But we still don't know who put her in the barrel or how she died. And we also don't know how long she's been there, although, from the looks of it, it's been a while."

Crockett lowered his voice, adopting a conspiratorial tone.

"We don't plan to tell anyone her remains were found in an Atkins barrel. We'll hold that information back from the press and public in case some nutcase tries to falsely confess. Only the real perp will know the truth."

Kinsey winced as she thought of the conversation she'd just had with Frankie Dawson. There was at least one innocent man in the area who knew about the barrel.

But, of course, there's no need to share that little detail with the sheriff, is there? Not if I tell Frankie to keep it to himself.

Biting her lip, she made a mental note to follow up with

the P.I. as soon as possible.

"Who was it that found the remains?" she asked.

"The construction crew working on the new Starbound Casino. They found it buried at the site along the Mississippi River," Crockett said. "Mr. McEwan was pretty upset. Looks as if the whole project is in jeopardy now."

"Mr. McEwan? You mean the real estate developer?"

Kinsey glanced out the driver's side window toward the porch, watching as Frankie paced back and forth.

"That's right," Crockett confirmed. "Ralph McEwan's behind the Starbound Casino project. He wants to compete with Enrico Sombra, who runs the only other gambling establishment in Buford County. Guess he's out of luck."

Wondering if the sheriff knew about McEwan's recent acquisition of Atkins Barrel Works, she opened her mouth to ask when she saw Ranger emerge onto Evelyn Wright's front porch. He spotted her and frowned.

"Sorry, Sheriff. I'm at a scene and I've got to go," she said, already opening the door. "Maybe we can talk later."

Ending the call, she climbed out of the SUV and jogged up to the house. Ranger was waiting for her at the door.

As soon as she stepped inside, he held up a camera.

"This must be the camera Evelyn used for the photo shoot," he said. "There're photos of the barrel works and-"

"Ralph McEwan bought the barrel works," Kinsey cut in.

Ranger raised an eyebrow.

"What are you talking about?"

"Frankie told me that he sold the barrel works to Ralph McEwan," she said. "You know, the hotshot developer who's building the Starbound Casino over in Buford County."

She lowered her voice.

"And Sheriff Crockett just told me they found an Atkins barrel at the Starbound construction site. The remains of a woman named Valentina Rojas were inside it."

"So, you're thinking whatever happened to Evelyn Wright after she left the barrel works yesterday may be connected to the remains they found in Buford County last week?"

Kinsey nodded.

"I know of one connection for sure," she said. "And his name is Ralph McEwan."

She looked toward the door, wondering when the medical examiner would arrive, then turned back to Ranger.

"Why don't you go and find Mr. Hotshot Developer and see what he has to say?" she suggested. "I can stay here with the CSI team and wait for Rosalie."

CHAPTER FOUR

Rosalie Quintero gripped the steering wheel of the Barrel Creek Medical Examiner's van as her tired eyes searched for the turn-off to Overland Road. She'd stayed up too late the night before, reviewing the latest findings from the forensic archaeologist who'd examined the most recent batch of bones recovered from the Wolf River.

The first of the bones had been discovered by conservation volunteers tasked with collecting debris and clearing out invasive plants during the recent effort to restore the habitat along the riverbank.

What they'd suspected to be animal bones or ancient remains had since been proven to be the human remains of at least three different women.

Rosalie herself had determined the cause and manner of death for each of the victims to be homicide by a single gunshot wound to the back of the head, and she was satisfied that the assigned task force of local police and FBI agents had identified and taken down the man responsible.

But the death of Bill Brewster, a.k.a. the Wolf River Killer, hadn't closed the case for Rosalie. While she had managed to piece together three sets of skeletal remains belonging to females in their late teens or early twenties, the question as to the victims' identities remained unanswered.

The knowledge that there were families out there still wondering what had happened to their loved ones kept Rosalie up late most nights.

Worst of all, more bones had been recovered in the months since Bill Brewster's death, which meant more unidentified bones had been added to the cooler back at her office.

"Turn here," Marty Prince said.

The forensic technician leaned forward in his seat as Rosalie made a wide turn onto Overland Road.

By the time she brought the big van to a stop by the curb, Marty had already zipped up his coveralls and pulled the hood over his close-cropped hair.

Jumping out of the van, he hefted out his bulky case of supplies and equipment and started up the path to where Detective Kinsey was waiting on the porch.

Rosalie zipped up her own coveralls, tucked her dark hair under the protective hood, and pulled on a pair of gloves, before hurrying after Marty.

She caught up just as he pulled out his camera and began taking photos of the dried blood on the front door.

"Looks like it could be arterial spray," she said as she studied the stain running down the doorframe. "It's at eye level and there's some on the wall over there, as well."

She met Marty's eyes.

"You thinking carotid?" he asked.

"I'd say it fits," she agreed. "If someone opened the door and their assailant cut the carotid artery..."

Moving into the hall, she felt Kinsey's hand on her arm.

"The worst of it's in there," the detective said, pointing toward the closet. "Someone tried to clean up, but I guess they realized it was pointless and panicked. They dumped everything inside."

Kinsey turned away as Marty pulled open the closet door.

Rosalie looked in at the grisly pile of bloodstained towels with a sinking sensation in the pit of her stomach.

"It only takes a few minutes for someone to bleed out if a major artery has been severed," she told Kinsey as Marty took photos of the puddle of congealed blood on the floor. "I'm pretty sure that's what happened here."

"There's no sign of a body," Kinsey said. "Frankie Dawson found the blood and he said the front door was open when he arrived. And we found footprints and tire tracks in the back. It looks as if the victim may have been attacked and then dragged to a waiting car."

Wondering why Frankie had come to the house in the first place, Rosalie moved into the living room and looked around. Everything in the little room appeared to be in order.

She continued down the hall toward the bedroom and peered inside. A queen-sized bed with a patchwork quilt and matching pillow shams had been neatly made.

"Ranger looked in there when he secured the house," Kinsey said, following behind her. "He didn't see anything, and the CSI team didn't find anything of interest either."

Rosalie turned at the mention of Kinsey's partner.

"Detective Ranger is here?" she asked, feeling her pulse tick up a notch. "I didn't see him when I came in."

"He was here earlier, but he went to question a person of interest," Kinsey said. "Someone we think may have been the last person to see Evelyn Wright alive."

The news prompted a flutter of disappointment.

During the last few months, Ranger had served as the assigned liaison between the local police department and the medical examiner's office regarding the investigation into the bones recovered from the Wolf River, and Rosalie had developed something of a crush on the handsome detective, although she had yet to do anything about it.

I bet half the women in town have their eye on him.

After all, Barrel Creek wasn't exactly known for its abundance of eligible bachelors. Most of the good-looking men were already spoken for, and in her line of work, Rosalie was unlikely to run into the few single men they had left.

She'd discovered too late that working as a medical examiner offered limited opportunities to meet people.

At least, people who are still alive.

Which was probably why she was still single, although her mother insisted she was just too picky and set in her ways.

Forcing her mind back to the scene, Rosalie headed into the en suite bathroom, glancing into the clean, empty tub before checking the medicine cabinet.

Among the lotions and pills, she found a single, pink

toothbrush in a ceramic cup.

"The toothbrush should allow us to pull a DNA profile we can match against the blood we found by the door," she said. "That'll help us confirm it is in fact Evelyn Wright's blood."

As she started to turn away, her eyes fell on an inhaler lying on the laminate counter.

"We should also check with Evelyn's doctor to see if her asthma is severe," Rosalie added. "Although it's unlikely, there's still a chance she's out there somewhere."

She looked back at Kinsey.

"Which means you should include information about her asthma in any missing or endangered person alert that you send out," she said. "Just in case she's found alive."

Before Rosalie could leave the bathroom, Marty scooped up the inhaler in a gloved hand and held it out to Rosalie.

"Did you see who prescribed the inhaler?"

Squinting at the little device, she saw Dr. Gordon Habersham's name on the prescription label.

Catching the gleam of amusement in Marty's eyes, she sighed and shook her head, wondering why she could only manage to attract men like Habersham.

It's like I'm a magnet for narcissists.

She should have known better than to go out with the self-important doctor, no matter how desperate she was to have a social life. Now she was having to avoid his calls at work and had been forced to ask Marty to tell the persistent man she was unavailable for the foreseeable future.

Deciding she was destined to stay single, Rosalie stepped

back into the bedroom just as a familiar voice called out from the hall.

"Hello? Anybody in here?"

Frankie Dawson appeared in the doorway, his hair damp with sweat as he nodded at Rosalie and Kinsey.

"You're not allowed in here," Marty said, scowling at Frankie's shaggy hair, baggy clothes, and scuffed-up tennis shoes. "You need to leave before you contaminate the scene."

"I'm afraid that ship has sailed," Frankie replied with a shrug. "I've already been through here once."

He craned his head to look past the forensic technician.

"I came back because I forgot to mention the safe."

"What safe?" Kinsey asked.

Stepping forward, she ushered Frankie back into the hall.

"The one at the bottom of the kitchen pantry," he said. "I saw it when I went to look in the back yard."

He bent over to rub a bloodstain on the leg of his jeans.

"I slipped on some blood and fell. At that level, I could see the safe under a shelf. It was open and it was empty, which makes me think maybe this was a robbery gone bad."

A hopeful tone entered his voice.

"Maybe they've taken Evelyn with the intention of asking for a ransom, or maybe they'll try to get her to withdraw money from her bank," he said. "You should check the local ATM cameras. You could still track them down."

Rosalie spoke up before Kinsey could.

"I hate to break it to you," she said. "But based on the blood evidence we found, if Evelyn Wright is the victim here, I wouldn't expect her to be up and walking around, much less going into a bank anytime soon."

Marty Prince nodded in agreement as Rosalie continued.

"The intensity and pattern of the blood spray on the wall suggests a severed carotid artery," she said. "And based on the consistency and color of the blood, I'd say it's been congealing for at least twelve hours."

"So, you're saying Evelyn Wright is dead?" Frankie asked. "And that she was likely killed sometime last night? Sometime after she left that voicemail?"

"What voicemail?" Rosalie asked, suddenly alert.

"What time was it sent?" Marty added. "The timing could help us narrow down the time of death."

Frankie pulled out his phone.

"Evelyn tried to call Dusty Fontaine around nine o'clock last night. When he didn't pick-up, she left this message."

He tapped on the display.

Rosalie frowned as the recording of a woman's voice began to play. She wasn't sure what she was listening to.

Then her eyes widened.

"Wait, play that part again."

"Which part?" Frankie asked.

"The part about the bones in the river."

Tapping again on the screen, Frankie moved back through the message. Again, Rosalie heard Evelyn Wright's voice.

"*...that got me thinking about Maisie. I was just wondering, have you ever heard anything more from her? What about those bones in the river? Could they be connected somehow?*"

As the voicemail ended, Rosalie mused aloud.

"What if Evelyn Wright was on to something? What if she was killed because she'd discovered some of the bones from the river *do* belong to Maisie Guinn?"

She looked first at Kinsey and then at Frankie.

"If one of you can get me a DNA sample from Maisie, I can run a comparison with the bones back in my cooler," she said. "That'll help us figure out if she ended up in the river."

CHAPTER FIVE

Frankie descended the porch steps and was halfway back to his Mustang when he heard footsteps coming up behind him. Glancing over his shoulder, he saw Kinsey following him down the walkway. The detective's face was tense and her shoulders were stiff under her suit jacket.

He slowed his long stride, allowing her to catch up.

"Are you planning to open an official investigation into Maisie Guinn's disappearance?" he asked as she fell into step beside him. "I'm only asking because I've been hired to find her, and I don't want you and your partner accusing me of interfering with police business again."

Kinsey considered the question, then shrugged.

"I can't see Chief Pagano giving Ranger and me the okay to open a missing person case for a woman who left town twenty years ago," she admitted. "Not unless we can show it's directly connected to this new homicide investigation."

Her voice hardened imperceptibly on Pagano's name.

"I'm sure he'll want us to spend our limited resources looking for Evelyn's body. Not to mention her killer."

Detecting a glint of resentment in her eyes, Frankie

wondered if Kinsey had gotten off on the wrong foot with Barrel Creek's new chief of police.

"Sounds like the new chief keeps you guys on a tight leash," Frankie said as they reached the Mustang, where Sherlock was patiently waiting. "But he's got to be an improvement over Shipley, right?"

He imagined few bosses could be worse than the town's late chief of police, who had been mixed up in the same smuggling enterprise as Dwight Atkins and Bill Brewster.

"Pagano is still settling in."

Kinsey's voice remained carefully neutral.

"And he's been tasked with earning back the trust of our community. That won't be easy for any of us."

Sensing her reluctance to discuss her new boss, Frankie moved on to the more pressing matter at hand.

"Well, I can't help you with that one," he said. "But maybe while you and Ranger are looking for Evelyn Wright I can track down a sample of Maisie Guinn's DNA."

He lifted a hand to shield his eyes from the blazing mid-morning sun and felt a drop of sweat roll down his forearm.

"If I manage to get hold of a sample, I'll deliver it to Rosalie for testing," he said. "Maybe those bones will tell us what happened and save us both from further investigation."

Kinsey nodded reluctantly as she bent to scratch Sherlock behind his soft, floppy ears.

"I guess that'll work," she said. "I can't stop you from investigating your missing person's case in any event."

She sounded resigned.

"Let me know if you manage to find a DNA sample," she said. "And I'd be interested in hearing about any other progress you make in your search for Maisie."

The detective surveyed the street, which had remained surprisingly quiet considering the array of official vehicles that now lined the curb.

"I'd better start canvassing the neighborhood before the press beats me to it," she said. "Hopefully someone saw something last night."

"Where'd your partner run off to?" Frankie asked. "I saw Ranger race out of here like he was chasing a hot lead."

Leaning forward, Kinsey exhaled and lowered her voice.

"He went to talk to Ralph McEwan," she admitted. "The guy's building the Starbound Casino on the site where the human remains were found over in Buford County, so..."

Frankie frowned.

"So, you think that whatever happened to Evelyn here last night might have had something to do with McEwan?" he asked, sounding doubtful. "You think he could have something to do with the remains in Buford County, too?"

"We've got to follow every lead," Kinsey said as she began to back away. "And right now that's about all we have, which is why I need to go coordinate search efforts."

She started to walk away, then stopped, and looked back.

"Oh, and by the way, Sheriff Crockett isn't releasing the information about the remains over in Buford County being found in an Atkins barrel to the public or press, so be sure to keep that to yourself."

Her words replayed in Frankie's head as he opened the

door to his Mustang and allowed Sherlock to climb in. He decided he was glad the detail about the barrel wouldn't be made public.

After all, if the press heard the remains at the Starbound had been dumped in an Atkins barrel, reporters and news crews might descend on Barrel Creek, searching for photos and sound bites to accompany the sensationalized story as it made its way through the content-hungry twenty-four-hour news cycle.

It was better to keep the spotlight off the town and the barrel works if at all possible.

Backing the Mustang onto Overland Road, Frankie rolled down the windows and began to mentally sort through everything that had happened since Dusty Fontaine had walked into his office that morning.

Within the space of a few hours, he'd gotten himself involved in a missing person case, a probable homicide, and a complicated cold case murder with a troubling connection to the barrel works.

"How do I get myself into these situations, Sherlock?"

He glanced back at the Labrador, but the dog had his head out the window and didn't appear to be listening.

It all started with Evelyn's voicemail, right? That's what got Dusty thinking and that's why he came to see me.

But what had prompted Evelyn to start asking questions about Maisie after all these years? Had those questions gotten her killed?

Stopping at a red light, Frankie recalled a snippet of Evelyn's voicemail.

"...the guy who hired me was asking about Maisie Guinn."

Maybe it hadn't started with Evelyn after all. Maybe Ralph McEwan had poked the sleeping hornets' nest.

And what is McEwan's story, anyway?

Frankie suddenly wondered if the man had played him for a fool. Could the real estate developer's purchase of the barrel factory have been motivated by something other than its potential resale value?

What exactly did McEwan know about the barrel of human remains found on the site of his future casino?

Looking into the back seat to check on Sherlock, his eyes fell on the cardboard box Dusty had given him, which was full of items recovered from Maisie's desk.

He saw a thick manila envelope under the black leather CD case and reached for it just as the car behind him honked.

The light ahead had turned green.

Dropping the envelope into his lap, he stepped on the gas, sending the Mustang surging forward as he used one hand to steer the car and the other to open the flap and pull out a stack of photos.

A blue ballpoint pen had been used to label each photo.

Frankie glanced down at the first photo in the stack, read the handwritten label on the back, and then flipped to the next.

His chest tightened at the sight of a familiar face.

Sliding the entire stack back into the manila envelope, he fixed his eyes on the road ahead, squinting against the unrelenting glare of the summer sun as he headed toward the state line.

CHAPTER SIX

The construction site appeared to be deserted when Detective Sheldon Ranger parked the black Ford Interceptor next to the locked gate. Climbing out of the vehicle, he looked through the chain link fence at the silent excavators, backhoes, and bulldozers scattered around the property. They reminded him of the hulking dinosaur skeletons on display at the Museum of Natural History.

A reflective aluminum sign hung on the gate bearing the Starbound Casino's logo and the optimistic assertion that *Buford County's Biggest Casino is Coming Soon!*

To the left of the sign, a notice listed the phone number to be called in the event of an emergency at the site.

Ranger considered calling the posted number and asking to be connected with Ralph McEwan, then decided against it.

The interview he planned to conduct with McEwan would hopefully advance the investigation into Evelyn Wright's murder, but it could hardly be considered an emergency.

He strained to see past a dump truck, still half filled with dirt, to where a strip of yellow crime scene tape had been strung out between a series of orange and white barricades.

That must be where the barrel of remains was found.

Leaning against the fence in an effort to get a better view, Ranger quickly jerked his hands away with a grunt of pain.

"That metal gets about as hot as fire come summer," a voice said from somewhere to his left. "But I guess that's a good way of keeping people from climbing over it."

Turning toward the voice, he saw a white-haired man in a baggy uniform and dusty black boots ambling toward him.

A black cap with the words *Security Officer* embroidered on the rim was perched jauntily on his head and a name tag reading *Officer Zuckerman* was affixed to his polyester shirt.

"If you're one of them reporters looking for-"

"I'm Detective Sheldon Ranger with the Barrel Creek PD," Ranger interjected, producing his badge. "I was hoping to speak to Ralph McEwan. I'm guessing he's not here?"

"Barrel Creek? Isn't that over in Tennessee?"

Ranger nodded.

"Yes, it is. But I'm working a homicide investigation and I have a few questions for Mr. McEwan. I don't imagine you have a way of getting in touch with him, do you?"

Zuckerman studied Ranger's badge, then pulled a phone out of a pouch on his thick, nylon security belt.

After tapping on the phone, he held it to his ear.

"I've got a Detective Sheldon Ranger over at the site looking for Mr. McEwan," he said into the phone. "Says he's from Barrel Creek, Tennessee and he's working a homicide investigation. Needs to ask the boss a few questions."

He lifted his eyes to Ranger's as he answered several questions from the person on the other end of the call.

"Yes, sir...no, sir...okay, sir. I'll let him know."

Expecting the security guard to tell him McEwan wasn't available, Ranger was already taking a step back when Zuckerman cleared his throat.

"Mr. McEwan will meet you here shortly," he said, inserting the phone back in its designated pouch. "He bought a house just a few minutes away, so it shouldn't be long."

He pulled a keyring off of his belt and unlocked the gate.

"You can wait in Mr. McEwan's trailer. No need for a hard hat. We haven't had any work going on for over a week. Not since they found those remains and closed down the site."

Ranger turned his head toward the highway at the sound of a car engine approaching, wondering how McEwan had managed to get there so quickly.

His surprise turned to annoyance when he saw Frankie Dawson's black Mustang pull into the site.

The P.I. brought the car to a stop beside Ranger's Interceptor and climbed out.

"You're gonna get sunstroke standing out here," Frankie called in a cheerful voice as he approached. "Weatherman says it's gonna get close to a hundred degrees. And that's in the shade."

Putting both hands on his hips, Ranger squared his broad

shoulders and glared at the skinny detective.

"What are you doing here, Dawson?"

Frankie ignored the question, still smiling.

"Did you get lost, Detective Ranger?" he asked. "Cause I'm pretty sure you're out of your jurisdiction."

He hooked a thumb over one thin shoulder.

"Barrel Creek is back that way."

Officer Zuckerman cleared his throat.

"You two aren't gonna cause any trouble, are you?" he asked with a frown. "Cause Mr. McEwan will be here any minute and I need to get on with my patrol."

"I'm not here for any trouble," Frankie assured the security guard. "I just want to talk to Ralph McEwan about a missing person investigation I'm working on."

The guard cocked a doubtful eyebrow.

"You're a cop, too?"

"I'm a private investigator," Frankie said. "Which means I can go where I like. I'm not stuck in a specific jurisdiction."

Ranger rolled his eyes.

"I'm free to travel anywhere an investigation leads, and I can talk to anyone I choose. Not that I need to explain myself to the likes of you."

He turned his attention back to the security guard.

"Feel free to get on with your duties, Officer Zuckerman. I'll be fine waiting here for Mr. McEwan on my own."

The old guard nodded slowly, then pointed to a trailer sitting back against the fence.

"That's Mr. McEwan's office when he's on-site," he

said. "You can wait for him there if you like. I'll be close by if you need anything."

Ranger waited until the older man had walked out of earshot, then spun back to face Frankie.

"What are you playing at, Dawson?"

The sound of tires crunching over gravel drowned out Frankie's answer.

A large white Escalade had pulled up behind Frankie's Mustang. The driver's door swung open and a tall man with a headful of copper-colored hair emerged.

Before Ranger could step forward to introduce himself, the man turned to Frankie with a wide smile.

"I'm surprised to see you here, Mr. Dawson! I didn't expect our paths to cross again so soon. I'm not interrupting a private conversation, am I?"

He cocked a questioning eyebrow as he turned to Ranger.

"Mr. Dawson was just leaving," Ranger said stiffly.

"Well, he doesn't have to leave on my account," McEwan replied. "In fact, I wouldn't mind having someone here to witness whatever shakedown you have planned."

Ranger frowned.

"Shakedown?"

"You are Ike Ranger's son, aren't you?" the developer asked. "I knew him well, and apples usually don't fall far from the...well, you know the saying. So, I'm assuming you've called me out here to demand some sort of payoff?"

A red flush of anger warmed Ranger's cheeks.

"I'm *nothing* like my father," he gritted out. "And I came out here to ask you a few questions about an investigation.

If you don't like the location, I'm perfectly happy to interview you at the Barrel Creek police station."

Cocking his head, McEwan scoffed.

"I'm sure that would suit *you* just fine. But my lawyer might have a differing opinion. He tends to frown on me giving statements to the cops without him being there to keep me in line."

"Listen, McEwan, we're not here to bust your-"

Ranger lifted a hand to stop Frankie from saying whatever it was the P.I. planned to blurt out.

"There is no *we*," he said, shooting a furious look in Frankie's direction before fixing hard eyes on McEwan. "I need to ask you about your connection to a woman in Barrel Creek. Someone who has been the victim of foul play."

McEwan's eyes narrowed.

"What woman?" he asked.

"The woman you met at Atkins Barrel Works yesterday," Ranger said. "Evelyn Wright is missing, presumed dead."

His words wiped the smug look from the real estate developer's wide, freckled face.

"What do you mean *missing*?" he asked. "I saw her-"

"Yes, we know," Ranger interrupted. "You saw her yesterday at the barrel works for some type of photo shoot. She left a message for a friend telling him all about it."

Frankie piped up before Ranger could stop him.

"I showed up at her house this morning and found blood everywhere, but no sign of Evelyn."

"I'm...sorry to hear that," McEwan said, raking a hand through his thick hair. "I hope she's alright."

The initial concern on his face quickly morphed into an indignant frown as Ranger continued to stare at him.

"What makes you think I'd know what happened to her?"

"According to Evelyn Wright's voicemail, it seems you might have been the last person to have seen her," Ranger said. "And you also happen to own this building site, where another victim's remains were discovered just last week."

He gestured toward the pile of dirt beside the crime scene tape, giving Frankie an opening to add his two cents.

"You gotta admit it's a pretty strange coincidence," the P.I. said. "Especially since the remains were dumped in a barrel from the Atkins' factory."

Scratching at the stubble on his chin, Frankie seemed oblivious to the glare Ranger was sending in his direction.

"And just why were you so damn eager to take the place off my hands, McEwan?" Frankie continued. "Was there something at the factory you were hoping to find?"

"What if I was?"

The real estate developer clenched both fists by his side.

"When I saw that barrel come out of the ground...and when I saw the bones inside it..."

He shook his head as if trying to dislodge the memory.

"I'm not a fool. I knew my whole project was at risk," he said. "I was familiar with the barrel works, and I'd seen the news about what went down in Barrel Creek last spring."

His eyes flicked to Frankie.

"The property was for sale, so I contacted Mr. Dawson. When I saw the price, which was extremely reasonable, I thought it would be less hassle to simply buy what I wanted."

"And what was it you wanted?" Ranger asked.

A flush of emotion filled McEwan's face.

"I wanted to find out who bought the barrel and who put the body inside, of course. I wanted to search the property and look through sales records without having to beg the owners or police for permission."

He exhaled in frustration.

"I was hoping to resolve the matter quickly, so my casino project could continue without further delays. I wanted the Starbound to open as scheduled."

He glared at Ranger as if the situation were his fault.

"Nothing I did is a crime."

"No, but interfering with an official homicide investigation is," Ranger shot back. "And your little plan to investigate the origin of the barrel on your own could compromise any evidence you may have found."

McEwan lifted a hand as if waving away his concerns.

"The Buford County Sheriff and his deputies couldn't find evidence if it bit them on their backsides," he said. "I knew I'd have to act if I wanted to save my project."

"And Evelyn Wright?" Ranger asked, not quite buying McEwan's story. "We believe you were the last person to have seen her. Are you saying you have no idea what happened to her? No idea where she is?"

Without hesitation, McEwan shook his head in denial.

"I left Evelyn at the barrel works just before dusk last night," he insisted. "She was taking photos of the place for me. I was planning to put it back up for sale."

"Already? Didn't you just buy it last week?"

Ranger's eyebrows shot up in surprise.

"I admit I acted rashly. I made a mistake," McEwan said. "I purchased the property and business sight unseen. It wasn't until I inspected the buildings and had my team go through the books that I realized Atkins Barrel Works was just a shell of a company.

"There were no records, no real inventory. Just old buildings filled with rotting wood. I was no closer to finding out who'd purchased the barrel we found, so I decided to cut my losses and unload the property as quickly as possible."

He turned troubled eyes toward the crime scene tape.

"You think we'll ever know whose remains were in that barrel?" he asked. "Or who dumped them there?"

"I'm pretty sure we will," Ranger said. "In my experience, the truth usually comes out sooner or later."

He chose his words carefully, wondering how long it would take for the Buford County Sheriff's office to release the news that the remains had been identified as Valentina Rojas.

"Although, from what I've heard, details about the Atkins barrel aren't being shared with the press or the public."

Glancing back at Frankie, Ranger pinned the P.I. with a meaningful look as he spoke.

"I recommend you keep that information to yourself."

Both Frankie and McEwan nodded.

"But I didn't come here to discuss the barrel," Ranger said, feeling as if he knew little more than he had when he'd arrived. "I came to find out what you know about Evelyn."

"I told you, I don't know anything," McEwan insisted. "I mean, who would want to kill her? And why?"

He sounded genuinely perplexed.

"That's what we came here to find out," Ranger said.

Frankie cleared his throat.

"Actually, I came here looking for a missing person named Maisie Guinn," he said. "She was a former coworker of Evelyn Wright's, which is why I went over to her house this morning hoping to find her."

Before Ranger could cut him off, Frankie pulled two photos from his pocket. He held one out toward McEwan.

"Does this ring any bells?"

McEwan stared down in silence as Ranger craned his neck to get a look at the photo, which showed two men standing in front of Sombra's Gambling Hall & Casino, deep in conversation. The photo was labeled with two names.

Henry and Ralph.

One of the men was obviously a much younger Ralph McEwan. The other man looked vaguely familiar.

"Henry's my father," Frankie said. "You were with him."

"Where'd you get that?" McEwan asked.

Keeping the photo out of reach, Frankie cocked his head.

"Maisie Guinn was a reporter and this photo was taken right around the time she went missing."

His voice hardened.

"Right around the time my old man left town for good."

Ranger glanced at Frankie in surprise, then turned his bright blue eyes back on McEwan.

"A lot of people around you seem to disappear, don't they, Mr. McEwan?" Ranger said. "You have any idea why that is?"

"My own father always told me, that if you want to understand a man's character, you have to look at the people he surrounds himself with," McEwan murmured. "In the past, I surrounded myself with some very bad men. I didn't listen to my father's advice until he was gone. By then..."

His voice trailed away as he stared down at the picture still clutched in Frankie's hand.

"Are you saying that my father was one of these bad men you associated with?" Frankie asked.

"Not at all," McEwan said. "Sure, Henry Dawson was a drinker, but he was a good man at heart. Like me, he just had questionable taste in his business associates. But then, we all make mistakes."

Frankie held out the second photo, which showed his father standing beside a young woman with long, dark hair.

"What about *Valentina*?" he asked.

He pointed to the name that had been written across the back of the photo with a blue ballpoint pen.

"Who was she? Another one of my father's mistakes?"

McEwan's eyes darkened as he studied the picture.

"Valentina Rojas was Enrico Sombra's mistress," he said. "Many years ago, before she left town. I hardly knew her."

Ranger gaped at the photo, trying to make sense of what he was hearing. Had the dark-haired woman been buried in the barrel only yards from where they now stood?

Questions swirled through his head.

"Do you know why Valentina left town?" he asked. "Do you know where she went? Do you know when?"

"It's been a long time," McEwan said as Frankie put both photos back in his pocket. "I'd say she's been gone for close to twenty years."

Lifting a hand to his beard, he ran his fingers over the coarse, reddish hair as if he were trying to soothe himself.

"As far as why she left? My guess is she was trying to get away from Sombra," he added. "Either that or Sombra decided to get rid of her. He is a ruthless man. So, I'd say if you really want to know what happened to Valentina, you'd have to ask him."

* * *

Ranger stood at the edge of the muddy grave beside Frankie. As he looked down into the yawning darkness, a feeling of dread settled into the pit of his stomach.

"How did you get a photo of the victim in the barrel?" Ranger hissed, his eyes following McEwan who had stepped away to answer a phone call. "How did you know the woman was Valentina Rojas? That information hasn't been released to anyone outside law enforcement."

Turning to Ranger, Frankie stared at him with wide eyes.

"What do you mean?"

"Come on, stop screwing around," Ranger said. "Kinsey must have told you that prints in the barrel were matched to Valentina Rojas' prints in AFIS."

Frankie shook his head slowly from side to side.

"I swear, I didn't know the woman in the barrel was Valentina," he said. "I recognized her because she was with my old man the last time I ever saw him."

He swallowed hard and scratched at his chin.

"I always figured they ran off together."

The soft words hung in the air.

"And Maisie Guinn had that photo?"

Frankie nodded.

"I found those two photos in a box of stuff Maisie left behind when she split town...or when she was taken."

"Why would some reporter have a photo of your father and this woman?" Ranger asked.

The P.I. hesitated as if he hadn't considered the question.

"Well, Maisie was investigating Enrico Sombra prior to her sudden disappearance," he said. "So, I'm guessing she was taking photos of the people around him."

"Okay, so where's your father now?"

When Frankie didn't answer, Ranger tried again.

"Sheriff Crockett is going to want to talk to him. He'll want to find out what your father knows about...*all this*."

He motioned to the grave and the photo in Frankie's hand.

"I don't have a clue as to where my old man is right now," Frankie finally said. "He skipped out on my mom twenty years ago, leaving me and my sister behind. At least, that's what I always thought."

Pulling out the photo of Valentina, he studied it.

"But if Valentina has been in the ground all this time, then I might have been wrong," he murmured. "And if I was, that means my father might...he might be out there somewhere. Or he could be buried in that field, too."

He stepped back from the hole, his face pale and drawn.

"Maybe it's time I find out the truth."

Frankie turned and hurried back to the Mustang, leaving Ranger standing on the curb, still thinking of the photo and the young woman's dark, flashing eyes.

Who buried Valentina alive in the barrel, and why?

CHAPTER SEVEN

Albert Sharkey glided through Sombra's Gambling Hall & Casino with the relentless compulsion of a real shark searching for prey. The self-professed high roller had been on edge ever since the Atkins barrel had been discovered at the Starbound Casino construction site the week before, and he was still furious with himself for his impulsive visit to Evelyn Wright's house the previous evening. It had all gone so terribly wrong.

Expecting to feel a tap on his shoulder at any minute, Sharkey reminded himself to stay calm and act rationally.

Another mistake like the one he'd made last night could lead to the revelation of secrets he thought he'd successfully buried long ago. It could also mean he'd spend the rest of his life in a cage.

But the restlessness inside wouldn't let him stand still.

Just as a real shark was destined to move ceaselessly through the water in a never-ending quest for oxygen, Sharkey was compelled to glide through the intoxicating atmosphere of the gambling hall in search of his next big bet, his next much-needed fix.

Heading toward the long row of blackjack tables situated

in the main pit area, Sharkey reached into his pocket, feeling for the stack of smooth, black chips he'd dropped in earlier.

He scanned the tables, spotted an empty stool, and made his way down the aisle, threading his way through the crowd.

Before he could claim his seat, Sharkey noticed a tall, skinny man with a stubbly beard and brown, shaggy hair walking toward him. His heart skipped a beat

What the hell is Frankie Dawson doing here?

The private investigator frowned up at the sign hanging over the aisle as if looking for directions, then continued past Sharkey without making eye contact.

Did he come all the way over here looking for Maisie Guinn? If so, he's about twenty years too late.

An ugly sneer spread across his face at the thought, then vanished again at the next thought.

Or maybe he came here looking for me. Maybe he figured out what I did with Evelyn Wright.

Melting into the crowd, Sharkey turned and followed the P.I. past the blackjack tables and the empty stool, sticking close behind him as he moved toward the side exit.

With his eyes glued to the man's shaggy hair, he didn't see the small figure beside him until a bony hand reached out and grabbed his arm.

He looked down to see a pair of bloodshot eyes staring up at him. The eyes belonged to one of the junkies who roamed the casino, looking for handouts from the gamblers who were on a lucky streak and feeling generous.

"Hey, man. You're a high roller aren't you?" the man slurred. "You must have a few bucks to spare for-"

Responding with a sharp shove, Sharkey watched as the emaciated man staggered backward, knocking into one of the blackjack tables, causing several drinks to spill and sending a stack of chips scattering over the felt-covered table.

The gamblers standing around the table turned to see who had caused the commotion, then quickly turned away again when they encountered Sharkey's rage-filled face.

Sharkey met the wide, startled eyes of the pretty, young dealer standing behind the table, noting that the name tag pinned to her white button-up shirt read *Darcy Doyle*.

A start of recognition got his feet moving again, but by this time he had lost Frankie Dawson somewhere in the crowd.

Making his way toward the cashier's booth near the exit, Sharkey stifled a curse and pushed his way into the stairwell.

He needed a few minutes alone.

Just enough time to get a grip on himself before he lost all control. Although, to be fair, demonstrating a lack of control wasn't usually a problem for him.

In fact, his ability to rein in and mask his emotions had enabled him to win big at the tables again and again.

He had developed a reputation as a card shark at an early age and had chosen the moniker Albert Sharkey as his gambling name accordingly.

He'd even gone so far as to use the name in the course of

other money-making schemes and whenever he thought it would be prudent to hide his true identity.

But every once in a while, he lost hold of the reins and his mask slipped, just as he'd done the night before. Just as he'd done that night two decades earlier when he had followed a different Dawson out of the casino.

That had been the night he'd discovered Henry Dawson was not only a snitch and an informant, but also a threat to his freedom. On that rare occasion, Sharkey had given into his true nature. He had released the darkness within.

Sharkey followed at a safe distance as Henry Dawson strode toward the back of the casino and pushed his way through the exit into the dimly lit parking garage.

While Henry waited for the elevator, Sharkey slipped into the stairwell, taking the stairs two at a time until he reached the second floor, where his car was parked halfway down the first row.

Sliding behind the wheel, he slammed the door shut and locked it but didn't turn the engine on.

Seconds later, the elevator at the far end of the garage slid open, and Henry stepped out. Looking neither left nor right, he hurried to a white Dodge pickup parked near the exit and climbed in.

As soon as the truck's headlights flashed on, Sharkey started his own engine. He waited until Henry's taillights disappeared down the exit ramp, then pulled out of his parking space.

Following the Dodge down the ramp, he tightened his hands on the steering wheel, trying to control the anger that had been brewing ever since he'd learned Henry had not only been passing information to the Gazette, ensuring the paper would have the dirt they needed to run a hatchet job on the casino but was also acting as an FBI informant.

Sharkey wasn't sure what he planned to do just yet, but he knew Henry presented a threat that he couldn't ignore.

He would follow the troublemaker and see where he went and what he was up to, sure that if he bided his time, he would find a way to eliminate the threat Henry presented once and for all.

Assuming the Dodge would head for the highway, Sharkey prepared to switch lanes, then hesitated and tapped on the brakes.

Instead of heading back toward Barrel Creek, Henry was circling the casino, heading around to a side service entrance where barrels were loaded and unloaded when a special shipment was being processed. However, it was rare to have those shipments go in or out at night when the casino was busy.

The risk that someone would see something and start asking questions was too high considering the barrels' illegal contents.

But then, maybe Henry wasn't worried about getting caught. After all, he'd been talking to the feds and telling tales, right? Maybe he wanted to get caught. Maybe that was the plan.

Turning off his headlights, Sharkey pulled alongside the curb and watched as the Dodge slowed to a stop.

Seconds later the service door opened and a slim figure stepped out into the night. Sharkey stared in surprise as a beautiful dark-haired woman climbed into the pickup's passenger seat.

Valentina?

A flame of jealous rage ignited in his chest. What the hell was Valentina Rojas doing with Henry Dawson? Was she back to her *old habits? Was she turning tricks again?*

But if it was money she was after, why waste time with a drunk who usually didn't have two cents to rub together?

Was it possible she'd actually developed some sort of feelings for the man, even though he was twice her age? Didn't she know that Henry was a snitch and an informant?

Or had he recruited her to be an informant as well?

The sudden thought alarmed him.

Valentina Rojas knew enough to bring his whole world crashing down around him. All she had to do was tell what she knew to the wrong person, to someone who wasn't being paid to keep their mouth shut, and he'd lose everything, including his freedom.

Of course, there were men inside the casino who were paid to take care of informants. He could whisper in the right ear and set the wheels in motion. But who could he trust?

Right now, it felt as if everyone around him was a threat.

It would be best to take care of the matter himself.

Watching the Dodge pull away from the curb and head back toward the highway, Sharkey noticed that several large oak barrels were loaded in the bed of the truck.

He had no doubt the barrels contained evidence that would be delivered to the feds. Evidence that would be used to take the casino down once and for all.

Lowering his foot on the gas with a new sense of determination, Sharkey kept his eyes fixed on the taillights ahead, allowing the car to creep closer to the Dodge as Henry merged onto the exit.

Suddenly, Sharkey knew where they were headed.

"The traitorous bitch is taking him home," he muttered into the car's quiet interior. "She really has gone over to the other side."

He balled his hand into a fist and smashed it down onto the dashboard with a snarl of fury as he watched the pickup turn onto Lombard Street.

Speeding past the narrow, winding road, Sharkey drove to the next cross street and made a clumsy U-turn, circling back in time to see Henry Dawson slipping into Valentina's cozy little house.

Lights flashed on behind the blinds and two shadows passed in front of the window as Sharkey parked the car under an overhanging tree branch and lowered his hand to his belt, feeling for the sheath of the switchblade he always carried with him.

After sucking in a deep breath and counting slowly to ten, he reached for the handle, preparing to step out into the humid night air, when the front door to the little house swung open again.

Henry Dawson appeared on the doorstep, looked up and down the street, then hurried back to the Dodge. Seconds later, the truck roared to life and began backing down the driveway.

Adrenaline pulsed through Sharkey as the truck's tires bumped onto the street and its headlights illuminated his car's interior.

Ducking down in his seat, he closed his eyes and gritted his teeth, praying that Henry wouldn't see him cowering behind the wheel.

He wasn't sure if the man was armed, but a switchblade would be no match for a gun, especially without the element of surprise.

His rush of fear turned to anger once the lights had faded into the distance, along with the rumble of the Dodge's engine.

Lifting his head, he looked toward the house. The lights behind the blinds cast a soft, welcoming glow.

Was Valentina in there waiting for Henry to come back?

Sharkey hesitated, unsure if he should follow the snitch in the truck or take care of the traitor in the house first.

A shadow passed by the window and was then gone again as if the woman inside was taunting him.

Did she know he was watching? Did she think this was some sort of game? Was she in there laughing at him, thinking her bluff had actually worked? Didn't she know who she was dealing with?

Suddenly he was out of the car, stalking up the front walk, lifting one fist to knock on the door as he tightened his other fist around the handle of his switchblade.

Footsteps sounded inside, and then the door opened and Valentina was there, her eyes wide and startled as she saw the blade clutched in his hand and the gleam of death in his eyes.

Turning to run, she made it into the living room before Sharkey could grab a handful of dark, silky hair and yank her back against his chest. He brandished his knife, hoping to scare her into silence, but she lifted a sharp elbow and knocked it from his hand.

The switchblade dropped to the floor and spun out of reach.

"Fine, then we'll do this...the hard way," he grunted as he flung her to the ground and fell on top of her.

His hands reached for her slender neck with a will of their own, squeezing harder and harder until her struggling stopped.

Getting back to his feet, he looked down at her motionless body, his cold eyes showing no sign of remorse.

She had brought this on herself with her own treachery. And until he'd disposed of her, she was still a threat.

If anyone found her dead on the floor, there would be a search and an investigation. Someone might have noticed his car outside the house. And his phone had been in his pocket the whole time. If they bothered tracking his activity...

Dread started its heavy climb up his spine as he looked around for something to drape over her body. He would have to take Valentina with him. He couldn't allow her to be discovered.

He needed to make her disappear.

With any luck, everyone would think she'd finally gotten sick of Buford County and left town. Sharkey figured that, for those who knew the place, it wouldn't be very hard to believe.

Wrapping Valentina in a blanket, he carried her to the car, dumped her in the trunk, and slammed the lid shut.

As he climbed back behind the wheel, he told himself he'd have to find a safe place to dispose of her soon.

But first, he needed to find Henry Dawson and-

Sharkey's mind jerked back to the present as the heavy door swung open and Darcy Doyle stepped into the stairwell.

"Oh, sorry," the young blackjack dealer said in a breathy voice. "I was just going on a smoke break."

She produced a guilty smile as she held up a pack of cigarettes and took a lighter out of her pocket.

"And I was just looking for someone," he said, which wasn't exactly a lie. "An old family friend."

Suspecting she'd been following him, Sharkey studied her flushed face, nervous blue eyes, and messy blonde ponytail.

Darcy's cheeks reddened as his eyes dropped to her name

tag, but he wasn't fooled by the shy routine.

In fact, he was almost certain that being a nosy troublemaker ran in the Doyle family and that the pretty dealer was planning to pick up where her aunt had left off.

"Go on, don't let me stop you," Sharkey said, waving toward the exit. "Enjoy your smoke."

With a relieved nod, Darcy pushed through the exit door, leaving Sharkey staring after her with cold hard eyes.

CHAPTER EIGHT

All of Frankie's senses were on high alert as he walked through the main pit area of Sombra's Gambling Hall & Casino looking for the man Ralph McEwan had described as ruthless. According to the real estate developer, Enrico Sombra was the one man who might know what had happened to Valentina Rojas after Frankie had seen her driving away from the casino that night with his father.

It was the last night he had ever seen his old man.

At the time, Frankie had been too young to come through the casino's main door without being spotted by the security guards stationed throughout the lobby, so he had slipped in the side entrance where his buddy Dwight sometimes dropped off barrels of what Frankie had assumed to be whiskey or bourbon.

But after quickly burning through the hard-earned cash he'd brought with him, Frankie had made his way back to the side entrance with empty pockets and a head aching from all the ringing bells, spinning wheels, and animated noises spewing nonstop from the slot machines.

Moving toward the exit, Frankie had seen a young, dark-haired woman in a blood-red dress and matching heels slip through the side door.

When Frankie had pushed through the exit only seconds later, vowing to himself that he would never gamble again, he'd come to a sudden stop.

The dark-haired woman was climbing into a white Dodge pickup that looked exactly like his father's truck. He hadn't realized it *was* his father's truck until he'd seen Henry Dawson's shaggy brown hair through the back windshield.

That brief glimpse of his father's hair, along with a quick flash of his profile as he'd turned to greet his lovely young companion, had hit Frankie like a sucker punch.

After everything they'd been through as a family, after all the ups and downs caused by his old man's drinking, his father had betrayed them.

Henry hadn't been out working after all. He had been catting around behind his wife's back. And when both Frankie and his mother had left angry voicemails on Henry's phone telling him not to bother coming home, his old man had taken them at their word.

They had never heard from Henry Dawson again.

He hadn't cared enough to even try to explain.

At least, that's what Frankie had thought back then. Only now, he wasn't so sure Henry had ever gotten the chance.

Doubt had set in as soon as he realized the dark-haired woman he'd seen with his father was the same woman who'd been buried in the barrel. That doubt was making him question the story he'd been telling himself all these years.

The story featured Henry Dawson as the evil villain who'd deserted his family to run off with a temptress half his age and Frankie starring as the hapless victim who had been betrayed and abandoned by his own father.

Had it all just been a fairytale he'd told himself? If so, was the real story darker than he'd ever imagined?

Suddenly questioning everything he had believed to be true about his father, Frankie strode toward the casino's management office in search of Sombra.

Not only did he want to ask the man what he knew about Valentina Rojas' demise, but he also wanted to find out what the casino owner knew about his own father's fate.

Is my old man out there somewhere living a life free from the responsibility of a nagging wife and a couple of kids as I always imagined...or maybe boozing it up every night in a flophouse?

A small, unsettling voice spoke in his head.

Or has he been six feet under all this time?

Clenching both hands into fists at the thought, Frankie made his way through the maze of gaming tables, brushing precariously past a waitress carrying a tray of complimentary drinks toward the high-stakes poker room.

Frankie figured it was too early in the day to be drinking, but without any windows or clocks as a reference, he imagined few people in the room were aware of the time.

As he passed the sports betting bar, he scanned the bank of flat-screen TVs mounted along the wall.

Most of the wide screens displayed some sort of race or sporting event. But the screen nearest the bartender showed the local news. A *Breaking News* banner scrolled along the bottom of the screen.

Remains found at Starbound Casino construction site identified as former Buford County resident Valentina Rojas.

Frankie stopped in mid-stride and stared up at a headshot of Valentina Rojas. She was beautiful, even in the stark, brightly lit photo, which appeared to be a mugshot.

Moving into the bar, he strained to hear the reporter over the shouts and groans inspired by the horse race taking place on the next screen over.

"The Buford County Sheriff's Department released a statement today regarding the remains discovered at the Starbound Casino construction site last week."

The meticulously groomed and coifed reporter spoke in a grave tone that belied the exhilarated gleam in her eyes.

"The remains have been identified by the medical examiner's office as Buford County resident Valentina Rojas, who is seen in this mugshot taken back in 2004. Foul play is suspected, and a homicide investigation into the death is underway."

There was no mention of the Atkins barrel or the victim's alleged connection to Enrico Sombra or his casino.

"Can I get you a drink?"

Frankie lowered his eyes to the bartender, who was staring at him expectantly.

"I don't drink," Frankie said.

He tried not to look at the bottle of Jack Daniels calling to him from behind the bar.

"I'm looking for Enrico Sombra," he added before the bartender could turn away. "Know where I can find him?"

A guarded expression fell over the man's face.

"Go out the doors and turn to your right, then follow the signs to Administration," he said. "But I'm not sure you'll be allowed back to the boss' office."

He glanced up at a camera mounted above the bar.

"They've got eyes everywhere, so they'll see you coming."

Following the man's gaze, Frankie stared up at the lens without concern. All casinos had a network of security cameras streaming real-time video of the gaming area back to a control room, but he was sure the security staff would have their hands full looking for real threats.

I'm not even gambling, much less counting cards, so why would they waste time tracking a small fish like me?

Reassured by the thought, Frankie followed the signs to the administration office just as he'd been instructed and soon found himself standing in an opulently furnished lobby.

He crossed to the reception desk, surprised to find it unmanned, and noted that the door to the inner office was open and that deep voices were spilling out into the lobby.

"Who are you?"

The woman's voice came from behind him.

Spinning around, Frankie faced a tall, willowy woman with long, caramel-colored hair and thick, showgirl-style lashes. She held a wine glass in one hand.

Based on her silk dress and fancy heels, not to mention the drink in her hand, he decided she wasn't the receptionist.

"I'm Frankie Dawson," he said. "And you are?"

The woman raised a perfectly arched eyebrow, ignoring his question as she looked him up and down.

"I thought you looked familiar. Just like your father."

"You knew my old man?"

Her red lips curled into a knowing smile.

"Yes, I knew Henry," she said. "Of course, I was just a girl then. Barely legal at the time. But I have a good memory."

"Yolanda? Who's this?"

The woman's smile vanished as she looked past him to where a man with shoulders the size of a linebacker stood in the doorway to the inner office.

"This is Frankie Dawson," she said. "Henry's son."

Her eyes flashed back to Frankie.

"I can see you haven't yet met the casino's Chief Operating Officer, Cordero Torres," she said dryly. "Cordero is what you might call my husband's *second-in-command* and I'm sure he'd be happy to help you with your little investigation."

"So you're married to the boss?" Frankie asked with a frown, wondering how the woman had known he was conducting an investigation. "I was actually hoping to talk to your husband if I could just –"

He didn't get a chance to finish his sentence as Cordero Torres stepped forward, his broad face and dark eyebrows creased with rage.

"You won't be talking to anyone," the big man said. "In fact, you were just leaving, weren't you?"

Grabbing Frankie by the arm, he steered him roughly

toward the door and deposited him in the hall.

"Mr. Sombra doesn't need any more troublemakers around here. No more reporters and no P.I.s."

"Then maybe I should take my questions to Sheriff Crockett," Frankie said, jerking his arm free. "Maybe Sombra can tell *him* what he knows about Maisie Guinn. And about Valentina Rojas for that matter."

Cordero smirked at the threat.

"Take your questions to Sheriff Crockett if you want," he said with a nasty laugh. "Just be sure to tell him I said hello while you're there."

The words were still ringing in Frankie's ears when he stepped out into the parking garage ten minutes later.

He'd almost made it back to his Mustang when he heard heavy footsteps coming up behind him.

Looking back, he saw a big fist coming at him and tried to duck, but it connected solidly with his cheek, sending him stumbling into the side of a souped-up Cadillac.

By the time he'd regained his balance and limped over to the Mustang, the man who'd attacked him had gone.

* * *

The cut on Frankie's cheek was starting to bleed again as he pulled the Mustang onto the driveway of what he still thought of as the Atkins house on Ironstone Way.

Using a crumpled napkin he'd found in the glove compartment to clean off the blood, he grabbed the cardboard box of Maisie's things out of the back and walked into the big, two-story house.

As he made his way into the kitchen, he greeted Sherlock, who was waiting patiently by his food bowl.

He set the box on the counter, then turned to frown at the backpack lying on the kitchen table.

Had Josie skipped school again?

He knew the teen wasn't happy about having to go to summer school when all of the other kids in Barrel Creek where hanging out at the lake or going to the mall, but she had little choice after missing over a month of school following her parents' murders.

Worried that she would be forced to repeat the ninth grade if she missed too many days and too much work, he went to the bottom of the stairs, intending to call up to Josie and demand to know what was going on, when his eyes fell on the clock on the wall.

It was three o'clock, which meant the school day had already ended. She must have dropped her backpack on the table when she'd come in for an afterschool snack.

There had been no need to worry, after all.

At least not this time, although lately, it seemed as if he was always worried about Josie. And if Frankie was honest with himself, he had good cause.

The girl was struggling to cope.

The sudden loss of the teenager's parents, and the revelation that Dwight Atkins wasn't her biological father, had been devastating.

Once the initial shock had worn off, and the cold reality of her loss had kicked in, Josie had become argumentative and moody, often withdrawing to her room, giving Frankie the impression she suspected he was somehow responsible for everything that had happened.

But he didn't really mind the attitude. In fact, it sort of made sense.

After all, the worst week of Josie's life had ended with the startling revelation that her biological father was a lanky, gum chewing P.I. who struggled to stay sober.

It was only natural for her to associate him with the grief and anger she was feeling.

But like it or not, he was the only family she had left, and his new role as her father and the executor of her parents' estate meant they would have to find a way to get along.

Determined to help his daughter regain some sense of normalcy, he'd taken her to see Dr. Beth Hurley and the therapist had explained that the teen was understandably grieving and confused. She also appeared to be suffering a serious case of PTSD, exacerbated by survivor's guilt.

Dr. Hurley had warned Frankie that he would need to be patient. His daughter's healing process would take time.

"Getting over something like this can take years. It can leave lifelong emotional scars. But with love and patience, she can heal."

"I just hope Dr. Hurley is right," Frankie muttered to Sherlock as he poured food into the dog's bowl. "Cause I don't know what else I can do. You know what I mean?"

"Who are you talking to?"

Frankie looked up to see Josie standing in the doorway with her arms crossed over her chest.

Her disdainful expression instantly morphed to concern when she saw the angry cut on his cheek.

"What happened to your face?"

Lifting a hand to his busted cheek, he winced and looked down at his fingers. The cut had opened again. Leaving a dark stain of blood on his fingers.

Josie hurried to the sink and ran a cloth under the tap, then crossed to him and held it to his face.

"I'm working a new case," he said. "I guess somebody didn't like the questions I was asking."

A shine of interest lit up Josie's blue eyes.

"What's the case about?" she asked as she wiped away the last of the blood. "Can I help?"

"No, you can't help," Frankie said, gesturing to his cut. "You think I want you to end up with one of these?"

He winced in pain to emphasize his point.

"Dusty Fontaine hired me to look for an old friend of his who went missing twenty years ago," he said. "She was a reporter with the *Gazette*. That's a box of her stuff right there, although I'm not sure what good it'll do me."

"Why would that make somebody punch you?"

It was a good question.

"I guess they want me to stop asking questions," he told her. "Which means they probably have something to hide."

Walking over to the box, he picked up the leather case full of discs, reminding himself he needed to look at the files Dusty had backed up.

"So, you think Maisie Guinn is dead?" Josie asked.

Frankie turned to her with a frown.

"How'd you know her name is..."

His question died on his lips as he saw the reporter's name written across a notebook in the box.

"I didn't know for sure," Josie said with a grin. "But now I do. So, do you think she's dead?"

It was the first smile Frankie had seen on her face in a while and the first time she'd shown interest in what he was doing in weeks.

"I'm not sure," he admitted, not sure how much he should share with a fourteen-year-old girl. "I've not done much looking around yet. But it's nothing for you to worry about."

The shine in Josie's eyes started to fade.

"The M.E. suggested some of the bones they pulled out of the Wolf River might belong to Maisie," he found himself saying. "She went missing back when Bill Brewster and his gang were shipping barrels to a casino Maisie had been investigating. Maybe she figured out what was going on."

Staring at the box with wide eyes, Josie nodded slowly.

"And you think there could be some kind of evidence in that box that could prove if those are her bones?"

Frankie shook his head.

"We'd need DNA for that, and I doubt there's anything in there that still has Maisie's DNA on it."

"I could look through it and see what's in there," Josie offered. "I could help you with the case if you want."

She gave him a beseeching look that reminded him how young she was, and how much she'd been through.

"Peyton's coming on Saturday," he said, wishing he'd

never told her about Maisie. "She'll help me with the case."

He pointed to the backpack on the counter.

"Now, forget about that box," he said. "You've got more important things to worry about. Like your homework."

Taking out his phone, he began to tap on the screen, updating Dusty on his progress.

"Now, I'm going to go back to the office. Ma will pick you up and take you over to Granny Davis' house for dinner. You and Sherlock stay out of trouble in the meantime."

CHAPTER NINE

Josie waited until the Mustang had backed out of the driveway and sped out of earshot before she crossed over to the kitchen table and peered into the cardboard box. Feeling Sherlock's reproachful eyes watching her, she lifted the box, which was disappointingly light, and carried it up the stairs to her bedroom.

She didn't want to be surprised by Arlene Dawson, who could show up at any time. Best not to let Frankie's mother find her rummaging through the box without first knowing what was inside.

Setting the box on her bed, she looked over her shoulder and saw that Sherlock had followed her up the stairs and was standing in the doorway,

The Labrador had his head cocked, and the sun coming in Josie's bedroom window illuminated the scar under his eye.

"I'm not doing anything wrong," she said. "I just want to help with the investigation. Especially if it turns out the Wolf River Killer had more victims than we thought."

Sherlock didn't look convinced as she reached into the box and pulled out the first thing her fingers settled on.

It was a bright yellow envelope addressed to Maisie

Guinn.

Inside was a birthday card and a wallet-sized school photo of a little girl who looked to be about ten years old. Someone had written *Cousin Darcy* on the back.

Childish handwriting had been used to write out the message inside the card.

> *Dear Maisie,*
> *Hope you have a happy birthday.*
> *Come see me soon. I miss you!*
> *Love, Darcy*

Studying the return address on the envelope, Josie could see that the sender was from Mississippi.

Josie set the card carefully on her desk, then reached back into the box and pulled out a leatherbound journal.

As she opened it, a slip of paper fell out.

It was a clipped copy of an obituary.

> *Ms. Lottie Mae Doyle, age 42, unexpectedly passed away on July 26, 2002. She leaves behind her loving husband, Clark Doyle, and their ten-year-old daughter, Darcy Anne Doyle.*

> *Lottie was born and raised in Buford County, Mississippi. She graduated from Buford High School and then went on to work at Sombra's Gambling Hall & Casino. She was a member of the First Methodist Church of Buford County. Services will be held Saturday at 10:00 a.m.*

Placing the newspaper clipping on top of the birthday card, Josie opened the journal and skimmed through the notes Maisie Guinn had written on the pages within with a blue ballpoint pen.

Her eyes caught a familiar name halfway down the page.

Last night I finally got a chance to speak to Henry Dawson alone. I followed him from Atkins Barrel Works all the way to Sombra's Casino. I asked him if he knew what was in the barrels and he said whiskey. I think he actually believed it.

Josie felt her stomach squeeze as she realized she was reading about Frankie's father.

"Henry agreed to meet with Boone. Now I've got to arrange a day and time. I'm starting to think we might be able to find out what really happened to Aunt Lottie after all."

Running an excited finger under the words, she read the entire passage again, then turned to her laptop, which was open on the desk.

She typed *Darcy Anne Doyle* in the search box, thought for a minute then added *Buford County, Mississippi*.

Within minutes she was combing through an online profile, surprised to see that Darcy also worked at Sombra's Casino, just as her mother had before she'd died unexpectedly, according to the obituary.

Darcy's latest post to social media showed a pretty blonde woman wearing a white collared shirt with a red silk vest and matching bowtie.

Her dark blonde hair had been pulled into a high ponytail and her wide friendly smile displayed a slight gap between her two front teeth.

As she was scrolling through the woman's recent posts, Josie heard the front door open, followed by the unmistakable sound of footsteps in the foyer.

Fear washed over her as frightening images of the night the Wolf River Killer had come into the house and killed both her parents flashed through her mind.

Creeping out into the hall, she looked over the banister to see Arlene Dawson standing in the foyer.

"You look as if you've seen a ghost," the woman called up as she caught sight of Josie's scared face. "It's just me, Granny Arlene. Or would you rather call me Grandma?"

Josie hesitated, willing her thumping heart to slow down as she considered the question.

She knew that biologically speaking, Arlene Dawson was her biological grandmother, but she couldn't imagine calling the woman Granny or Grandma.

Just as she couldn't see herself calling her biological father anything but Frankie, regardless of any blood test.

Dwight Atkins had been the only father she'd ever known and she wasn't about to dishonor his memory by calling another man Dad.

"I'll stick to Arlene," Josie said after an awkward pause.

Accepting the decision without further comment, Arlene motioned for Josie to join her at the bottom of the stairs.

"Frankie asked me to bring you over to the house for dinner," Arlene said. "You can bring your backpack and do your homework over there."

They drove in Arlene's blue sedan toward Chesterville, a suburb outside Memphis.

"You do know that Peyton will be staying with Granny Davis when she arrives on Saturday, don't you?"

When Josie didn't answer, Arlene cleared her throat.

"She'll use the attic room until...well until she leaves."

A surge of resentment pulsed through Josie, who had grown used to staying in the attic room whenever she spent the night. Not only would Peyton be taking on the case Josie wanted to work on, but she'd also be taking over her room.

Arlene sighed.

"I just hope Frankie isn't getting ahead of himself," she said. "Peyton might be coming to help with the agency, but that doesn't mean she's ready to reconcile."

She raised a penciled-on eyebrow in Josie's direction.

"Not everyone wants to take on someone else's child."

Josie's cheeks grew hot with embarrassment and anger.

Was Arlene right? Did Peyton consider her an unwanted burden? Is that why she was staying in Chesterville instead of moving into the house in Barrel Creek?

Another more troublesome thought followed.

If Peyton asks Frankie to choose between me and her, who will he choose? And if he chooses her, where does that leave me?

CHAPTER TEN

The ends of Peyton Bell's short dark hair stuck to her forehead and clung to the nape of her neck as she picked up the last of the boxes and added it to the neat pile intended for storage. Tucker Vanzinger, her former partner at the Willow Bay Police Department, had agreed to come by later to help her transport some of the heavier items before she left Willow Bay on Saturday.

Everything was now ready to go.

Looking around the stripped-down, cleaned-out living room, she felt a wave of panic threaten to wash over her.

Her whole life had been reduced to a pile of boxes and a few suitcases shoved in the trunk of the used Dodge Charger she'd purchased at the police auction the month before.

"What the hell am I doing?" she whispered as she stepped onto the balcony and looked out at the Willow River beyond.

But there was no one there to hear her. No one to assure her she was doing the right thing, even if it meant uprooting her life for a man she had already served with divorce papers three months earlier.

Her mother had died the year before, and the friends and

coworkers she had in town were busy with their own lives. They had their own families to worry about.

Lifting her face to catch the hint of a breeze coming off the water, Peyton sucked in a deep breath, reminding herself that she would need to be patient in the days to come.

Hopefully, the trip to Tennessee would help her figure out if she, too, had a family to worry about.

Of course, she knew the tragedies and traumas that she, Frankie, and Josie had all endured in their own way over the last year would take time to heal.

It would take time to adjust to their new reality and time to figure out how to best move forward, which was why Peyton planned to stay at Granny Davis' house when she arrived on Saturday.

She'd shot down Frankie's unrealistic suggestion that she should move right in without any kind of warm-up.

There is no such thing as an instant happy family. No way to just add water and stir. No easy way to make the past and all the baggage that comes with it just disappear.

There was also no guarantee all their efforts would work in the end. Hence the two small suitcases and the stack of boxes heading for storage.

If it doesn't work out, then I can always come back.

But the thought felt like a lie.

In some cases, there is no going back. Sometimes, if you make a mistake and take the wrong road, you end up lost and broken.

The depressing thought was accompanied by another warm draft of air blowing in from the river but it offered little relief from the heavy, humid air weighing down on her.

Stepping back into the apartment, Peyton shut the sliding glass door and turned on the air, wondering if the current heat wave would follow her all the way up to Memphis.

She took out her phone and typed *Memphis Weather* into her search app and ended up on the *Memphis Gazette* site.

Her heart sank at the headline on the Weather page.

Record-Setting Heat On Its Way to Memphis.

Hoping the Charger's air conditioner would hold out on the drive, Peyton was just about to close the site when she saw the *Breaking News* bulletin at the top of the page.

Woman's Remains Identified at Starbound Casino Building Site.

She quickly scanned the *Gazette* article, which stated that the remains of Valentina Rojas had been found at the site of a new casino being built in Buford County, Mississippi.

Well-known real estate developer Ralph McEwan was funding the project, which was now at a standstill due to the resulting homicide investigation being carried out by the Buford County Sheriff's office

Ralph McEwan's building a casino?

The name triggered a rush of foggy memories.

McEwan had been an up-and-coming real estate developer in Memphis when Peyton had worked for the Memphis PD.

While rumors of shady business dealings had swirled around him, her sole encounter with McEwan involved a frantic 911 call that had ended with Peyton being called to investigate an unnatural death.

She tried to think back to the day she'd responded to the scene but her memories were blurry. It was often hard to remember those days.

Had I been drinking the night before?

She grimaced at the thought.

Of course, I'd been drinking. What night didn't I drink back then?

She'd been a mess at the time, hanging on to her job by a thread as she worked within a Major Crimes task force.

That was around the time I first met Kade.

An image of Special Agent Kade Mabry's thick dark hair and intense blue eyes hovered in her mind. Back then, he'd been new to the Bureau and easier to talk to than the seasoned agents on the task force.

Eventually, they'd become an item. At least, for a while. But her drinking had made it hard to maintain a relationship.

So much hiding and so many excuses and lies.

When she'd gotten the call from her mother asking her to go back to Willow Bay, telling her she needed help getting through her cancer treatments, Peyton had almost been relieved to break things off with Kade.

He had deserved better. Or at least someone who was sober. Someone who wasn't overcome with guilt and regret.

She hadn't actually gotten sober until she'd met Frankie. Not until she'd started going to AA meetings and had finally come to terms with her past.

The fact that she hadn't relapsed again after everything that had happened in the last nine months was a miracle.

Her hand dropped to her midsection at the thought.

"Nine months," she whispered, swallowing hard. "You would have been here by now, if only..."

A stab of loss and longing pierced her heart as she looked toward the spare bedroom that was meant to be a nursery. With a heavy sigh, she crossed the room and closed the door.

CHAPTER ELEVEN

Thunderclouds were gathering outside the office on Winchester Way as Frankie sat at his desk frowning at the browser on his computer screen. Trying to take his mind off his father, he'd been searching for clues to Maisie Guinn's whereabouts for over an hour, trolling through the most popular social media and networking sites without luck.

The reporter hadn't left the usual trail of digital footprints for him to follow and he'd been unable to find any sign of her within the online community.

Although Dusty Fontaine had given him the contact information for Anders Nielson, in hopes the editor-in-chief of the *Memphis Gazette* could provide him a copy of Maisie's resignation letter and a forwarding address, thus far Nielson had ignored his messages and sent his call to voicemail.

Refusing to be ignored, Frankie tapped in another message and was about to press *Send* when the office door opened and Josie stepped inside.

"What are you doing here?" Frankie asked. "Aren't you supposed to be in Chesterville?"

He took in her flushed face and limp, blonde ponytail.

"And where's Sherlock?"

"He's with Granny Davis," Josie said. "Arlene dropped us off at the house then went to the store for ingredients. She said something about making your favorite dinner tonight."

Frankie's frown deepened as he wondered what his mother was planning to cook. Her skills in the kitchen were limited, and he suspected her memory of what he had liked to eat as a child was very different than his.

"How did you get here?" he asked, looking toward the window and the darkening sky.

"There was an old bike in the garage," Josie said. "It was in pretty good shape after I pumped up the tires and put the chain back on. I even found this helmet. It fits perfectly."

She held up a powder pink helmet that Frankie immediately recognized.

"That was Franny's helmet," he said, swallowing the lump that had suddenly materialized in his throat. "It's probably her bicycle out there, too. My little sister was just about your age when she used to ride her bike all around Chesterville and Barrel Creek. She loved that old thing."

Frankie summoned a stern expression to hide the ache that had started up in his chest.

"Just be sure to take care of it," he said. "Now, why'd you want to come over here anyway?"

"I wanted to tell you what I found in Maisie's box," Josie said. "I didn't think it was safe to just leave it on the counter so I took it to my room, and...I found these."

She held up a yellow envelope and a leather journal.

"This is a birthday card from her cousin Darcy Doyle," Josie said. "I already looked her up online and she works at the Sombra Gambling Hall. I was thinking maybe you could ask her for a DNA sample. You know, to test against the bones they found in the river."

Frankie stared at her for a long beat, not sure if he should be mad at her or grateful. He'd forgotten all about the box.

"I was planning to go through that box tonight," he lied. "And if there were any fingerprints on there-"

"We don't even know if she's missing," Josie cut in, sounding hurt. "I doubt the CSI team will be swarming in to have a look at her old notebook anytime soon."

Opening the leather journal, she pulled out a newspaper clip and handed it to Frankie.

"Although, it is kind of weird that her Aunt Lottie worked at the Sombra Casino, too," she said. "Her aunt's obituary said she died *unexpectedly* a year or so before Maisie dropped out of sight, but it doesn't say how she died."

As Frankie read the obituary, Josie tapped on her phone.

"I just sent you a pic of Darcy," she said. "I downloaded it from her socials."

The phone in Frankie's hand emitted a loud *ping*.

Staring down at the image of the smiling blonde woman that had appeared on his phone, Frankie was torn between grounding the teen for riding her bike all over town without permission and asking her if she could go through the rest of the items in the box.

"Good work," he finally managed to say and earned a pleased smile in return. "But next time, I need you to stay put. I don't want anything to happen to you."

He expected Josie to protest, but she only nodded as if her prickly attitude had momentarily been put away.

"I better ride back to the house before it rains," she said, heading for the door. "Maybe I can make it back before Arlene even knows I left."

Frankie lifted a hand to stop her, planning to tell her he would give her and the bike a ride back in the Mustang, but his phone began to buzz in his hand and he saw that Anders Nielson was calling him back.

"Hello, Mr. Nielson?"

By the time he'd arranged a meeting with the editor, Josie had slipped out of the office and was gone.

* * *

The address Nielson had given him matched one of a dozen small commercial warehouses situated downtown on Drummond Street. Frankie checked the street number again, parked the Mustang in front of the building, and climbed out.

A tall man with fair hair and a thin, almost gaunt face was waiting for him at the bottom of a concrete flight of stairs that led up to a little office flanking the warehouse.

"Mr. Dawson?"

Anders Nielson held out a hand, which Frankie shook.

"I'm pleased to finally meet you in person," the editor said. "The *Gazette* has certainly printed enough about you to make me feel as if I already know you."

He patted his pockets as if searching for keys.

"The series of articles on the Wolf River Killer alone increased our circulation by more than ten percent," he said.

Producing a pleased smile, he started up the stairs as Frankie stared after him with raised eyebrows.

Anders Nielson obviously wasn't bothered that the increase in circulation had only been possible thanks to the work of a serial killer and the death of more than a few innocent men and women.

"Well, seeing that I may have helped you sell a few extra papers, I'm hoping you'll help me with a case I'm working."

Frankie tried to keep the sarcasm out of his voice.

"As I said on the phone, I'm looking for a reporter who used to work at the *Gazette*. She seems to have vanished off the face of the earth about twenty years ago. Her name is Maisie Guinn."

The editor reached the landing and turned to look down at Frankie. The smile on his narrow face had dimmed.

"Maisie left the paper a long time ago. She wasn't very happy with us at the time. Felt we weren't supporting her *journalistic integrity* or some such nonsense."

Digging a hand into his pocket, he pulled out a set of keys.

"We closed the *Gazette*'s office over on Arcadia Street a few years ago. Everyone works remotely now, and we outsource printing and delivery, but we rent this warehouse to store our records and archived copies of-"

Nielson's words ended abruptly as he gaped at the lock.

"It's...broken," he said. "Someone's *been here*."

His voice dropped to a panicked whisper as if whoever had broken the lock might still be inside.

He lifted a hand and pushed open the door, which creaked ominously as it swung open.

"Maybe we should call the cops," Frankie suggested.

But Nielson was already stepping into the dark interior of the building, his bony hands balled into fists.

Deciding he had little choice but to follow, Frankie hurried up the steps, wishing he'd thought to take out the Glock that was nestled in the Mustang's glove compartment.

Light flooded the room as Nielson reached for a switch on the wall and led Frankie through a small office that opened onto the bigger warehouse beyond.

Long racks of metal shelves lined the cavernous room, holding box after box of what Frankie assumed to be old files and copies of every edition the *Gazette* had ever published.

"At least they didn't ransack the place," Frankie said, looking around the warehouse, which appeared to be in perfect order. "Maybe they were looking for electronics or something they could sell. Something of value."

He figured the vandals had taken one look at the rows of dusty file boxes and had turned back around.

"You want to call the cops and report the break-in?"

Nielson shook his head.

"Calling the Memphis PD would be pointless," he said.

"Whoever did this is long gone. And I doubt the police would waste much time on a complaint from the *Gazette*. Not after all the stories we've posted about them lately."

A smug smile fluttered on his lips and then was gone as he began to hurry down the aisles, inspecting the long racks of identical-looking boxes.

"I can't see anything missing," he admitted, coming back into the office. "I don't know why anyone would...wait a minute. Someone's been in the HR files."

He stood in the office doorway, staring with dismay at a heavy steel filing cabinet situated against the far wall. The second drawer from the bottom was slightly open.

Crossing the room, he pulled the drawer all the way out and peered inside. After scanning the files, he looked back at Frankie, his face a mask of confusion.

"This doesn't make sense. Maisie Guinn's file is empty."

"Are you sure?" Frankie asked, coming to stand behind the editor. "How can you..."

He looked down at the empty file in Nielson's hand.

"You don't think Dusty could have..."

The words slipped out before he could stop them.

"What does Dusty Fontaine have to do with this?" Nielson asked, instantly on alert.

"Dusty's the one who hired me to find Maisie," Frankie admitted. "He hasn't seen the woman in–"

Nielson held up a hand to stop him.

"I can't believe this," he said, slamming the drawer closed. "I've warned that man that he needs to focus on his own beat. I made it quite clear that I'd given him his last warning after he went rogue on the Wolf River Killer case."

"This isn't business for Dusty, it's personal."

Realizing he'd said more than he should have, Frankie spoke quickly, trying to explain.

"Dusty's not planning to write a story about Maisie. At least, I don't think he is."

But Nielson wasn't listening as he pulled out his phone and tapped furiously on the screen.

"That cat's on his ninth life, and he doesn't seem to realize it," he said, holding the phone to his ear. "You know, Dusty actually asked me if he could cover the story on the remains at the Starbound Casino site over in Buford County. I nixed that idea quicker than-"

He held up a finger, motioning for Frankie to be silent as he left a curt message on Dusty's voicemail asking the reporter to return his call.

Once his phone was back in his pocket, he turned to Frankie and sighed dramatically.

"Dusty Fontaine is an entertainment reporter and a staff writer. Not an investigative crime reporter," he said with a tut of disapproval. "For stories like the one in Buford County, we use stringers. In fact, I've already assigned someone to follow up so that Dusty won't be tempted."

"What's a stringer?" Frankie asked, eager to draw the conversation away from Dusty.

Speaking over his shoulder, the editor led Frankie back toward the office door.

"A stringer's a freelance journalist who writes for different media outlets," he said. "Nowadays you have to be able to take some good photos and videos, too."

He ushered Frankie back onto the landing and looked down at the broken lock with a resigned sigh.

"The *Gazette* can't afford to send out staff writers to remote locations for on-the-ground coverage, so we use freelancers. In the case of the human remains found in Buford County, I've already assigned a reliable stringer."

Nielson headed down the steps with Frankie on his heels.

"This guy's expensive, and he works for a variety of newspapers, so he's busy. We can't afford to use him very often, but he always delivers. And from what I can tell, he has connections within law enforcement, including the FBI. Believe me, Sharkey will get the story if there's one to find."

His phone buzzed just as Frankie opened his mouth to ask Nielson another question.

"That's Dusty," the editor said, his voice hard.

Putting the phone to his ear, he didn't give Dusty a chance to speak before he began his rant.

"I don't know if you broke into the warehouse yourself, or just caused the break-in by running your mouth, but this is your last warning."

He cut off Dusty before the reporter could offer a defense.

"Don't forget there are plenty of younger reporters out there dying to take your spot," he said bluntly. "I've asked Al Sharkey to cover the remains found at the Starbound construction site. And if you aren't careful, I'll be asking him if he wants a job as our next entertainment reporter."

Frankie could hear Dusty's yell of protest as Nielson

tapped on the display to end the call.

"Listen, I know those files are gone," Frankie said as they reached the Mustang. "But you worked with Maisie. What can you tell me about her? You think she split town, or could she have been silenced for writing that story on Sombra?"

Nielson's eyes narrowed.

"That was her big mistake," he said, clenching his fist around the keys in his hand. "I tried to talk her out of going after Sombra. I warned her the man was dangerous."

He shook his head as if still frustrated by her stubborn refusal all these years later.

"The problem was, she had this aunt. I think her name was Lola or Lottie. Something like that. Anyway, her aunt was a dealer at the casino, and she'd told Maisie that Sombra and his associates were dealing in drugs and stolen goods."

Frankie raised an eyebrow.

"And were they?"

"That's what Maisie wanted to find out. She said her aunt was going to help her from the inside, but then she had that freak accident..."

He hesitated as if he wasn't sure he wanted to go on.

"What accident?" Frankie prompted.

Nielson exhaled and rubbed a hand over his narrow jaw.

"Her aunt fell from the roof of the parking garage at Sombra's casino," he finally said. "Maisie really lost it after that. She was sure Sombra was involved. She let it become a personal vendetta and lost all perspective."

"Did the police investigate the fall?" Frankie asked.

He was picturing the newspaper clipping of the obituary Josie had found for Lottie Doyle.

"The local Sheriff, who is still out there as far as I know, was unwilling to call it a suspicious death," Nielson said. "I had no choice but to take the story away from her. When I said I was going to pass it on to Al Sharkey, she hit the roof."

The editor checked his watch again, clearly ready to leave the warehouse and the past behind.

"In the end, Maisie said she would write the story on her own and sell it to the highest bidder. I never saw her again after that, although she did send me a resignation letter a few weeks later. It was in her file."

He looked back at the warehouse, his face grim.

"You know, I always thought she'd come back. Thought she'd come walking through the door of the newsroom someday after making it big. But that never happened, and now the newsroom doors are permanently closed to us all."

"Did the *Gazette* ever print an article on the criminal activity at Sombra's casino?" Frankie asked, not quite buying the man's sentimental routine. "Or on Lottie Doyle's unexplained fall from the parking garage?"

Nielson's shoulders stiffened as Frankie continued.

"Did you just let the story go? Let Sombra off the hook?"

A red flush crept up the editor's neck.

"I didn't trust the police to protect my reporters," he said. "With your past, you should know better than most that you can't always put your trust in local law enforcement."

He turned to meet Frankie's eyes.

"I wasn't willing to have anyone's life on my conscience, so perhaps I did let Sombra and his associates get a free pass from the *Gazette*," he admitted. "But in the end, it's law enforcement's responsibility to stop organized crime. That's what I tried to tell Maisie, but she wouldn't listen."

Something that sounded like bitterness colored the man's voice. Or maybe it was frustration at not being able to change the way the world worked.

Frankie knew that feeling too well.

"What do you know about the remains found at the Starbound Casino site?" he asked as Nielson began to walk away. "Did Maisie ever mention Valentina Rojas when she pitched the Sombra story to you?"

Nielson shook his head, then frowned.

"Are you thinking there's some sort of connection between Maisie Guinn and Valentina Rojas?" he asked. "Maybe a connection that links back to Enrico Sombra?"

The idea seemed to intrigue him.

"I'll run the idea past Al Sharkey," he said. "He's the stringer I mentioned. Maybe he can look into it. Now, I'm on a deadline. I've got to go."

CHAPTER TWELVE

Enrico Sombra sat back in the leather swivel chair and puffed thoughtfully on one of the Cohiba cigars he always kept a ready supply of in the rosewood credenza behind his desk. Normally the sweet, woody aroma of the thrice-fermented Cuban tobacco soothed him, but today the smoke drifting around his head only served to strengthen the headache that was brewing behind his eyes.

As he stubbed out the cigar, he kept his eyes focused on the wide-screen television mounted on the wall, watching yet another special news bulletin on the recent discovery of Valentina's remains.

"...the Starbound Construction project is temporarily on hold as authorities investigate the scene where Valentina Rojas..."

Jamming a wide finger on the remote beside him, he switched off the television just as a black and white mugshot flashed onto the screen.

"That stupid picture...can't they find anything better?"

Valentina had been a gorgeous woman, but now everyone would only remember her as a criminal.

A dead criminal.

Sombra stood and stalked over to the sideboard, pouring

himself a long shot of Kentucky bourbon, savoring the smooth, sweet taste as it slid down his throat.

Crossing to the window, he looked out into the private courtyard he maintained for his personal use, studying the angry, gray storm clouds that had gathered over the wide, muddy river beyond.

Soon it would rain, and the darkness of night would fall over the casino, bringing with it the endless stream of gamblers who had turned his once modest gambling hall into a world-class money-making enterprise.

Despite the opulent office and luxurious surroundings, Sombra never forgot that he'd started out as a penniless nobody running shipments for Joaquin Alvarez.

At the time, Alvarez had been a well-connected drug and weapons smuggler who was feared for his brutal tactics throughout Latin America and the southern United States.

When Sombra had met and married Alvarez's daughter, Yolanda, his new father-in-law had sent him up to Mississippi to open a gambling establishment intended to act as a front for their expanding operations.

But Sombra had bigger ambitions than being a puppet dancing on his father-in-law's strings, and he was soon leading his own syndicate with deep ties in cities all along the Mississippi River and the surrounding states.

Eventually, he'd earned, stolen, and laundered enough dirty money to go clean, and for the last decade, he'd been building a reputation as a legitimate business owner.

He liked to think he'd gone straight, at least for the most part, and he made sure his hands and accounts stayed clean.

In the event he needed a problem solved the old-fashioned way, he would call on certain resources he had at his disposal. People he liked to think of as fixers.

Just as politicians and celebrities relied on fixers to solve their problems and clean up their messes, Sombra used his own network of associates to keep his reputation clean.

But recently the feds had turned up the heat on his operation, coming down hard on the local police and politicians who had long been a part of Sombra's network.

He had to be careful if he didn't want to spend his old age in a federal prison instead of on the golf course.

The news about Valentina had unsettled him, but he couldn't allow himself to react without thinking things through. He couldn't make another mistake.

Looking out at the roses in the courtyard without really seeing them, Sombra thought back to the last time he'd allowed his emotions to take over.

Had it really been twenty years ago when he'd hired young Valentina Rojas to work in the casino as a cocktail waitress?

Of course, he'd known there were rumors. More than one person had whispered in his ear, telling him Valentina had been arrested for solicitation. Accusing her of turning tricks.

But he'd shut down the jealous rumors, unwilling to listen to the ugly lies spread by people who didn't even know her.

She had been special, and he had done what he could to take care of her, despite the risk that Yolanda would find out, regardless of all warnings from those around him.

Valentina had told him that she loved him and that she was grateful for his protection. And then, she'd betrayed him.

At least, that's what he'd thought all these years.

He believed she had turned her back on him without so much as a goodbye. But now he knew the truth.

Or at least, part of it. Now he knew she hadn't left him willingly. She had been *taken* from him. She'd counted on his protection and he'd let her down.

I let someone kill the only woman I ever loved.

The guilty thought stabbed through him like a knife.

And the bastard just left her there to rot in the dirt.

His dazed grief was beginning to simmer into anger.

All these years he'd suffered, thinking Valentina had left him, imagining her with another man.

Pouring himself another long shot of the bourbon, Sombra walked back to his desk and sank into his chair, remembering the night Valentina had disappeared.

I had business to take care of and asked Henry Dawson to take her home, just as he had done a dozen times before.

Dawson had been little more than an errand boy. Someone who picked up shipments and followed orders. And Sombra had trusted him to take Valentina home.

It had been the biggest mistake of his life.

They had run off together, or so his many sources had told him. They'd been seen driving away together, and Henry's truck had been found at the airport.

Neither one had ever come back. They'd probably been

too scared of his reprisal. He had a reputation as a ruthless man.

But I never would have hurt her, even if she wanted to leave. If she'd told me she was unhappy, I would have let her go.

After all, he'd been a married man and a Catholic who went to church every Sunday and confessed his sins to a priest at least once a month. He'd had no intention of leaving his wife or the church for Valentina.

He'd known from the beginning it couldn't last forever.

And after she had gone, after the initial heartache and shock had passed, he had almost convinced himself that Valentina's betrayal had been a blessing and that her actions had saved his marriage and possibly even his soul, if that was still possible.

Jerking up his head as someone knocked on the door, Sombra set his empty glass down.

"Come in," he called, standing as Cordero Torres entered the room. "What did Crockett tell you?"

He stared impatiently at the younger man, whose dark, spiky hair and broad shoulders were covered in raindrops.

The storm must have started.

"The sheriff said the remains were found in a barrel."

Torres couldn't seem to meet Sombra's bloodshot eyes.

"He said they identified her because of fingerprints inside the barrel. They think she tried to claw her way out."

A terrible image filled Sombra's head, and for a moment he thought he was going to throw up all the bourbon he'd sucked down.

Valentina was buried alive in a barrel? Her beautiful body was left to rot over the years, leaving only bones and fingerprints behind to prove that she had ever existed?

Sombra forced down the bile that had risen in his throat.

"There was only one barrel?" he asked. "Only one body?"

"Yep, according to Crockett, that's all they found."

A jolt of fury surged through him at Torres' words.

"So, that means Henry Dawson must still be out there somewhere," he said between gritted teeth. "He must have killed Valentina and then panicked. That must be why he left town and never came back."

He stared at his second-in-command with blazing eyes.

"Now we need to find him and make him pay."

"You do remember that we already looked for him and couldn't find him, right?" Torres asked. "I found out he'd been talking to a reporter in Memphis and I even went to see her, but she hadn't heard from him either."

Sombra reached out and grabbed the front of Torres' shirt, jerking him forward.

"Don't talk to me like I'm some kind of *pendejo*," he spat out. "It was you who told me Valentina left town. You who fell for the lies Dawson fed you before he left."

Releasing his grip on the shirt, Sombra turned away, suddenly unable to catch his breath.

"You okay, Boss?" Torres asked.

He put out a hand but Sombra brushed it away.

"I'm fine," he said, drawing in a wheezing breath. "But Valentina is not. She's dead, and I think Henry Dawson killed her. Now, you find him and bring him to me."

Sombra pointed to the door but Torres hesitated.

"Dawson's son was in here earlier," he said. "He wanted to talk to you and I asked him to leave. I didn't think you-"

"I'd forgotten Henry had a son," Sombra interrupted impatiently. "I want to see him, too. I want to find out everything he knows about his father."

CHAPTER THIRTEEN

Darcy Doyle sat on a wooden bench just outside the employee entrance, smoking a cigarette, and staring out into the rainy evening. She'd only made it halfway through her shift at Sombra's Gambling Hall & Casino and her feet were already killing her. She should have known better than to wear a brand-new pair of pumps when she'd have to be on her feet for eight hours straight.

Taking off her left shoe, she looked down at a tender pink patch of skin on the back of her foot with a grimace.

Her shift didn't end until midnight, and by then she was sure the blister on her heel would be bleeding.

"Are you Darcy Doyle?"

A skinny man with shaggy brown hair and a five-o'clock shadow stood on the sidewalk under the awning, trying to shield himself from the downpour.

"Depends who's asking," Darcy said, eyeing him up and down with suspicion. "And if you're selling something or looking for a date, you can sling your hook somewhere else."

"I'm Frankie Dawson. And I'm a private investigator, not a fisherman, so I don't have a hook."

Darcy lifted an eyebrow.

"You're really a private investigator, like in the movies?" she asked. "Cause you don't look like one."

"What's a P.I. supposed to look like?"

He lifted a hand to wave away a puff of smoke.

"You think I should be wearing a trench coat and a fedora?" he asked. "Or maybe carrying a magnifying glass?"

Resisting an urge to smile, Darcy cocked her head.

"You any good at your job?"

"I found you, didn't I?"

She nodded, now curious as well as impressed.

"What did you say your name was?"

"Frankie Dawson."

He held out a hand but she pretended not to see it. She knew better than to get too friendly with strangers.

"So, Frankie, why'd you want to find me?" she asked, reluctantly sliding over to make room for him on the bench. "And how'd you know I'd be out here?"

"One of the bartenders inside said you'd probably be out here smoking. You do know cigarettes will kill you, right?"

Reaching into his pocket, he pulled out a pack of gum, removed a piece wrapped in shiny foil, and offered it to her.

"I used to smoke, too," he said. "These helped me stop."

"Goodie for you."

Darcy grabbed the stick of gum from his hand and slid it into the pocket of her vest for later.

"I gotta get back inside," she said, stubbing out her cigarette in the ashtray beside the bench. "I'm not sure what you wanted from me, but-"

"I wanted to ask you about Maisie Guinn," he said as she started to get to her feet. "An old friend of hers has hired me to try to find her."

He held out a wallet-sized school picture.

"You're Cousin Darcy, right?" he asked as he turned over the photo to reveal the name written on the back. "Which means your mother was Maisie's Aunt Lottie."

Darcy stared at the photo, not sure what to say.

"I haven't heard from Maisie in over twenty years," she finally managed. "You see, my mother died not long after that photo was taken. And she was the one who kept in touch with Maisie. She was a good aunt...and a good mom."

She struggled to keep the pain off her face. No need to let this stranger know how much those words hurt.

"After Mom died, my father...well, let's just say he wasn't very good at remembering birthdays and sending cards."

Wishing she hadn't stubbed out her cigarette, she took the piece of gum from her pocket and opened the wrapper.

"Dad wasn't very good at much of anything, come to think of it. I guess Maisie and I just sort of fell out of touch."

Frankie nodded slowly.

"It doesn't seem like Maisie kept in touch with anyone," he said. "In fact, there's been no sign of her since she quit the *Gazette* back in 2004."

He lowered his voice.

"That's when she started researching a story on Enrico

Sombra and...disappeared."

Darcy frowned.

"What do you mean, *disappeared*?"

"I think your cousin may have been a victim of foul play," he said. "She was investigating some very dangerous people. Maybe she got too close and they decided to silence her."

The possibility that Maisie could have been killed because of a news article she'd been writing seemed preposterous, only Darcy felt as if she'd heard something similar before."

"Maisie was at my mother's funeral," she said, closing her eyes in an effort to recall that terrible, long-ago day. "I overheard her telling my dad that she thought Mom had been killed. She said she had been asking too many questions."

Darcy imagined she could still hear her cousin's voice.

"Lottie didn't fall off that roof, you know. She was pushed!"

For some reason, those words and the conviction behind them had stayed with Darcy all this time.

"I know it sounds crazy, but she said some very bad men had pushed Mom off the roof. She was convinced of it, but my dad wouldn't listen. He just told her to leave."

Looking into Frankie's eyes, she could see he didn't think it was crazy at all. He believed her. He also looked worried.

"You think Maisie's dead, don't you?" she said. "You think someone killed her like they killed my mom."

He didn't deny it.

"I think it's possible," he admitted. "In fact, I suspect she might have ended up in the Wolf River, along with the bones of some other women I helped to find."

"So, why'd you come here then?" she asked, suddenly angry. "Why come here and stir all this up if she's dead and there's nothing I can do about it?"

"I think there is something you can do," he said.

Holding out a plastic bag, he pointed to the blonde ponytail that was hanging over her shoulder.

"Give me a couple of hairs, preferably with a root attached, and the medical examiner can tell us if Maisie ended up in the river, or if she could still be out there somewhere."

* * *

Darcy shifted on her feet, trying to take the weight off the blister on her heel which was now throbbing, as was the back of her head where she'd yanked out several long, blonde hairs by the root to give to Frankie Dawson.

His words continued to echo through her head as she tried to concentrate on the blackjack table in front of her.

There were three players sitting across from her, all of whom she recognized as regulars, and she was doing her best to keep up with the usual banter.

Shuffling the cards, she watched as the regulars placed their bets, then looked up with a start as Cordero Torres took a seat at the table, setting a stack of black chips in the betting box in front of him.

The casino's chief operating officer kept his eyes on her hands as Darcy pulled a card from the top of the deck and slid it across the table, turning it face up in front of the first player to her left.

Her hands felt strangely clumsy as she dealt face-up cards to the rest of the players, then placed a face-down card in the dealer's box. She risked a quick glance up at Torres as she started to deal another face-up card to every player.

The big man was now staring at her face, assessing her with narrow, suspicious eyes.

Glancing down at the table, he grimaced as she laid a six of hearts over the ten of diamonds in front of him and motioned that he would stand.

"Tough luck," the man beside Torres gloated when Darcy turned over her face-down card, revealing the queen of hearts to go with her nine of spades.

She scooped up the stack of chips in front of Torres, not quite daring to look up into his face, and after he'd set down another stack of chips, she dealt another game.

This time, he busted, earning a snicker from the man beside him, who had gotten lucky with two face cards.

As the couple to his right stood and gathered their chips, and the man to his left turned to order a drink from a cocktail waitress, Torres leaned forward and lowered his voice.

"What did Frankie Dawson want with you earlier?"

His face was as hard as stone.

"I don't know anyone-"

"One of the bartenders told me he was asking about you," he snapped. "I know he was out there...what did he want?"

Darcy froze in mid-shuffle.

She was saved from answering by the arrival of a trio of women wearing *Here Comes the Bride* sashes and carrying two drinks each. As the women settled in at the table, Torres stood, his hand clenching around the few chips he had left.

"I guess I'll have to catch you later."

Watching as he disappeared into the crowd, she checked her watch, relieved to see she only had thirty minutes left until she could clock out.

When she finally pushed through the door into the parking garage, Darcy was limping, her left heel a raw patch of pain.

Once she'd slipped behind the wheel of her little cherry-red Honda, she slid off her pumps with a relieved groan, then dropped her purse on the passenger's seat.

Before she could start up the car, she saw a woman scurry past, her head covered in a red scarf as if she were a movie star who didn't want to be seen or recognized.

But the long, caramel-colored hair that peeked out from under the silky material gave her identity away.

What is the boss' wife doing out here in the parking garage?

Following Yolanda Alvarez with her eyes, she watched as a white Escalade pulled up beside the woman, stopping only long enough to allow her to climb into the passenger's seat before it continued down the exit ramp.

Darcy had gotten only a quick glance of the man behind the wheel but it was enough to make her doubt her senses.

Were her eyes playing tricks on her?

Cause, if I really just saw who I think I saw, then Enrico Sombra's wife must have some sort of death wish.

The thought reminded her of Frankie Dawson's theory.

Had Maisie's investigation into Enrico Sombra caused someone to get angry? Was that why her cousin had disappeared? Was that why her mother had died?

The storm was still raging outside as Maisie drove out of the parking garage and headed toward home, still troubled by the questions and fears that swirled through her mind.

She had often thought of leaving Buford County behind but had never had the courage to take that step. It was all she'd ever known. But maybe now was the right time.

Maybe she should leave town before she had an accident and ended up lying dead and broken on the casino grounds just like her mother had.

Tightening her hands around the steering wheel, she merged the little Honda onto the exit ramp and took the next right onto Cowley Highway.

As she sped along the rain-slicked street, headlights appeared in her rearview mirror.

The car behind her was gaining on her fast.

Darcy checked her rearview mirror and automatically lightened her foot on the gas pedal, realizing she'd been cruising along at ten miles over the speed limit.

Could the car behind her be a police cruiser?

She glanced again in the rearview mirror, well aware that the Buford County Sheriff's Department was notorious for giving exorbitant speeding tickets to boost the department's otherwise modest income.

Seeing no lights on top of the vehicle behind her, Darcy decided the driver must just be in a hurry to get home, and she couldn't really blame them.

It was past midnight and the storm was showing no signs of letting up or stopping anytime soon.

As the shadowy vehicle made a move to overtake her, Darcy kept the Honda's speed steady, giving the car behind her a safe opportunity to pull ahead.

But as the vehicle pulled up beside her, the driver made no move to accelerate past the Honda.

Instead, the car veered sharply toward her.

Darcy wrenched the wheel to the right in a desperate attempt to avoid a collision, causing her front wheels to lock and skid across the slippery pavement.

The car plowed into the soggy bank that separated the road from the woods beyond, eventually jerking to a hard stop that caused Darcy's head to whip back against the headrest.

Staring through the rain-spattered windshield with stunned eyes, she forced her hand to reach for the handle.

The idiot who ran me off the road must be drunk. I'll need to call the police and get them out here to-

The thought was interrupted by the appearance of a man in a black rain parka standing by her window.

He was holding a switchblade.

Darcy instinctively jabbed at the lock, but it was too late. The man was already pulling the door open.

Rain poured in as he dragged her out of the car. Slipping

in the mud, he fell to one knee, pulling her down with him.

Managing to twist out of his grasp, Darcy jumped to her feet and tried to run despite the fact that her shoes were still in the footwell of her car.

As she sprinted barefoot along the muddy ground, she slipped again, this time falling into a rush of rainwater flowing through a ditch beside the road.

When she looked up, the man in the black raincoat was looming over her. He grabbed Darcy's blonde ponytail and forced her head under the fast-moving stream of water, holding it down while she kicked and struggled to break free.

Managing to land a solid kick to the man's knee, she felt his grip loosen, and then she was up and running again, gasping for air as she headed closer to the woods, hoping to lose him in the dark army of trees.

But the ground had grown soggy with thick, heavy mud that sucked at her bare feet, making Darcy feel as if she were running in slow motion.

She screamed out in frustration, willing her tired legs to move, cursing the merciless rain that continued to pelt down all around her as she looked toward the shelter of the trees.

"I can't turn back now. I'm almost there."

The thought was accompanied by the unmistakable sound of wet, sucking footsteps somewhere behind her.

Then an arm was circling her throat. It began to squeeze, and squeeze, and squeeze. And then the rain was gone and Darcy's world went dark.

CHAPTER FOURTEEN

Sherlock lay in a patch of sunlight by the upstairs window, keeping an eye on Frankie, who was still sleeping after coming in late the night before, damp from the rain and smelling of blood. The Labrador had immediately caught the sharp scent of blood from the fresh cut on Frankie's cheek as well as the fainter scent of dried blood on his tennis shoes.

Looking over at the shoes now, which still lay where they had been kicked off just before Frankie had fallen into bed, Sherlock could see the faint rust-colored stains in the tread on the soles to go along with the distinctive odor.

The smell reminded him of the little house with the wilted roses on the porch. The house smelled like fear, blood, and death.

He knew the smell of death better than most dogs, having encountered it at the house where he'd gotten his scar, then again at the Atkins house not long after Frankie had taken him from the shelter.

Now that he was living in the house, the scent of blood had been cleaned away, but the memory of it remained.

As a phone began to buzz nearby, Sherlock lifted his head

and surveyed the small room, which lay between Josie's room and the master bedroom, which had remained empty and unused ever since Frankie and Sherlock had moved in.

Something about the room seemed to make both Frankie and Josie feel sad, and they rarely went inside it.

Reaching out a hand, Frankie felt for the phone buzzing on the bedside table. His voice was dry and hoarse as he tapped on the speaker option and croaked out a greeting.

"Hello?"

"Sounds as if I woke you up."

The caller spoke in a soft, high-pitched voice Frankie seemed to recognize. Sitting up in bed, he rubbed his eyes.

"Rosalie? What time is it?"

"It's after nine and I can't imagine Sherlock hasn't wanted to go out for a walk by now. I figured you'd be up."

Hearing his name and the mention of a walk, Sherlock stood and trotted toward the bed, more than ready to begin his usual morning routine.

"I also thought you'd want to hear the results from the analysis done on the blood found at Evelyn Wright's house," Rosalie said. "We were able to match the DNA from the blood to the DNA found on the toothbrush as well as DNA from her inhaler. There's no question the blood was hers."

Frankie was now sitting on the bed running a hand through his messy hair. He yawned and scratched at the stubble that had grown thick on his chin overnight.

"Well, at least that's one question answered," he said. "We've confirmed the victim was Evelyn Wright. Which we pretty much already knew. Now all we've got to do is find out who attacked her, and why."

Inching closer to the bed to make sure Frankie saw that he was up and ready to go, Sherlock sniffed at a plastic bag lying on the bedside table next to Frankie's phone.

There were several strands of long, blonde hair in the bag, which carried with it a faint but distinct scent of cigarette smoke and shampoo.

"Oh, by the way, I managed to get a DNA sample from Maisie Guinn's niece," Frankie said as he stood and looked down at the bag. "I'll bring it over to you later today if-"

"Hold on, Frankie, Marty's trying to reach me on the other line," Rosalie said. "Just give me a minute."

Frankie sighed and rolled his eyes, but he quickly snapped to attention when Rosalie came back on the line seconds later, her voice suddenly tense and serious.

"We just got a call from the Barrel Creek PD," she said. "A body's been found floating in Shadow Lake. I've got to go."

Lowering the phone, Frankie looked down at Sherlock.

"She hung up on me," he said with a sigh. "You believe that? She calls and tells me they found a woman's body in Shadow Lake and then leaves me hanging. Doesn't even tell me if they have identified the victim yet."

Looking up at Frankie with pleading eyes, Sherlock turned and stared meaningfully at the stairs, but Frankie ignored the look and made his way down the hall to Josie's room.

The dog watched as Frankie quietly opened the door, only

to find the bed empty and Josie's backpack gone.

Returning to his room to pull on jeans and a t-shirt, Frankie shoved his feet back into the blood-stained tennis shoes before going into the bathroom to brush his teeth and wash the dried blood that had crusted on the cut across his cheek.

"I think I may end up with a scar like yours, Sherlock."

He studied his face in the mirror, then shrugged.

"Okay, boy, let's go for a walk."

With relief, Sherlock followed him down the stairs and out the back door into the already sweltering heat.

The puddles of rain from the day before had evaporated, leaving the sidewalk along the road hot and dry against the soft pads of Sherlock's feet.

As they moved along Ironstone Way, Frankie seemed distracted and kept checking his phone.

He didn't seem to notice the car parked along the street a few houses down, although Sherlock looked back several times, curious about the man sitting quietly inside the vehicle watching them.

Once they got back to the house, Frankie poured food into Sherlock's bowl and made himself a cup of coffee.

Turning on the television, he quickly turned up the sound.

"Look at that, Sherlock," he called out. "The news about the body at Shadow Lake has already gotten out."

He sipped at his coffee, then looked down at the Lab.

"Are you thinking what I'm thinking?"

Sherlock didn't look up. He continued eating the food in

his bowl as Frankie began to pace back and forth.

"Because I have a feeling I know who was in the lake," he said, grabbing up his keys. "And there's one way to find out."

* * *

Sherlock was still licking his jowls when the Mustang backed out of the driveway onto Ironstone Way.

He looked out the open window as Frankie stepped on the gas and saw that the car that had been parked along the road earlier was gone.

Sticking his head out the window, Sherlock reveled in the warm breeze as they sped west, turning onto Shadow Lake Trail just short of the state line.

A crowd of reporters and onlookers had already arrived as Frankie opened the door for Sherlock and followed him toward the calm, mirrored surface of Shadow Lake.

"Hold up! That's a crime scene!"

Frankie stopped and turned to stare at a man running toward them. It was the detective who had been at Josie's house the first time Sherlock had seen her.

The scent of death and blood had filled the air that night and the dog associated the man with the pungent scent.

"Where do you think you're going?" the detective asked as he approached. "Why are you even here?"

"It's a free country, Ranger. I can go where I like, and this is public property," Frankie said. "Now, I see your partner over there. Maybe she'll be willing to fill me in on what you guys have found. After all, I am working on a missing person case, and a body has just been found."

Turning on his heel, Frankie continued toward the lake, calling out and waving to a woman standing on the shore.

"Detective Kinsey?"

She glanced up with a grim expression.

"It's her," Kinsey said as Frankie drew closer. "The woman in the lake is Evelyn Wright."

Frankie stopped walking and stared at the detective.

"Are you sure?"

Kinsey nodded.

"We'll need DNA to confirm it," she said. "But I'm sure. Her body was found in the marshy area west of the lake along with several broken strips of oak."

She pointed to a piece of shattered wood on the ground.

"It looks as if they're staves from an oak barrel."

Looking past Frankie, she pointed to a woman in white coveralls at the water's edge.

"Rosalie says she appears to have been in the water for about forty-eight hours," Kinsey said. "Her throat was cut."

"That sounds like Evelyn alright," Frankie said, shaking his head. "What a damn shame."

Picking up a familiar scent on the breeze blowing off the water, Sherlock lifted his nose and let out a plaintive bark.

Death was in the air.

CHAPTER FIFTEEN

Rosalie Quintero knelt next to the dead woman lying on the muddy shore of Shadow Lake and untangled a sharp splinter of wood that had gotten stuck in her dark, matted hair. She held it out to Marty, who had already collected a bag full of similar shards, along with larger pieces of wood that appeared to be broken staves from an oak barrel.

"It looks as if she was put into a barrel and thrown into the lake," she said. "Some of the wood has rotted and I imagine it likely couldn't withstand the pressure."

She looked over her shoulder at Detective Sheldon Ranger.

"Once the barrel started to break apart, splinters of wood got tangled up in her clothes and hair, so it's possible the lab will be able to lift prints. I can also make out some numbers on one of the pieces."

Getting to her feet, Rosalie stared out at the water.

"It looks as if she was killed during a struggle at her house and then dumped in the lake."

"When will you be able to do the autopsy?" Ranger asked. His blue eyes remained fixed on her face as if he were reluctant to look down at Evelyn Wright's body.

"We actually have a heart attack and a drug overdose waiting back at the office," Marty said. "So, I think-"

"We'll do the autopsy this afternoon," Rosalie cut in. "You and Detective Kinsey are welcome to observe."

Ranger nodded, then watched as she and Marty loaded the body onto a gurney and wheeled it toward the van.

"You really like Detective Ranger, don't you?' Marty asked as they hefted the gurney into the back. "Poor Dr. Habersham doesn't stand a chance now."

"Habersham never did stand a chance," Rosalie shot back, her cheeks suddenly hot under her mask. "And I didn't agree to expedite the autopsy because I *like* anyone."

She slammed the door shut and glared up at Marty.

"Whoever killed Evelyn Wright is still out there," she said. "And we need to do everything we can to help the police catch her killer before anyone else ends up in the back of this van."

On the way back to the medical examiner's office, Rosalie remained quiet, finding it hard to process everything that had happened over the last few days.

Could Barrel Creek really be facing another serial killer so soon after Bill Brewster had been taken off the streets?

Pulling up to the medical examiner's office on Sandstone Boulevard, she and Marty unloaded the gurney, bypassing the cooler and taking Evelyn's body straight back to an empty autopsy suite.

"I'll get her prepped," Marty said. "That way we can start the postmortem directly after lunch."

Rosalie checked her watch.

"I'd rather get started as soon as possible," she said, confident she wouldn't have enough of an appetite to eat anytime soon. "Let me know when you're ready to start."

An hour later she was wearing fresh white coveralls and had secured her dark hair under a blue, disposable cap.

Snapping on a new pair of gloves, she positioned herself at the head of the metal autopsy table. Before she could pull back the sheet covering Evelyn Wright's body, a soft knock sounded behind her.

Ranger's big shoulders filled the doorway.

The detective was holding a hand under his nose as if trying to block out the smell of death that permeated the room. Kinsey peered over his shoulder, her eyes wary.

"There are masks and coveralls in the room to your right," Rosalie called out. "We were just getting started."

As the detectives pulled on protective gear, Rosalie folded back the sheet to reveal Evelyn Wright's swollen, discolored face and lacerated throat.

"You can start the recorder now, Marty," she said once Ranger and Kinsey had crossed to stand on the other side of the dissecting table. "I think we're ready."

Marty pressed the RECORD button on a voice-activated device mounted beside the table and she began to speak.

"The decedent is a white female measuring sixty-eight inches and weighing one hundred twenty-eight pounds," she said. "External appearance is consistent with the victim's age, which is known to be forty-two years."

Starting at Evelyn's feet and working her way up, Rosalie

described several minor abrasions and contusions on her body but found no obvious defensive wounds on her arms or hands and no visible blood or tissue under her fingernails.

As she reached the head and neck, Rosalie noted the absence of foam on Evelyn's nose and mouth.

"I doubt she was alive when she went in the water, but we'll look at her airway and lungs when we open her up to see if she sucked in any water."

Finally, she studied the gash across Evelyn's throat.

"Decedent has a sharp force injury to the left side of the neck, transecting the left internal jugular vein," she said. "The cut measures approximately four inches in length beginning on the left side of the neck, at the level of the mid-larynx, with hemorrhaging visible along the wound and in the adjacent subcutaneous tissue."

Motioning for Marty to turn off the recorder, Rosalie glanced up at Ranger and Kinsey, who had both remained quiet throughout the external examination.

"We'll need to open her up and continue with the internal examination, of course," Rosalie said. "But I'm confident the cause of death was exsanguination, which means she suffered a massive loss of blood. Her assailant cut her throat with a very sharp blade, slicing open the jugular, which caused her to bleed out within minutes."

Ranger nodded at her words.

"I'd say the evidence we found at her house certainly supports that scenario," he agreed. "Her killer tried to clean up, then panicked and threw her in the lake."

"Don't forget the barrel," Kinsey added. "Whoever did

this tried to hide the body in a barrel before disposing of it. That certainly is a coincidence considering Evelyn was last seen at the old Atkins Barrel Works the night she went missing."

Her brown eyes were grim over her mask as she spoke.

"And, although the information hasn't been released to the public yet, the remains found in Buford County last week were dumped in a barrel made at the Atkins factory."

Rosalie lifted a surprised eyebrow.

"So, Atkins Barrel Works has a connection to both homicides? That's good, right? It gives you guys something solid to work with, doesn't it?"

Ranger frowned and shrugged his wide shoulders, his blue eyes doubtful as he pulled off his mask and turned away without answering.

By the time Rosalie had finished the autopsy, leaving Marty to prepare the collected tissue and specimen samples to give to the lab, Ranger had left the building.

She thought Kinsey had gone with him until she found her waiting all alone in the hall outside her office.

There was something furtive in the way the detective was pacing back and forth and Rosalie got the impression that Ranger didn't know she was there.

"I wanted to give this to you," Kinsey said. "So you can test the hair for DNA and see if it's a partial match for any of the Wolf River bones."

Looking over her shoulder as if someone might overhear, she held out a clear plastic bag with what Rosalie presumed were human hairs inside.

"Frankie Dawson gave this to me," the detective continued. "He got a voluntary sample from a relative of the reporter he's looking for. A first cousin, I think he said. Maisie Guinn hasn't been seen in twenty years, so-"

"So, he thought she might have ended up in the Wolf River," Rosalie finished for her as she reached for the plastic bag. "I remember talking to Frankie about that."

Studying the strands of long blonde hair inside, she was pleased to see that the roots were still attached.

"I'll get our lab on it right away," she said. "Now that we have our very own rapid DNA machine, we can usually get a profile in a couple of hours instead of waiting weeks for the state lab in Jackson to come back with results."

She turned and unlocked her office door.

"The machine has been a huge help, although we've still got plenty of bones to identify in our cooler," she admitted. "But I'll see if I can get these hairs added to the front of the queue for testing. Once I have the results, I'll let you know."

* * *

It was almost time to go home for the day when Rosalie got the results back from the lab.

She had managed to convince the lead technician to fast-track the testing of the hair sample Kinsey had given her, but her efforts had come to nothing.

"DNA from the hair Frankie gave you doesn't match any of the Wolf River bones," she said, once she'd gotten Kinsey on the phone. "Will you give Frankie the news?"

"Wow, that was quick," the detective said, sounding glum. "I'm actually back at the Shadow Lake scene now working with the CSI team, but I'll let him know as soon as I can. I know he'll be disappointed."

Looking down at the results, Rosalie shrugged.

"Well, there's not much you can do about that. The DNA doesn't lie. And besides, he should be glad. It means there's a chance his missing reporter is still alive."

But Kinsey didn't sound convinced.

"Evelyn Wright was a friend and co-worker of Maisie Guinn,' she said. "And we both saw firsthand what happened to her after she started asking questions."

Rosalie raised her eyebrows.

"You think Maisie Guinn's disappearance twenty years ago really could be related to Evelyn Wright's murder?" she asked. "Isn't that a long time for a killer to lie dormant?"

"Who said he was lying dormant all this time?" Kinsey replied. "Maybe he just hasn't been caught."

The words sent an uneasy shiver down Rosalie's spine.

"Over the last few days I've heard about three women who have gone missing or turned up dead," Kinsey added. "And they all seem to have some sort of connection to each other.

"Think about it. Evelyn Wright went to the Atkins Barrel Works only days before her body washed up on the shore of Shadow Lake alongside a barrel. And her friend, Maisie Guinn, went missing around the same time as Valentina Rojas, who was found buried in an Atkins barrel."

Sitting back in her chair, Rosalie frowned.

"So, there's two women dead and one still missing?" she mused. "Sounds as if we may have a serial case."

"Don't let Chief Pagano hear you say that," Kinsey warned her. "According to him, Maisie Guinn hasn't been designated a missing person. And he doesn't want us to reopen any cold cases right now in any event."

She exhaled in frustration.

"I can try talking to him again, but he already said we have enough fresh cases to keep us busy, and I don't see him willingly changing his mind anytime soon."

Once Kinsey had ended the call, Rosalie slowly lowered the phone, mulling over their conversation, and thinking through the report on Evelyn Wright's autopsy she needed to write up before she could go home.

What had led to the woman's sudden, brutal end?

Impulsively, she tapped on the display and scrolled through the names in her contact list, glad to see she hadn't deleted the number she needed.

She expected the call to go to voicemail, but it was answered on the second ring.

"Agent Mabry? It's Rosalie Quintero calling," she said, adopting the no-nonsense tone she used on official business. "I'm hoping you have time for a quick chat. I want to ask you about a missing woman. A reporter named Maisie Guinn."

CHAPTER SIXTEEN

Detective Nell Kinsey waited until Barrel Creek's small CSI team had finished combing the Shadow Lake shore line and surrounding area before making her way to the gravel parking lot where Ranger was sitting in the driver's seat of the Interceptor typing up his initial report.

Frowning at the laptop screen in concentration, he didn't seem to notice her as she slid into the passenger's seat.

"I'd say it's impossible to know where the barrel went in the water," he said, looking up at the big lake, which was calm and glassy under a hot afternoon sun.

"I've got officers out canvassing the neighborhoods with a public dock or ramp nearby," she said. "If someone was seen dumping a barrel into the water, we'll hear about it."

Her optimistic words contrasted with the bleak tone of her voice, causing Ranger to look over and raise an eyebrow.

"You feeling okay?"

It was the kind of question she didn't expect to hear from her partner. Although they'd been partnered together for almost six months and had developed an amiable working relationship, personal conversations were rare.

"Yeah, I'm *great*," she said, folding her arms over her chest. "Our new chief is treating us like a couple of rookies who can't be trusted to run our own investigation but does that bother me? Not at all. Everything's hunky dory."

Stunned into momentary silence by her sarcastic outburst, Ranger started the engine and pulled out onto Shadow Lake Trail, heading east toward Hastings Highway.

They'd made it halfway to the Barrel Creek police station before he dared to try again.

"Listen, I know Chief Pagano is a little uptight, but he did inherit the mess Shipley left behind, so I imagine he's just trying to get the department back on the straight and narrow. He'll loosen up eventually."

Wondering when Ranger had become the voice of reason, Kinsey opened her mouth to give him a reality check about the odds of Pagano ever becoming a nice guy, then decided not to waste her breath arguing about their new boss.

Only time will tell which one of us is right.

She kept the thought to herself as they pulled into the lot beside the station and caught sight of the tall, lanky figure standing by the front entrance.

"Why is Dawson here?" Ranger asked under his breath. "As if this day hasn't been tough enough."

"If it wasn't for Frankie, we might never have found the scene at Evelyn Wright's house," she reminded him. "We wouldn't have a clue right now who she was or how she ended up in Shadow Lake."

Ranger didn't reply. He just wrenched the door open and climbed out, striding up to the station with only a curt nod of his head to Frankie as he pushed into the lobby.

"What are you guys doing to find Evelyn Wright's killer?" he asked Kinsey as she walked toward the door. "I'm guessing Rosalie did the autopsy today, so did you learn anything new? Anything that points to who did this?"

His reference to Rosalie reminded Kinsey about the news she'd agreed to deliver.

"We're doing everything we can," she assured him, knowing even as she said them that the words were hollow. "We plan to analyze the oak from the barrel. If it's an Atkins barrel, that would link Evelyn's death to Valentina Rojas."

She lowered her voice as two uniformed officers exited the building and walked past them.

"I was meaning to call you," she said. "About the DNA results on Darcy Doyle's hair. It wasn't a match for the bones. Not even a partial. Which means Maisie Guinn wasn't one of the victims in the Wolf River."

Frankie lifted a hand to his chin and rubbed at his stubble.

"I guess that could be considered good news and bad," he said. "She could still be alive. But we don't know for sure."

The lobby door swung open behind her and Kinsey turned to see Barry Pagano standing at the entrance.

The chief of police was taller than Frankie and almost as thin. His jet-black hair was parted in the middle and hung down straight, reaching just past his chin.

The style was unflattering, emphasizing his long narrow

nose and close-set eyes.

"Detective Kinsey, I need to see you and your partner in my office asap," he said, flashing a hostile glance at Frankie. "Don't keep me waiting."

As he spun on the heel of his shiny, black leather shoe and disappeared into the station, Kinsey resisted the urge to give him the one-finger salute.

It wouldn't do for her to let a civilian like Frankie see how much she detested the city's new chief of police.

"I guess I better go," she said, wondering where Ranger was. "I'll touch base with you later."

Frankie hesitated as if he was about to protest, then nodded and made his way down the sidewalk.

As Kinsey went into the station, she stopped by her office, but Ranger wasn't there.

Cursing under her breath, she continued on to Pagano's office, thinking up an excuse for Ranger's absence.

But she needn't have worried. Her partner was already sitting across the desk from Pagano, as were two other men, one of whom she recognized as Special Agent Kade Mabry.

"Why is the FBI interested in Evelyn Wright's homicide?" Ranger asked as Kinsey sank into an empty chair in the corner. "She's a Barrel Creek resident and was found within our city limits, so-"

"We have reason to believe Evelyn Wright's death is related to the murder of Valentina Rojas," Kade said.

He looked over at Kinsey and lowered his head in a nod.

"It's good to see you, Detective Kinsey," he said. "You

missed the introductions. This is my colleague, Special Agent Trent Boone with the Bureau's Memphis Field Office."

Kinsey nodded a greeting at the man, who looked too old to be an active agent considering the fact that the FBI's mandatory retirement age was fifty-seven.

His face was a mask of wrinkles, and his hair, what there was left of it, was gray and straggly, as was his beard.

"Agent Boone, this is Detective Nell Kinsey," Kade continued. "She and Detective Ranger partnered with me on the Wolf River Killer task force."

"I understand you two got Otto Shipley killed," Boone said with a yellow-toothed smile. "Of course, he had it coming."

Leaning forward before Kinsey could respond, Pagano slapped his hand impatiently on the desk.

"Enough talk, the decision's been made," he said, "The FBI and the Buford County Sheriff's office will work together to investigate Evelyn Wright's homicide. End of story."

A flush of anger washed over Ranger's clean-shaven face at Pagano's blunt declaration.

"Can you at least tell us what evidence you have to link the two homicides?" he asked.

"Both women were disposed of in barrels from the Atkins Barrel Works," Kade said without hesitation. "And we've been able to confirm both barrels had the same lot number charred into the wood."

Ranger looked stunned.

"How did you manage to confirm that?"

"I got a call today from Rosalie Quintero, the medical examiner who performed the autopsy on Evelyn Wright," Kade explained. "She found some pieces of oak with the body and was able to relay the lot number to me. I matched it to the lot number on the barrel recovered out at the Starbound Casino where Valentina Rojas' body was found last week."

Turning to Ranger, Kinsey saw that he was just as surprised by the information as she was.

"As I said, I've agreed that we'll partner with the Bureau on this one," Pagano said, narrowing his eyes in Kade's direction. "But I don't want it to get out to the press that these two deaths might be related until we have irrefutable proof. The last thing Barrel Creek needs right now is another serial murder case."

"We'll do our best to keep the possible connection under wraps for now," Kade agreed. "But I should tell you that Rosalie Quintero mentioned there may in fact be a third woman linked to our unsub."

Pagano's forehead creased into a deep frown.

"What woman?"

"A reporter named Maisie Guinn from the *Memphis Gazette*. Apparently, she went missing around the same time as Valentina Rojas," Kade explained. "I ran a search on the name and found some interesting results. That's why I brought Agent Boone along."

All eyes turned to the grizzly man beside him.

"I worked undercover at the casinos along the

Mississippi for years," Boone said as he rubbed a fist over one baggy eye. "That's how I met Maisie Guinn. She was researching a story on Enrico Sombra at the same time I was following up a lead I'd gotten from an informant who worked for Sombra. A man named Henry Dawson."

He shook his head as if the memory still pained him.

"What happened?" Kinsey asked. "With Henry I mean."

"He let me down," Boone said. "He and Maisie both did."

CHAPTER SEVENTEEN

The sun was sinking quickly toward the horizon, leaving a humid, stifling heat in its wake as Frankie drove away from the Barrel Creek police station. He had intended to head over to Granny Davis' house in Chesterville where Josie and Sherlock were waiting, but instead of heading south toward Monarch Avenue, he turned the Mustang's wheels west.

I'll stop by the casino first and give Darcy an update in person. She'll want to know those weren't Maisie's bones in the river.

He'd been stewing over the news that Darcy Doyle's DNA wasn't a match ever since Kinsey had given him the update and he'd already tried calling Darcy's number twice but both calls had gone straight to voicemail.

No doubt she's busy dealing some poor punter a losing hand.

But when he walked into Sombra's Gambling Hall & Casino forty-five minutes later and scanned the row of blackjack tables for her blonde ponytail, she wasn't there.

Stepping into the sports bar, he nodded to the bartender, who was holding a bottle of Kentucky bourbon.

"What will you have?" the bartender asked as he poured a generous amount of the golden liquid into a tumbler.

Tempted to point to the glass of bourbon on the bar, Frankie pulled his eyes away and smiled.

"I was hoping Darcy was dealing over at the blackjack tables tonight," he said. "But I don't see her over there."

"That's because she never showed up for her shift," the bartender replied. "I heard the pit manager trying to find someone to cover it. Now, do you want a drink or not?"

Frankie cocked his head.

"Sure, I want one," he said, pushing back a strand of light brown hair that had fallen into one eye. "But that doesn't mean I should have one."

Turning on the heel of his tennis shoe, he walked out into the pit area and looked down the aisle in the direction of the administration offices.

Sombra might be in there right now. And the casino boss might have the answers to all of Frankie's questions.

He glanced down at his watch, thinking he really should head back to Chesterville.

Josie will be waiting and...

A heavy hand dropped on his shoulder, interrupting the thought. With a hard yank, the hand spun Frankie around to face Cordero Torres.

The casino's COO looked like a bull getting ready to charge. His eyes were narrowed and his nostrils flared in an angry red face that hovered over tense, balled-up shoulders.

"Didn't I already throw you out of here once?"

Speaking in a low, dangerous voice, Torres began to propel Frankie down the aisle.

"I guess you didn't learn your lesson the first time."

Frankie's hand automatically reached up to touch the cut on his cheek, which was still tender

"I'm not looking to cause any trouble," Frankie said, offering no resistance as Torres used his broad shoulders to plow a path for them through the crowd. "I was just looking for one of the dealers who-"

"I know who you were looking for."

The words were gritted out between clenched teeth.

"And I know why you're here. You want to stir up old problems that we buried a long time ago."

The man's breath was hot in Frankie's ear.

"You want to stick your nose in our business, just like your old man did. But he made a mistake...and so have you."

Before Frankie could ask him what he was talking about, Torres pushed him forward into the reception area of the administration office.

The door to Sombra's inner office was open.

A slim man in an impeccably tailored suit stood in the doorway. His dark hair was slicked back from a face so hard Frankie thought it could have been chiseled from granite.

"Where's your father?" the man asked.

The question hung heavily in the quiet room as Frankie stared at Enrico Sombra with a dumfounded expression.

"Mr. Sombra asked you a question," Torres growled behind him. "He wants to know where your father is."

"Join the club," Frankie said, shaking his head. "I haven't seen the man since I was seventeen years old."

Taking a step back from the anger he saw in Sombra's

eyes, he bumped into the stone wall of Torres' chest.

"Join me in my office, Mr. Dawson," Sombra said. "I believe we have business to discuss."

He turned and walked back toward a large, polished desk that sat in the place of honor near the back wall like a judge's bench in a courtroom.

Only in this courtroom, I get the feeling Sombra is gonna be judge, jury, and executioner all rolled into one.

Following the older man into the luxurious office, he suddenly wished he had told someone where he was going.

Peyton wasn't scheduled to arrive in Memphis for two more days, and his mother and Josie probably thought he was at his office, or over at the Atkins' house on Ironstone Way.

If he didn't show up by bedtime, they may even wait until the next morning to send out an alarm.

By that time, he might be the one floating in a barrel.

"How much is it going to cost me?" Sombra asked as he took a seat behind the big desk. "What's the going rate these days for ratting out your own father?"

Torres put a hand on Frankie's shoulder, pushing him onto a chair across from Sombra's desk before taking up a position behind him.

"I told you I don't know where my old man is," Frankie said, anger now mixing with his fear. "And if I did, I wouldn't tell you. I don't want your dirty money, and I'm no snitch."

The casino owner leaned back in his big leather chair and studied Frankie with assessing eyes.

"Maybe not," he finally said. "But your father was. He not only was a snitch, he was also a traitor. Maybe even a killer."

Frankie tried to jump up at the accusation but Torres put a heavy hand on his shoulder to keep him in the chair.

"You really don't know where your father is, do you?" Sombra asked. "Because he ran out on you, too. How old did you say you were, seventeen? Is that when he left town, leaving you and your mother behind? Do I have that right?"

A dull ache started up in Frankie's chest as the words conjured up memories he'd tried so hard to put behind him.

"I thought that was how it happened," he admitted as he reached into his pocket and pulled out a stick of gum.

Holding it in his hand, wishing it was a cigarette, he tried to decide how much he should say.

"For the last twenty years, I believed my old man skipped town with some young chick he'd picked up at the casino," he finally said. "I was pissed off that he'd cheated on my mom and left me and my sister behind. I told anybody who'd listen that I never wanted to see him again."

"And now...?"

Sombra lifted an eyebrow.

"You've had a change of heart?"

"I'd call it a change of mind," Frankie corrected him. "Ever since I found out that the woman I saw him with never left town after all, that she ended up dead in a field..."

He shook his head and looked down at his hands, not noticing the anguish that had taken over Sombra's face.

"After I saw the photo of Valentina Rojas on the news, I

recognized her as the woman my father had been with the last night I'd seen him," Frankie said. "She was the one I thought he'd run off with. Only, I was wrong. She hadn't run off with anyone. She was dead. All that time..."

Looking up at Sombra, Frankie was surprised to see the man's fists clenched on top of his desk, and his dark eyes blazing with emotion.

The calm, cool façade he'd been wearing was gone.

"So, you admit your father was with Valentina before she went missing," Sombra said. "You admit that after that day, he never dared show his face again."

He brought his fists down hard on the polished wood.

"He knew if I found out what he'd done...

"Hold on just a minute," Frankie said, throwing off Torres' hand and jumping to his feet. "There's no proof my old man had anything to do with her death. In fact, he could be dead, too, for all I know."

Sombra's mouth spread into an angry smile.

"Well, there's one thing I can promise you. If Henry Dawson's not dead now, he soon will be."

* * *

By the time Frankie pulled up to Granny Davis' house in Chesterville, full dark had fallen and his stomach was protesting the lack of any food since that morning when he'd scarfed down a bowl of the sugary-sweet cereal Josie had talked him into buying the last time they'd managed to make it to the grocery store.

Already salivating in anticipation of the lasagna Arlene had promised to keep warm on the stove for him, he climbed out of the Mustang and headed for the back door.

"Frankie?"

The voice came from a black SUV parked along the curb. In the darkness, and in his haste to get to the promised lasagna, he hadn't noticed the vehicle, or the two men sitting inside.

"Agent Mabry?"

Frankie stared at the dark-haired man who was smiling at him from the open driver's side window.

"What are you doing here?"

He hadn't seen the FBI agent since they'd closed the Wolf River Killer case. And the man in the passenger's seat didn't look familiar at all. Why would they be sitting outside his granny's house after dark?

"Call me Kade," the agent said. "I'd say we've been through enough together to be on a first-name basis."

"I guess you're right about that."

Looking back at the house, he could see a shadow passing by the lighted window. Someone was in the kitchen.

"You guys want to come inside?" he asked, hoping that his mother had saved a big enough piece of lasagna to split three ways. "I've got two old women, a teenager, and a hungry dog waiting inside for me, so-"

"No, we can't stay," Kade said. "Just wanted to let you know the Bureau's going to be partnering with the Barrel Creek PD on a case I hear you're working, too."

He motioned toward the back seat of the SUV.

"Take a load off. This shouldn't take long."

Reluctantly, Frankie climbed into the back.

"This is Special Agent Trent Boone," Kade said as the man beside him turned to nod at Frankie. "He's worked undercover all up and down the Mississippi. Turns out he knows that reporter you've been looking for. She'd been feeding him information before she went missing."

Frankie leaned forward, all thought of lasagna gone.

"You knew Maisie Guinn?"

He stared at the older man, who took out a cigarette then slowly set about lighting it and taking a long drag.

"I heard about a reporter asking questions at Sombra's casino," he said in a husky voice. "I was working undercover and in pretty deep with a group supplying drugs to dealers in most of the casinos and clubs along the river."

Cigarette smoke drifted into the backseat, making Frankie's eyes water as he listened.

"I made contact and tried to warn her that she was putting herself in danger," Boone said. "I risked my cover to tell her that she needed to back off before she got hurt."

He tapped the ashes of his cigarette out the car window.

"But she was on a mission. Wouldn't listen to me or anyone else," he said. "She was convinced Sombra was behind her aunt's death, and she told me straight out that she was set on exposing him for what he really was, regardless of the danger."

After pausing to emit a hacking cough, Boone continued.

"She started feeding me information she was getting about the operation," he said. "Turned out she was getting it from a low-level runner for Sombra's group. A guy named Henry Dawson. Kade tells me that's your old man."

Frankie nodded, feeling slightly nauseous from inhaling the second-hand smoke on an empty stomach.

"Eventually, I started getting info from Henry directly," he said. "He told me he had two kids and he wouldn't want these lowlife dealers selling them drugs. He said he wanted to take them off the streets and out of the clubs and casinos."

Another cough erupted, causing Frankie to wince.

Now I remember why I quit smoking that poison.

He waited until the fit had passed, wanting to hear the end of the story. The way Boone was telling it, he could almost believe his father had been trying to do the right thing.

"To make a long story short, I bought your old man's act hook, line, and sinker. I thought he was going to help me get the evidence I needed to bust the ring, including Sombra."

Boone suddenly sounded bitter.

"I even started talking to the federal prosecutor about bringing the case to a grand jury," he said. "I guess you can imagine it pretty much tanked my career when Henry suddenly bailed on me, leaving me looking like a sucker who'd been duped all along."

"What do you mean duped?" Frankie asked.

He glanced over at Kade, who wore a guarded expression.

"Are you saying my father set you up?"

"No, I'm saying he let me down."

Boone snorted with disgust.

"My SAC and the prosecutor were primed and ready to proceed, but I had jack-all to give them after your father split town. I told Maisie what he'd done and she begged me not to give up. Said she'd find Henry and talk him around."

Stubbing out his cigarette, he looked back at Frankie.

"I guess you know what happened next."

His face creased into a patchwork of lines and furrows as he frowned, exhibiting the inevitable fallout from a lifetime of heavy smoking and hard living.

"After she went AWOL, too, I stopped by her office and found out that she had resigned," he said. "Some skinny reporter wearing cowboy boots claimed she'd gone missing, but I saw the resignation letter in her employment file."

"You never suspected Sombra came after them?" Frankie asked. "You never opened up an investigation?"

Digging for another cigarette, Boone shook his head.

"I was sticking to Sombra like glue around the time Henry up and vanished," he said. "I had eyes all over. No way he put out a hit on the guy and no one spilled the beans."

He waved his lighter in the air for emphasis.

"Besides, when I called Henry's house looking for him, his old lady said he'd run off with a younger woman. Said she hoped he'd never show his face again."

Frankie's chest tightened at the words, but he stayed silent as Boone continued.

"And with Maisie officially resigning, saying she wanted to find new opportunities with a company who would support her values or some crap like that, I was left holding an empty bag," Boone said. "The operation pretty much fell apart after that and I was *reassigned.*"

Frankie watched with dismay as the agent stuck the new cigarette between his lips.

"And you never looked into Maisie's claims that her Aunt Lottie had been killed?" he asked. "Because Lottie's daughter works at Sombra's Casino now and she seems to think it's highly likely."

"I don't know anything about Lottie or her daughter," Boone said, sounding irritable. "But with the local cops on Sombra's payroll, I'm not surprised they would call any crime committed at the casino an *accident.*"

The comment earned a raised eyebrow from Kade.

"What do you mean the local cops are on Sombra's payroll?" he asked. "Which cops?"

"The Buford County Sheriff's Department," Boone said. "They were on the payroll back then and from what I've heard, Sheriff Crockett has carried on the tradition."

Figuring the agent was probably right about Crockett, Frankie still couldn't buy into the rest of the man's theory.

"I think you got it wrong, Agent Boone," he said. "I'm pretty sure you and I both did."

He leaned against the seatback and exhaled.

"Back then I was young and hot-headed. I guess I may have jumped to conclusions," he admitted. "When I saw my father leaving the casino with Valentina, I told my mom and she told you. She also left a pretty explicit voicemail telling him not to come home. He never did."

Echoes of his mother's angry voice sounded in his head.

"The woman I saw with my father was Valentina Rojas and we know she was murdered. Maybe she wasn't the only one. Maybe my old man was murdered, too."

Frankie was now certain he'd made a terrible mistake.

"What if Maisie found out what happened to them? Maybe whoever killed them decided to shut her up, once and for all. And when Evelyn Wright started asking questions, the killer could have panicked and killed her, too."

CHAPTER EIGHTEEN

Albert Sharkey stood beside the roulette table eyeing the black and red rectangles with greedy pleasure. Plucking a single hundred dollar chip off his stack, he placed a straight-up, inside bet on red fourteen, then rubbed his hands together, anticipating the thirty-five hundred dollar payout he stood to receive if the ball fell in his favor.

"Place your bets!"

His heart beat faster at the croupier's call.

Watching as the roulette wheel spun in one direction, and the ball flew around the outer track in the other direction, he eyed the dollar chips of his fellow gamblers with disdain.

Why bother betting if it won't hurt to lose? The pleasure is only intensified by the risk of pain.

"No more bets!"

The croupier waved a long arm over the table as the ball began to lose momentum, and Sharkey held his breath as it bounced several times and then landed in a pocket.

"Eight, black, even!" the croupier called in a cheerful voice as he set the marker on the four and swept away the hundred-dollar chip that had belonged to Sharkey only seconds before.

Scooping up his remaining chips, he turned away from the table just in time to catch a glimpse of Yolanda Alvarez, half-hidden in a noisy group of gamblers walking toward the exit.

Now, where is she going at this time of night? And why is she trying to use the crowd as cover? What's she hiding?

He picked up his tumbler of whiskey, drained the last few drops, then set it on the nearest table and headed after her.

She'd made it all the way to the parking garage before the crowd dissipated and she was left walking on her own.

Sticking to the shadows, Sharkey trailed after her, not sure who he was going to see until a familiar white Escalade glided into view and slowed beside Yolanda.

As she climbed into the big SUV, he wondered how he might use the information he'd discovered to his advantage.

Taking out his phone, he recorded a video of Enrico Sombra's wife leaning over to plant a kiss on Ralph McEwan's cheek, then watched as the vehicle disappeared down the exit ramp, shaking his head in disgust.

She's just like all the rest. Just another cheating, lying traitor who can't be trusted. But then, that might just work in my favor.

He dropped his phone into his pocket and walked back toward the casino, tempted to go back to the roulette table and try to win back what he'd lost.

But he was tired after the busy week, and he still needed to complete the article due for publication in the Sunday edition of the *Memphis Gazette*.

Best to go home and get some rest.

Circling around the side of the building, he flagged down a long, black town car waiting in the taxi queue.

"Charrington Road," he said to the driver as he climbed into the comfortable back seat. "Take the highway."

Fifteen minutes later they were pulling up to the big, comfortable house he'd bought with cash a decade earlier.

Surveying the property, he reminded himself that his winnings at the tables allowed him to live a lifestyle his work as a stringer could never provide.

The many risks he'd taken over the years, both at and away from the gaming table, had certainly paid off.

After giving the driver a twenty-five dollar chip in lieu of a tip, Sharkey crossed the lush yard to the porch and collected the unopened edition of the *Gazette* before letting himself into the house.

Once inside, he walked straight to the bar and poured a long shot of whiskey into a tumbler.

Sliding the *Gazette* out of its plastic bag, he opened the paper, looking eagerly for his latest article.

The pittance Sharkey earned from researching and writing freelance articles each month was laughable compared to the windfall he could take home from the casino on a single lucky night at the tables.

But the satisfaction of seeing his very own byline on the front page of a newspaper distributed to tens of thousands of people every week was priceless, as was the opportunity to put his own spin on any article he wrote.

Sharkey folded the paper and dropped it on the table, knowing he would clip out the article he'd written later and add it to the deep pile he kept in his study for posterity's sake.

But first, he wanted to take a quick trip out to the cellar, just to make sure everything was in order.

Heading through the kitchen and out the back door, he flipped on the lights in the backyard and crossed to the cellar doors, which had been recently painted a deep, forest green.

The double doors were secured with an old-fashioned padlock, which Sharkey deftly removed before pulling the right door open. He stepped onto the top step and gazed down into the dark space below with some trepidation, half-expecting something or someone to jump out at him.

But the cellar was quiet, and the only thing that rose up to greet him was a strong, pungent smell.

As he started down the stairs, he flipped the light switch, illuminating the long low space with the light from a single bulb, which hung from the ceiling.

Several barrels had been stacked along the wall.

The barrel he'd opened two nights earlier stood closest to the door. Stepping down onto the concrete floor, Sharkey crossed to it and laid a hand on the lid, tracing the words that had been charred into the wood.

Atkins Barrel Works
Lot number #ABW: B04C24

Bending over, he rested his ear against the side of the barrel, listening for any sound or movement from within.

"Darcy?" he whispered.

After a moment of total silence, he tried again.

"Can you hear me?"

Still nothing, just as he'd expected.

The barrel was still there and Darcy Doyle was inside, but she wouldn't be causing any more trouble.

All Sharkey had to do was wait until the heat around Evelyn Wright's death had cooled down and then he would think about taking the barrel somewhere he could bury it.

The barrel he'd used to bury Valentina Rojas hadn't been found for twenty years, so there were pretty good odds this one wouldn't be found for some time.

Of course, he knew he couldn't put it in the lake.

I learned my lesson about old wood and water with Evelyn.

The barrel Evelyn Wright had been in had broken apart almost immediately. But then, it had been sitting in the cellar for too long, without the proper care that barrels needed to stay strong and water tight.

No, he couldn't risk another screw-up like Evelyn. There were already too many people searching for him.

The police, the feds, and Frankie Dawson.

And once they realize Darcy Doyle is missing...

Running a hand over the scratched wood, Sharkey felt a pang of anxiety at the thought of Frankie Dawson.

The man had taken down the Wolf River Killer as well as Otto Shipley and his corrupt cronies. He didn't give up easily.

So, I'll have to come up with something I can use against him. Some sort of leverage.

Thinking back to the article he'd written and sold to

several local papers about the Wolf River Killer's crimes, he pictured the photo that had accompanied the article in the *Gazette*. The photo of the Atkins girl. The girl Frankie had risked everything to save.

"Josie Atkins," he whispered. "Yes, that was her name."

CHAPTER NINETEEN

Josie woke to the sound of birdsong and sunshine outside her bedroom window. Opening one sleepy blue eye, she looked at the clock on her bedside table, then sat up with a start. Had she missed her alarm? Or had it failed to go off for some reason? Her feet were already on the floor when she remembered it was Friday.

There's no summer school on Fridays, dummy!

Falling back onto the bed, she considered going back to sleep, then decided she might as well get up and make the most of the summer day.

Unlike most of the other kids in Barrel Creek, she hadn't gotten the chance to spend the summer swimming at the lake or going on a family vacation.

Even if I didn't have to go to summer school, I couldn't go on a family vacation. You need a family to do that.

The depressing thought followed her into the hall as she headed toward the bathroom.

She stopped in front of a framed photo of her standing with her mother and father under a giant tree. The photo had been taken two summers earlier, back when she'd still been a regular kid, and they'd gone to Redwood National

Park.

But that had been before her father had gotten sick and before the Wolf River Killer had ended his life, along with her mother's.

And mine. Don't forget Bill Brewster ended my life, too. At least, the life I had in that picture. That life died along with my parents.

Once she'd brushed her teeth, washed her face, and pulled on a pair of purple shorts and a *Girls Rock* t-shirt, Josie went downstairs to the kitchen, where Frankie had the television turned to the morning news.

Looking out the kitchen window, she could see the man she now privately thought of as her bio-dad pacing back and forth on the lawn, speaking to someone on the phone as Sherlock watched from the shade of the porch.

As she reached for a box of sugary cereal her mother had always refused to buy, Josie found herself listening to a live report from the shore of Shadow Lake.

"...woman found yesterday in Shadow Lake has been identified as Barrel Creek resident, Evelyn Wright, a former photographer with the *Memphis Gazette*," the reporter was saying. "Sources within the BCPD believe that she was in the water less than forty-eight hours and-"

Josie turned off the television and carried her cereal to the table, not ready to hear about another killer in Barrel Creek and another dead body found only a few miles away.

Before she could sit down, she noticed that Sherlock's food bowl was still clean and empty.

With a put-upon sigh, she crossed to the back door and

pulled it open, then froze as she heard Frankie leaving what sounded like a frantic voicemail.

"Darcy, I'm really getting worried now. I went by the casino last night and they said you never showed, and now this is the sixth time I've called and...wait, maybe it's seven times. Anyway, please call me back as soon as you get this message and let me know that you're okay."

"Has something happened to Darcy Doyle?" Josie asked as soon as he'd lowered the phone.

Frankie whirled around, revealing worried eyes.

"No, of course not," he said. "You know me, always worrying about stuff that ends up being nothing."

"I hope you weren't trying to play poker with that face when you went to the casino last night," she said, crossing her thin arms over her chest. "Cause it definitely wasn't made for bluffing."

She tried to summon a sarcastic smile, but it trembled and died away on her lips.

"This is my fault, isn't it?" she said. "I was the one who found the birthday card and the school picture. I was the one who told you to get the DNA from her."

"Nothing has happened to Darcy," Frankie insisted. "At least, not that I know of. But even if it had, it wouldn't be your fault. You were trying to help with a missing person investigation. You can't be blamed for that."

But Josie wasn't so sure.

She finished her cereal in silence and was still brooding when Frankie grabbed the car keys off the counter and looked at her expectantly.

"You ready to go?"

When she looked at him blankly, he raised an eyebrow.

"You have a therapy appointment, remember?"

Josie hadn't remembered, but she skipped her usual sarcastic comeback and followed him out to the Mustang, staring silently out the window as they drove to Beth Hurley's office.

But once she was seated safely behind the closed door of the therapist's session room, she could no longer hold back the tempest of grief and fear swirling inside her.

As Josie vented about everything from hating summer school to dealing with her recurring nightmares about the Wolf River Killer, Dr. Hurley sat quietly listening.

The therapist, an attractive blonde woman with a definite cool-mom vibe, never offered the pointless advice most adults were usually ready to hand out.

Instead, she asked questions that made Josie think. Questions that never seemed to have only one right answer.

"Before I go, can I tell you something else, Dr. Hurley?"

The therapist, who had been getting to her feet, settled back into her chair with an agreeable nod.

"It's just, I don't know how I feel about Frankie's wife moving up here," Josie said. "Her name is Peyton, and she'll be here Saturday."

She kept her eyes on her hands, which lay in her lap.

"I guess I feel like things might...change."

"What is it you imagine will change once she arrives?"

Josie bit her lip as she considered the question. She'd imagined a lot of things would change once Peyton showed up, and none of the changes were good.

"I guess, maybe I'm worried we won't get along," she said. "What if she doesn't like me? Or, maybe..."

Her cheeks turned pink as Dr. Hurley waited.

"Maybe Frankie won't have time for me anymore."

Once she'd actually said it out loud, the idea seemed childish and somehow selfish.

"I suggest you share your fears with Frankie before his wife arrives," Dr. Hurley said. "That might give him the opportunity to tell you how he's feeling, too. Less chance for miscommunication if you talk about it openly."

Josie nodded and got to her feet.

But when she climbed back into the car, Frankie was on his phone, and by the time he'd ended his call, she was feeling moody again.

"So, how'd the session go?' he asked. "Anything I should know about? Anything you want to tell me?"

"Not really," Josie said, turning again to stare out the window, her mind turning back to Darcy Doyle. "But if you don't mind, can you drop me off at the library? I need to do some research."

* * *

Josie sat in front of a microfiche machine at the Chesterville Public Library, scrolling through old articles in the *Memphis Gazette*, looking for any mention of Maisie Guinn's disappearance or Lottie Doyle's death.

Her shoulders and neck were aching, and her eyes were

beginning to burn when she saw an article about a drug bust down at a Biloxi casino. Her eyes stopped and studied the article's byline.

Albert Sharkey. Why does that name...

Suddenly, it came to her. Maisie had referenced that same name on the last page of the journal. Josie could still picture the words, which had been written in blue ink.

Follow up with Albert Sharkey.

She stared at the byline, wondering if the man named Sharkey had been involved in the research Maisie had been conducting prior to her disappearance.

After all, the article he'd written was focused on events in the regional casino industry.

Turning back to the microfiche machine, she began to look for other articles written by Albert Sharkey, expanding her search to include other major newspapers in Tennessee and Mississippi, hoping to find a headshot of the man.

Her head was beginning to ache by the time she pushed back from the machine and looked around.

She'd managed to find eight articles with the Albert Sharkey byline, although none of them offered an accompanying headshot of the writer.

All eight articles appeared to have some connection to the casino industry or organized crime, but the last article she'd found was the most troubling, at least to Josie.

The headline announced a new organized crime task force in the greater Memphis area that would include several local police departments and agents from the FBI's Memphis field office. But it wasn't the subject of the article that troubled Josie. It was the black and white photo that accompanied it.

At first, she hadn't recognized the much younger Peyton Bell standing next to a tall, dark, and handsome FBI agent.

But on closer inspection, she could make out Peyton's fine cheek bones and distinct amber eyes under her cap of dark hair. She could also see the strapping FBI agent's hand resting possessively on Peyton's arm.

Squinting to see the tiny caption under the photo, she realized that the man in the photo was Special Agent Kade Mabry, the same agent who had swooped in to help Frankie solve the Wolf River Killer case.

An uneasy feeling settled in Josie's stomach as she studied the lovestruck look on Kade's handsome face.

Deciding she'd had enough research for one day, Josie left the library, walking quickly back to the little house on Monarch Avenue where Granny Davis had lived for the last fifty years or more.

She stopped short when she saw a white Dodge Charger sitting in the driveway. She'd heard Frankie mention just such a car the day before when he was on the phone.

It could only mean one thing. Peyton had arrived early.

Anxiety surged through Josie at the unexpected surprise, sending her heading around the back of the house, hoping to delay the inevitable reunion and all the awkward small talk that would go with it.

Creeping through the back yard, she was careful to avoid the rose bushes Granny Davis still lovingly attended despite the dementia that made it more difficult every day.

She stopped and listened outside the open back window.

"Thanks for letting me stay here, Granny Davis."

Josie crouched down as Peyton's voice drifted out.

"I think I'll go upstairs and wash up before I go to the office. I was planning to get here until tomorrow, so he'll be surprised to see me."

After Peyton's footsteps faded up the stairs, Arlene came to stand at the window, looking out at the roses as she spoke.

"I can't tell if they're officially back together or not," she said, looking back to where Granny Davis sat at the kitchen table. "Sometimes she acts as if they're just business partners. She could be seeing someone else for all we know."

Her voice had taken on the disapproving tone Josie had come to know too well.

"I just hope she doesn't break his heart again," she added with a sigh. "I don't know if he'd survive another break-up like that last time."

Arlene turned away from the window, leading Granny Davis into the living room to watch the afternoon shows they enjoyed, leaving the coast clear for Josie to slip inside without being seen.

Before she could scurry across the room to the stairs, she heard a soft *ping*. Looking around, she saw a phone in a bright red case lying on the old wooden table.

Her eyes dropped to the message on the screen.

Let me know when you're free to talk.

Her eyes widened as she saw the name of the sender.

Kade Mabry certainly isn't wasting any time.

Footsteps on the stairs sent Josie running for the door. She wasn't prepared to face Peyton now. Not when it looked as if the ex-detective was set to break Frankie's heart.

She hadn't considered the possibility that Frankie and Peyton might never officially get back together, and she found the thought more than a little unsettling.

While only that morning Josie had been worried Peyton would take Frankie's attention away from her, she was now beginning to fear that Peyton might not take him at all.

Maybe she plans to work with Frankie and see Kade on the side.

The thought made her stomach hurt.

She didn't want her bio-dad's heart to be broken.

But what could she do? She was still just a teenager, and while her research skills were getting pretty good, the reach of her influence was limited due to her age.

You can only get so far and go so fast on a bicycle.

Walking back to the driveway, Josie checked the time, wondering if Frankie would be in his office.

She could ride Franny's old bike there and tell him...what?

There was no proof anything was going on. Just an old photo of Peyton and Kade together in the *Gazette* and a generic message asking to talk.

But as she stood next to Peyton's Charger and stared down at the passing time, she had a thought.

My watch has GPS tracking enabled.

She had used the feature once before when trying to

remember where she'd left the watch after taking it off to help Frankie give Sherlock a bath.

Maybe it could help me conduct a little remote surveillance.

Slipping off the watch, she leaned into the open window of Peyton's car and tucked it under the tattered owner's manual in the Charger's glove compartment.

–

CHAPTER TWENTY

The door to Dawson & Bell Private Investigations swung open to reveal Frankie Dawson sitting at his desk and Sherlock curled up in his usual spot underneath the air vent. Dusty Fontaine stood in the doorway, his eyes bright and his thin face flushed with emotion, as Frankie looked up in alarm.

"I guess you got my voicemail about Evelyn Wright?"

Striding into the room on his usual two-inch heels, the reporter slammed the door behind him and sank into the chair across from Frankie with a dramatic sigh.

"Even if I hadn't, it's all over the news," Dusty said. "Although, the *Gazette* was late to break the story."

He picked up a folder off the desk and began to fan himself vigorously as if overcome with heat and exertion.

"When you told me Evelyn had gone missing, I was sure she would turn up," he said. "I thought maybe she'd gotten scared and had decided to go into hiding."

Brushing back several long strands of gray hair that clung to his sweaty face, Dusty dropped the folder on the table.

"I'm afraid Evelyn Wright might not have been the only

victim of foul play this week," Frankie said. "It looks as if Maisie Guinn's cousin, Darcy Doyle, is missing. I haven't been able to reach her since she gave me some of her hair."

The creases on Dusty's forehead deepened.

"I needed the hair so the M.E. could compare Darcy's DNA to the bones in the Wolf River. I wanted to know if any of the bones were a partial match to Maisie," Frankie explained before the reporter could ask. "No luck."

"So, Evelyn Wright is dead, Darcy Doyle is missing, and you still have no idea what happened to Maisie Guinn?"

Frankie nodded glumly at Dusty's concise assessment.

"That about sums it up," he agreed. "And if you open that folder you were using as a fan, you'll find an invoice for my services, plus expenses."

"So, there's no suspect in Evelyn's death, yet?"

The reporter made no move to pick up the folder.

"If you're asking me, I think Enrico Sombra or someone at the casino is behind all this," Frankie said. "But the task force looking into it may have a different theory."

"There's already a task force?"

Dusty seemed surprised.

"Yep, the Barrel Creek PD, the Buford County Sheriff's Office, and the FBI's field office in Memphis are all on the case, although they haven't shared any of their theories with me, and I don't imagine they plan to."

He cocked his head.

"But Detective Ranger with the BCPD went out to question Ralph McEwan a few days ago, so he's likely their main suspect, at least in Evelyn Wright's murder."

Wiping at the sweat on his forehead, Dusty shook his head.

"I don't think either McEwan or Sombra have much of a motive to kill Evelyn Wright," he said. "Although, they may have plenty of reasons to want to kill each other."

A woman spoke from the doorway.

"McEwan? Are you talking about Ralph McEwan?"

The familiar voice sent Frankie's heart racing.

"Peyton, what are you doing here? It's only Friday!"

Jumping up from his desk, he crossed the little room in two long strides, pulling her into a bear hug.

"I thought you wouldn't get here until tomorrow," he said, unable to stop himself from beaming at her like an idiot. "I've been counting the hours. But you must have driven through the night. Is everything alright?"

Peyton grinned up at him.

"Everything's fine," she said. "And I see you've already put up a new sign. Dawson & Bell, is it? What was wrong with Bell & Dawson? Ladies first and all that..."

She turned to Dusty with an apologetic smile.

"I'm sorry to interrupt a meeting with our very first client," she said. "But, what's this about Ralph McEwan?"

Frankie sensed she wanted to divert the conversation away from her early arrival but decided to let the matter drop.

What was it Dad used to tell me and Franny? Don't look a gift horse in the mouth? But is it really wise to just accept people's actions at face value? Did that work out for him in the end?

The somber thought threatened to put a damper on his

excitement at seeing Peyton, so he brushed it away as he explained how Ralph McEwan had ended up as the task force's prime suspect in Evelyn's murder.

Once he had summarized the events of the last week, he turned curious eyes to Peyton.

"So, how do you know Ralph McEwan?"

"It's actually a sad story," she said, her grin now gone. "Back when I was with the Memphis PD, I responded to a scene where a car had gone off Harahan Bridge. It was a single-vehicle accident and alcohol was involved. I was the one who notified the driver's son, his next of kin."

Frankie suddenly realized where the story was headed.

"The drunk driver was McEwan's father?"

"That's right," Peyton said. "A subsequent investigation determined that the man committed suicide. If I remember correctly, he'd recently declared bankruptcy due to gambling debts and his wife had left him. Ralph was left on his own to pick up the pieces."

She fell silent for a long beat, then checked her watch.

"Enough with the depressing memories," she said. "The day's still young. Let's make use of it. Once you finish with Dusty, we could go talk to McEwan and see if a familiar face will convince him to open up. I'll drive."

* * *

Peyton was standing beside a white Dodge Charger when Frankie and Sherlock exited the office.

"Before you say anything, I have to remind you that I got

this baby at the police auction," she said. "And in my estimation, it was a very good deal. Unfortunately, the interior has some minor imperfections."

Climbing into the passenger seat, Frankie eyed the torn leather and dirty carpet without comment.

"Let's drop off Sherlock at the house and then drive over to the Starbound construction site in Buford County," Frankie said. "That's where I found McEwan last time."

The words were barely out of his mouth when Peyton stepped on the gas, apparently eager to get going.

When they pulled up to the construction gate forty minutes later, the same security guard who'd been there earlier in the week appeared beside the Charger's window.

"Mr. McEwan doesn't work Fridays," Officer Zuckerman said as he leaned forward to peer into the car.

"You have any idea where we could find him?" Peyton asked. "It's kind of important that we do."

The old man looked over his shoulder as if checking to make sure they were alone, then lowered his voice.

"On my way over here, I saw Mr. McEwan's Escalade turning into Sombra's Casino down the road. That big white tank of his is hard to miss."

He dropped a wink at Peyton.

"That wasn't more than twenty minutes ago, so you may still catch him there," Zuckerman said. "But if anyone asks, you didn't hear it from me."

Frankie waved a thank you to the security guard as Peyton pulled back onto the highway. She sped south, then merged into the exit lane as they flew passed a sign reading

Sombra's Gambling Hall & Casino Parking Garage.

Parking the Charger in the first empty space she could find, Peyton jumped out and made it halfway to the casino entrance before Frankie caught up.

"Slow down," he cautioned "I'm *persona non grata* around here, you know. If any of Sombra's men see me I'll be leaving here in the back of an ambulance...or a hearse."

Peyton looked back at him and grinned as if he was joking.

Before he could tell her he was deadly serious, he caught sight of a familiar figure slipping through the casino doors.

"Dr. Habersham?"

The name slipped out before he could stop it, but the man who had overseen Dwight Atkins' cancer treatment either hadn't heard him or pretended not to.

"Was that who I think it was?" Peyton asked as Gordon Habersham hurried away. "Wasn't he Josie's doctor?"

"Yep, and he also treated Dwight," Frankie said. "He's a bit of a jerk, but he's one of the only doctors in Barrel Creek. I get the feeling he thinks he's an expert in every field."

He turned his head to stare after Habersham but the crowd of eager gamblers inside had already swallowed him up.

Instead, he made eye contact with Cordero Torres, who immediately started in his direction.

"We've been spotted," he said, grabbing Peyton's hand and dragging her toward the door. "Let's go."

As they hurried back into the garage, Peyton pointed to

an oversized white SUV idling further down the row without his lights on.

"Isn't that McEwan?"

Frankie followed her gaze, his eyes landing on the Escalade just as the driver switched on the headlights.

He instantly recognized McEwan's thatch of coppery hair and bristly beard behind the wheel.

But the real estate developer wasn't looking at Frankie. He was staring at Peyton, looking as if he'd seen a ghost.

Just then a woman wearing a faux fur wrap and silk head scarf hurried past them and climbed into the Escalade.

As the big SUV rolled past them, Frankie got a clear view of the woman in the passenger seat.

"What's Yolanda Alvarez doing with McEwan?" he asked, pulling Peyton toward the Charger.

"I don't know. Who is she?"

The question remained unanswered until they were back in the car and driving down the exit ramp.

Only when he felt sure Cordero Torres and his goons weren't following them, did he turn to Peyton.

"Yolanda is Enrico Sombra's wife," he said. "And from what I know about her husband, if she's screwing around with his competition, she must have a death wish."

CHAPTER TWENTY-ONE

Ralph McEwan tried to block out the incessant chatter coming from the woman sitting in the passenger seat beside him. He was desperate for a few minutes of silence in which to think after the unexpected sighting of Detective Peyton Bell in the casino's parking garage.

Why had the former Memphis PD detective come back to the area after all this time? It couldn't have anything to do with him. Could it?

Gripping the steering wheel with both big hands, McEwan reassured himself that if Peyton was there with Frankie Dawson, it meant that she was looking for Maisie Guinn.

Hadn't that been what the skinny P.I. said he'd been doing the other day when he and the self-righteous Detective Ranger came to the Starbound building site?

The nerve of the big detective still stung. How could someone with a father like Ike Ranger be allowed to wear a badge and go around harassing people suspected of far lesser crimes than those perpetrated by his own family?

The blood of the father runs in the veins of the son, doesn't it?

Of course, if the saying was true, then that would mean

that McEwan himself would take after his own father, which was a prospect that had filled him with fear ever since his father's accident.

That's how he preferred to think about it. As an accident.

The crash off Harahan Bridge wasn't intentional. It was an accident. A simple mistake. Just a momentary glitch in Dad's reasoning abilities that was brought on by one too many losses at the gaming table and one too many whiskey sours.

It could have happened to anyone in that situation.

Perhaps something similar had even happened to Frankie Dawson's father, Henry, who had been a regular at the casino and a hard drinker.

McEwan's memory of Henry Dawson was foggy. The two men hadn't spent much time together, and what time they had spent had been infused with alcohol.

He couldn't remember when he became aware that Henry was no longer coming to Sombra's casino. No longer hanging out in the sports bar or vying for a seat in the poker room.

At some point, Henry was just not there anymore.

His father's accident hadn't taken place until several years after Henry had disappeared from the scene.

McEwan had sobered up after that, thanks in no small part to Peyton Bell, and one day it had occurred to him that his father hadn't been the only casino regular who was no longer with them. Henry Dawson was gone, too.

Once he was sober, McEwan could clearly see who was to blame for his father's death. He vowed to seek justice for his father by enacting revenge on the man who had ruined him.

Enrico Sombra had enriched himself off the suffering of addicts like his father for decades, making a living off those who were addicted to the gaming tables and to the bottle.

And he had shown those addicts no mercy, taking their money, their health, and their pride without remorse.

But after years of planning, McEwan was now poised to take his revenge. His casino would be bigger and better than Sombra's casino, which would soon be overshadowed and run out of business.

And Sombra's wife was preparing to leave him, just as McEwan's mother left his father once he'd hit rock bottom.

He'd promised himself that one day Sombra would stand by the ruins of his casino, alone and despised.

And I'm so close. So very close. If not for that stupid barrel...

"Are you okay?"

Yolanda put a diamond-encrusted hand on his arm.

"You haven't said a word the whole way home."

Turning to her with a fixed smile, he wondered if she really thought of the house he'd bought to use for their illicit hook-ups as home. If so, he'd done his job well.

"I was thinking that next time you should drive your own car over," he said. "We've been taking too many chances. We'll be seen and then..."

"And then what?" she asked lightly. "Are you worried I may end up a single woman?"

McEwan shook his head.

"Nothing would make me happier."

The words seemed to satisfy her, making up for his

inattentiveness on the drive, and she returned to her mindless prattling as they went inside.

But the unexpected sighting of detective Bell had shaken McEwan, and his mind returned to the past as he poured Yolanda a large glass of cabernet.

He knew that Peyton's quick response to the scene of the crash had made her the natural choice to notify the dead man's next-of-kin, but something about that choice had always seemed like fate to McEwan.

There he was, a young man who'd just lost his father due to an alcohol-related accident, and he was presented with an alcoholic looking for a reason to sober up.

He'd never been able to decide if it was the loss of his father, the conversation he'd had with Peyton, or a combination of the two, that had changed his life that night.

Whatever the reason, McEwan had sobered up, and he'd become wise to the fact that Enrico Sombra had destroyed his father and ruined his life.

After that, he worked hard to be in a position to return the favor. He'd spent years preparing.

And then, just when everything was finally in place and the wheels were ready to be set in motion, the Atkins barrel had been found at the building site and the bones inside were identified as belonging to Valentina Rojas.

That's when he'd panicked. He'd impulsively bought the barrel works, and then hired Evelyn Wright.

Now the photographer was dead, too.

McEwan was suddenly sure his plan wasn't just falling

apart. No, someone was taking great pleasure in slowly *ripping* it apart, piece by piece.

CHAPTER TWENTY- TWO

Peyton was still picturing the stunned look on Ralph McEwan's bearded face when she turned the Charger onto Monarch Avenue and brought it to a stop in the driveway of the little house she would be calling home for the foreseeable future. Granny Davis and Arlene had graciously agreed to put her up in their attic guest room on a temporary basis until certain decisions and arrangements were made.

But it was only her first day back in Memphis and those decisions and arrangements would have to wait for another time. Right now Peyton was hungry, and making herself a late afternoon sandwich was all she wanted to think about.

But as she opened the Charger's door and climbed out, a voice called out behind them.

"When did you get back in town?"

Peyton turned around to see two men sitting in a black SUV parked along the curb. Her eyes widened as she recognized the dark-haired man in the driver's seat.

"Kade? What are you doing here?"

"I came by to see Frankie," the agent said. "He's been helping us with a few cases that appear to be connected."

Bending down to look in the window, Peyton lifted a hand in greeting at the man in the passenger seat.

"That's Special Agent Trent Boone," Kade said as Frankie circled the Charger to stand beside her. "He was working undercover at some of the casinos along the Mississippi around the time Maisie Guinn went missing. That's the reporter Frankie's been looking for, right?"

"It's not just me," Frankie said proudly. "As of today, Peyton's a full-fledged partner in Dawson & Bell Private Investigations, so she's officially looking for Maisie, too."

Motioning for Kade and Boone to follow him, Frankie headed for the house.

"Come on in and have some coffee or a glass of iced tea," he said. "My throat's as dry as bone with all this damn heat. I need a drink and we can talk inside."

Peyton looked back and caught Kade's eyes, suddenly remembering how blue they were, and how intense they could be when they were searching for information.

"Is it okay with you if we come in?"

His voice had softened on the words.

"I don't want to intrude or-"

"Since when does the FBI worry about intruding?" Boone grumbled beside him. "Let's get in there so you can ask your questions and then get out of here. I've got things to do."

The older agent wrenched open the door and climbed out, squinting against the sun that was still blazing above them, despite the lateness of the day.

He followed after Peyton and Kade as they stepped into

the little house to be greeted by Sherlock, who sniffed at them with interest before following the group into the kitchen.

"This is my mother, Arlene," Frankie said as the men lowered themselves into chairs around the kitchen table. "She loves making coffee...don't you, Ma?"

Arlene Dawson raised an overplucked eyebrow in his direction but graced the agents with a smile.

"How about iced tea instead?" a high-pitched voice said from the doorway. "I made some for Franny earlier."

Peyton turned to see Granny Davis standing by the refrigerator, a big pitcher of tea in one small hand.

For a minute, Peyton wasn't sure who Frankie's grandmother was talking about, then she remembered what Frankie had told her the last time she'd visited.

Most of the time Granny Davis thinks Josie is Franny. The Alzheimer's can do that, I guess. But Josie doesn't seem to mind.

Stepping forward, she took the heavy pitcher.

"Tea sounds wonderful," Kade said as Peyton began to pour the icy tea into tall glasses. "I'm parched."

He gave Peyton a winsome smile as she filled his glass, and for a disturbing moment, she suspected he was flirting with her, but then he turned away and she decided she must be imagining things.

As she took a seat at the table, Agent Boone picked up his glass and drained it in one gulp, then set it back on the old wooden table with a careless *thunk*.

"Okay, let's get this show on the road," he said, checking the battered watch on his thin wrist. "I've got other fish to fry after this."

Peyton wasn't surprised to see Frankie's back stiffen. Boone was rude and insufferable. She couldn't imagine why Kade had brought him to Frankie's grandmother's house.

"What exactly did you want to talk about, Kade?" she asked in a cool voice reserved for people who inspired her wrath. "Agent Boone has things to do, and so do we."

A flush of what Peyton judged to be embarrassment fell over Kade's smooth-shaven face.

"I wanted to ask Frankie if he'd managed to track down Ralph McEwan. See if they had a chat," Kade said. "And find out if he has additional information to share with the task force. There's a meeting tomorrow and…

He saw Peyton frowning over at him and hesitated.

"My questions can wait if you're all too busy. We can schedule time tomorrow at the field office if that works."

Sensing the nervous energy behind Kade's explanation, she decided he must be hiding something.

What did he really come here for?

The question flitted through her mind as Frankie leaned forward and propped his bony elbows on the table.

"Chief Pagano doesn't want me on the task force, but I'm guessing he has no problem with you and Agent Boone here draining my brain for everything I know."

The words were said with a wry smile, and Peyton got the impression that Frankie was please they'd sought him out.

"Unfortunately, we didn't get a chance to speak to McEwan yet," he admitted. "We got a tip he was at

Sombra's Casino, but when we got there the only people we saw inside were Sombra's second-in-command, Cordero Torres, and Dr. Habersham from Barrel Creek. The doc blanked me and Torres chased me away, so it was pretty much a wasted trip."

"Dr. Habersham?"

Kade cocked his head.

"Why does that name sound familiar?"

"That's Evelyn Wright's doctor," Boone said. "His name was on the inhaler taken as evidence from her house. It was listed in the report from the medical examiner."

A gleam of recognition lit up Kade's eyes.

"That's right. And you saw this guy at the casino?"

"Yeah, but that doesn't mean much," Frankie said. "Lots of rich folks in Memphis and the surrounding area drive over to the casinos to lose their money on the weekend."

Taking out a cigarette, Boone pointed it toward Frankie.

"But are any of *their* names in Evelyn Wright's autopsy report?" he asked. "Coincidences happen all the time. But in homicide investigations, they need to be investigated."

Annoyed by his condescending attitude, Peyton leaned forward to pluck the cigarette from Boone's fingers.

"No smoking in here," she said, dropping the cigarette on the table beside him. "You think we want the place to smell like smoke? People live here, you know? Including me, at least for now. And there's a child in the house."

"I don't see any kids," Boone muttered, but he picked up the cigarette and returned it to the pack.

Kade appeared to be suppressing a smile as he wrote

something on a small notepad he'd taken from his pocket.

"I've made a note to look into Habersham if only to eliminate him as a person of interest," he said. "Now, I guess we'd better be going."

"Hold on a minute," Frankie said.

Reaching out a hand, he rested it on Kade's arm.

"Last time we talked, I told you about a blackjack dealer at Sombra's Casino. A woman named Darcy Doyle. She was Maisie Guinn's cousin and her mother was Lottie Doyle, the woman who took a tumble from the parking garage."

Kade nodded.

"Okay, what about her?"

"I think she's missing," Frankie said. "After I talked to her the first time, I could never get hold of her again."

Opening his little notebook, Kade jotted something down.

"I'll make it a point to speak to her," he said, then got to his feet. "Now, we'd better get going. Boone here must be dying for a smoke."

But as Frankie and Boone walked out the door and into the hall, Kade hung back and waited for Peyton, who was musing over the fact that Frankie hadn't told the agents they'd seen Ralph McEwan with Sombra's wife at the casino.

Is he holding back the information from the feds for some reason, or did it just slip his mind?

Deciding she should probably discuss the omission with Frankie before bringing it up to Kade, she stepped into the hall to find the agent's bright blue eyes pinned on her.

"Are you really staying here in Chesterville?" he asked. "I

would have thought you'd be staying out at the Atkins house in Barrel Creek with Frankie and Josie."

Caught off guard by the personal question, Peyton stared at him in surprised silence.

"It's just if you're single again..."

He lowered his voice, using an intimate tone that made her distinctly uncomfortable.

"I've never forgotten you...or what we had together."

Before she could respond, footsteps sounded on the stairs, and then Josie was there, staring at them with a hostile expression Peyton couldn't fail to understand.

"I think you had better go," she said to Kade, who was already heading toward the front door.

Once the agent had slipped outside, she turned to Josie, wanting to assure the teen that Kade had been out of line, and that she had in no way encouraged his rekindled interest.

But the girl had already disappeared into the kitchen without giving her a chance to explain. Peyton followed after her only to find the back door open.

Josie was gone.

–

CHAPTER TWENTY-THREE

Frankie stood on the driveway and watched the black SUV pull back onto Monarch Street and roll toward the corner. He couldn't deny that he was glad to see the back of Trent Boone. The man was a real piece of work, although he guessed it took a certain type of person to work undercover with criminals and drug smugglers.

The type of person I don't want sitting in my Granny's house.

Deciding he didn't like the agent regardless of any excuse or justification he might have for being a jerk, Frankie started back toward the house, then stopped again when he heard footsteps in the dry grass.

Josie appeared from around the side of the house, her face set in an expression Frankie recognized.

"What's happened to upset you now?" he asked as she started down the sidewalk. "Where are you going?"

"I'm going to the library," she called over her shoulder.

As he watched her stomp down the sidewalk, Peyton appeared wearing an expression that closely matched Josie's.

"Did something happen?" he asked. "You look upset."

Before she could answer, his pocket buzzed.

Pulling out his phone, he saw Rosalie Quintero's number on the display and immediately tapped to answer.

"I've just heard a rumor that the FBI lab managed to pull a print off the wood," she said, sounding unusually agitated. "But I've yet to receive an official update."

Frankie wasn't sure what she was talking about.

"Fingerprints on the wood?" he asked. "What wood?"

"You know, the broken wood that was collected along with Evelyn Wright's body at Shadow Lake," she said, not bothering to hide her exasperation. "Am I the only one with any sense of urgency to find that poor woman's killer?"

Understanding just how Rosalie was feeling, Frankie waited for her to finish venting.

"Chief Pagano insisted that I send the wood to the FBI lab for testing even though I assured him our lab was perfectly capable," she fumed. "But he said they had the best facilities and that they would run it through AFIS."

"Now days have passed and a friend of mine over in the FBI lab said they'd had success pulling a print. Supposedly the task force received the results, but I've heard nothing back. It's been complete radio silence on my end."

Frankie headed for the Mustang and motioned for Peyton to follow. By the time she'd climbed in and put on her seatbelt, Rosalie was starting to calm down.

He didn't realize that Sherlock had made it into the backseat until he was backing onto Monarch street.

"I think I know what's going on," he told the M.E. as he steered the car west into the setting sun. "I'm driving to the Barrel Creek police station now, but I need to hurry. They'll be closing soon if they haven't already. I'll let you know what I find out."

He ended the call and then looked over at Peyton.

"Rosalie Quintero's the medical examiner, and even she can't get answers out of the task force," he said. "I suspect Pagano is trying to keep her out of the investigation. After all, she was the one who turned Shipley into the FBI. I think she must be on the chief's blacklist, although I'm pretty sure I'm at the top."

Peyton sat back and let Frankie concentrate on the road as they left Chesterville and sped down Hastings Highway toward the Barrel Creek police station.

Parking beside a meter next to the curb, they hurried up to the door just as a uniformed officer was turning the lock.

"We close at six on Friday," she called through the glass.

"Officer Lang?"

Frankie rapped on the glass.

"You remember me, right?" he called out. "I need to speak to Detective Kinsey. Please, it'll just take a minute."

The young, female officer approached the door with a cautious frown that turned into a smile when she saw Sherlock standing on the pavement behind him.

"His name is Sherlock, isn't it?" she said.

Turning the lock, she opened the door and bent to ruffle the Labrador's soft, black fur.

"I remember you, little buddy," she said in a high-pitched voice as the dog lifted his head to better enjoy the soft scratching. "You're a good boy, aren't you? Yes, you are!"

She looked up with a smile and gestured to the lobby.

"Wait inside and I'll see if Detective Kinsey is available," she said, giving Sherlock a final rub before hurrying away.

Minutes later she was back, waving for them to follow her to a small conference room where Kinsey and Ranger sat at a table going through evidence and case files.

"I heard you found prints on the wood pulled out of the lake with Evelyn Wright," he said, getting straight to the point. "Was there a match in AFIS? Do we know who it is?"

Ranger's face tightened.

"Who told you?" he demanded, casting a suspicious glance at his partner. "That information hasn't been released yet."

"It doesn't matter who told me," Frankie said. "We're all on the same team, aren't we? We're all trying to find the sick bastard who sliced open Evelyn's throat and threw her in the lake. The same person who may have killed Valentina Rojas and taken Maisie Guin and Darcy Doyle."

He ran a frustrated hand through his shaggy hair.

"There are too many victims for you to keep this contained any longer," he added. "If that's Pagano's plan, it'll fail."

Turning to Kinsey, he met and held her eyes.

"If you know something that could help Peyton and me find whoever's doing this, you've got to tell us," he implored.

"Frankie's right," Peyton added. "The more people out there searching for the women who are still missing, and looking for the perp who killed the others, the better."

She sank into the chair next to Kinsey.

"I've been in your shoes plenty of times," she said. "I've been the assigned detective on a homicide, trying to find a perp before someone else died. And more than once Frankie or some other P.I. helped me close the case."

Kinsey threw a sideways look at Ranger, then sighed.

"The lab was able to pull a fingerprint off a piece of wood that was twisted up in some of Evelyn Wright's hair and clothes," she said, ignoring Ranger's groan of protest. "The print matched a man who was arrested at a Biloxi casino ten years ago on a drunk and disorderly misdemeanor."

She slid a print out toward Peyton.

"The man gave his name as Albert Sharkey, although he had no ID on him. He used an address that turned out to be a fake. He spent a night in jail, paid a fine, and was released on his own recognizance."

Her voice was grim.

"There's no other record of him in the system and as far as we can tell, he's not been in any trouble since."

Eyes widening at her words, Frankie leaned over the table.

"I think I know where-"

"What's going on here?"

Barry Pagano towered in the doorway, his close-set eyes blazing and his nostrils flared in his narrow face, which was framed by a slick sheath of inky black hair.

"What are they doing in this conference room with all this confidential information? And why is there a *dog* in here?"

Frankie opened his mouth to explain, but Pagano cut him off with a sharp exclamation.

"No! I was asking Detective Kinsey, not *you*."

He pointed a finger toward the door.

"Leave now, before I have you arrested for trespassing," he ordered. "And take that mutt with you or I'll call animal control and have him put down."

CHAPTER TWENTY-FOUR

Kinsey's blood felt hot and heavy in her veins as she watched Frankie and Peyton lead Sherlock out of the room. When the door had closed behind them, she looked up at Barry Pagano, her throat and chest so tight with anger and resentment that she wasn't sure she could speak.

"What do you have to say for yourself, Detective Kinsey?" Pagano asked in a cold voice. "I instructed you and Detective Ranger not to share any information outside the task force unless I gave you explicit approval to do so."

He folded his arms over his narrow chest.

"You defied a direct order by sharing that information, and now our entire investigation is compromised."

"I made a judgment call," she countered. "Which is what Major Crime detectives working multiple cases have to do."

Jumping to her feet, she looked up at the police chief with an unflinching gaze, unintimidated by his aggressive attitude and his height advantage of ten inches.

"Frankie Dawson is a private investigator who has helped this department before and-"

"I suggest you sit down and lower your voice."

Pagano's tone was imperious.

"Otherwise you may find yourself out of a job."

Kinsey gaped at him, momentarily speechless.

"And I suggest you treat the people who work for you with some respect," Ranger said, standing up beside Kinsey. "Or you'll find yourself in the middle of a homicide investigation with no detectives to run it and two unfair dismissal lawsuits on the docket. Now, let's take the threats down a notch."

The police chief opened his mouth, then snapped it closed as if suddenly unsure of his next move.

"I can assure you that the official task force has this investigation under control," Ranger said in a calmer tone. "Any information shared with a third party is done so only in an effort to move the investigation forward."

"Without Frankie Dawson's involvement, we may never have stopped the Wolf River Killer," Kinsey added stiffly. "And now that the task force is trying to solve two homicides while looking for a missing person, we can't afford to turn down any help Frankie Dawson is offering."

Drawing himself up to his full height, Pagano glared first at Kinsey and then at Ranger.

"And you agree with this assessment, Detective Ranger?"

"Yes, I do," Ranger said. "I trust Kinsey's judgment."

A lump rose in her throat but Kinsey swallowed it back, feeling both grateful for her partner's words of support and resentful that Pagano had required them.

"Fine," the chief said in a clipped tone that told her it was anything but. "Then it's on your heads if it all goes wrong and someone else gets killed."

As he turned on his heel to leave, Kinsey considered telling Pagano about Darcy Doyle. He was still the chief after all.

Shouldn't he know another woman is likely missing?

But then he was out the door and heading down the hall and the opportunity to provide an update had passed.

With a sigh, Kinsey decided the new chief would likely discount anything Frankie had told them, in any event.

"I'd say that went well," Ranger said dryly as he began to gather the folders on the conference table.

"I'm going after Frankie and Peyton," she said, heading toward the door. "Maybe they're still outside."

But when she pushed through the exit and looked up and down the street, it was clear they were already gone.

Walking out to the Interceptor, she climbed behind the wheel, forcing her thoughts away from Pagano and back to the investigation at hand.

They'd gotten a real break with the fingerprint. She should be happy with that. After all, Albert Sharkey, whoever and wherever he might be, could prove to be their killer.

Of course, they would have to find him first.

She thought for a long beat then pulled out her phone and tapped in a message to Kade Mabry, offering to stop by and discuss strategies for moving forward with the fingerprint evidence. Seconds later her phone pinged with his response.

Sure, come on over. I'll meet you outside.

She pulled up outside the FBI's Memphis field office as the sun was sinking into the west with a vivid splash of violet.

Kade was already waiting for her outside the five-story, redbrick building, his face showing signs of fatigue as she approached him in the waning light.

Leading her into the quiet building, he escorted her through security and led her upstairs to a conference room, offering coffee or bottled water.

"Water will be fine."

"Good decision," he said. "Our coffee is pretty awful."

She sank into an ergonomic desk chair as he left the room, enjoying the air-conditioned view of the splendid sunset taking place outside the big picture window.

"So, the fingerprint on the wood," Kade said as he returned, handing her the bottled water as he took a seat across the table. "There was a match in AFIS I hear."

Kinsey felt a yawn coming on and managed to cover her mouth just in time. When the yawn had come and gone, she saw Trent Boone step into the room and head for the table.

"Agent Boone, I thought you'd already gone home," Kade said, looking over at the newcomer in surprise. "Detective Kinsey and I were just discussing the print pulled off the wood they found with Evelyn Wright."

"Yes, the print matched a man with a misdemeanor conviction for drunk and disorderly down in Biloxi," Kinsey said. "His name was Albert Sharkey."

"Albert Sharkey?"

Boone repeated the name in a gravelly voice as he sat at

the table, bringing with him an unpleasant, smoky scent that made Kinsey want to hold her breath

"Yes, didn't you hear? Of course, there are lots of Al Sharkey's running around. I've already checked online," she said. "And we don't even know if that's his real name. But it's a starting point. Unfortunately, it looks as if the digital mugshot file is missing, which is weird. But..."

She hesitated as Boone stood and began to back toward the door with a distracted frown on his face.

"Is everything okay?" she asked.

"Yeah, but I've got to go check on something before it gets too late," he said. "I'm sorry. Continue without me."

Kade watched him go, then turned back to Kinsey with an apologetic smile.

"I think we're all a little tired this week with too much going on and not enough sleep. How about we pick this conversation up tomorrow? I'm planning to work through the weekend, although Agent Boone may not be available."

Agreeing to touch base with him the next day, Kinsey stood and allowed herself to be escorted to the door.

As she climbed back into the Interceptor, she didn't see Boone standing in the window of his office, watching as she pulled out of the lot and headed back to Barrel Creek.

CHAPTER TWENTY-FIVE

K
ade waited until Kinsey's taillights had faded into the distance, then turned and went back inside, seeking out Boone in his office, wanting to know what had triggered the agent's strange reaction when he'd heard the name Albert Sharkey.

"What happened in there?" Kade asked as he stuck his head into the small, windowless office Trent Boone shared with two other agents.

His office mates had gone home for the weekend, leaving Boone sitting at a desk by himself, brooding over a box full of old, yellowed files.

"Nothing happened," Boone said irritably.

There was a strict no-smoking policy in the building that even Boone knew better than to break, forcing him to resort to nicotine gum during office hours.

Grabbing the pack off his desk, he stuck a piece in his mouth and began to chew.

"I've got to quit the damn cigarettes," he said, glancing longingly at the pack peeking out of the pocket of his backpack. "It's a filthy habit."

Kade didn't disagree.

Cocking his head, he waited patiently as Boone chewed a few more times on the gum and then looked up at him with troubled, bloodshot eyes.

"A man going by the name Albert Sharkey was mentioned in a few of the reports I turned in between 2004 and 2005," he said. "At the time, the undercover operation we were running at casinos along the Mississippi was in high gear."

He stopped as a coughing fit took over.

Reaching for a cup of cold coffee on his desk, he grimaced as he took a sip, but the coughing fit started to abate.

"Anyway, like I was saying, I named a few of Sombra's cronies in my reports before the operation was called off. Before Maisie Guinn and Henry Dawson let me down."

His eyes darkened and he looked away.

"This Sharkey guy was a hardcore gambler. He was winning and losing big. Lots of high-stakes stuff. But in the end, we never had cause to bring him in. At that time, I don't believe he had a record."

"And you think this guy could be the same guy that got picked up in Biloxi?" Kade asked. "You think he could be our killer?"

Boone shrugged, but his face was tight with tension.

"I don't see why not," he admitted. "The Sharkey I knew was a bigtime risk taker and addict. He gambled, drank, you name it. And as a high roller, he made connections all along the river. Connections that included local cops."

"What are you saying?" Kade asked. "That he sometimes

paid off cops to look the other way?"

The question prompted a snort from Boone.

"Of course, he paid off the cops. But I'm thinking of that missing mugshot Kinsey mentioned. I'm wondering if he paid someone at the local station to delete the file after the fact, just to cover his trail."

He started to cough again and Kade stood and backed toward the door, figuring it was time for them both to get some rest.

"Listen, I may not be reachable over the weekend," Boone said. "I'm going to catch up with some of my contacts from my undercover days. See what I can find out about all this from behind the scenes."

Kade nodded and slipped back into the hall, feeling sorry for Boone, who at fifty-six was only a year away from mandatory retirement.

But as he got into his SUV and headed back toward his lonely apartment, he started to feel sorry for himself as well.

I could still be single and alone in another twenty years, only then I'll be old, too. Just like Boone.

He wondered what was wrong with him.

Here it was, Friday night in a lively city like Memphis, and he hadn't made any plans. To make matters worse, the only woman he wanted to see was married to someone else.

At least, technically.

Taking out his phone, he considered calling Peyton.

He'd been keeping in touch with her lately, sending her little updates about the case here and there, which may have been why she had come to town a day early.

She'd told him she was getting worried and it sounded as if Frankie needed her help.

Then today, when Kade had heard she was in town, he'd made up an excuse to go see her, telling Boone he wanted to give Frankie an update, feeling awkward when it was obvious he'd had no good reason for stopping by.

But then Peyton said she would be staying at the house in Chesterville, not with Frankie.

That must mean they aren't together anymore, right?

The thought lingered in his mind, prompting him to drop the phone back in his pocket and change course.

He wouldn't go home quite yet.

First, I'll drive over to Chesterville and tell Peyton what I learned about Albert Sharkey. I'll give her the update in person, and maybe see if she wants to grab a bite to eat. It'll all be very innocent...

But as he headed west, he wondered what he was doing.

Why was he driving across town to see a woman who had dumped him years ago? A married woman who'd given him no reason to think she would welcome his attention?

He thought back to earlier that afternoon when he'd asked her if she was single. She'd had a strange look on her face.

Did that look mean yes or no?

He knew an FBI agent should be able to figure out these types of things. He'd been trained in interrogation tactics and had learned how to detect when someone was lying.

But for some reason, when it came to Peyton, he seemed

to lose all perspective.

By the time he reached Chesterville and pulled up to the little house on Monarch Avenue, he was pretty sure he'd made a mistake.

The feeling was compounded when Granny Davis opened the door with a wide, welcoming smile.

"I'm sorry to stop by without calling first," he said. "But I was hoping to speak to Peyton."

A voice called out from behind the frail-looking woman. He looked past her to see Frankie's mother standing in the hallway wearing a flowered housecoat and curlers in her hair.

"Peyton's not here," Arlene Dawson called out. "Can I give her a message for you?"

"No, thanks, I'll just send her a text."

He held up his phone, feeling foolish.

"I think she's gone to see Frankie," Granny Davis said.

Her small face creased into a delighted smile.

"She's head over heels for my grandson you know. Even I can see that. It's just as clear as day."

Kade nodded awkwardly and started down the steps.

Frankie's grandmother was right, even if he didn't want to admit it. Peyton had never looked at him the way she looked at Frankie. Not even when they were dating.

And she certainly didn't look at him that way now.

No, he had to accept the truth.

It was time to move on.

"I'll tell her you came by," Granny Davis said in a small voice. "She'll be sorry to have missed you."

But Kade didn't hear her.
He was already walking away.

CHAPTER TWENTY-SIX

Frankie stretched and turned over, then sat up with a start as he realized someone was in his bed. He rubbed his bleary eyes and stared down at a pale face framed with dark hair. His wife was lying on the pillow beside him, her beautiful amber eyes closed in sleep, her warm body tucked beneath a soft white quilt.

"I hope this isn't a dream," he whispered to Sherlock, who was sitting on the floor beside the bed, staring at Peyton with a startled expression.

As if feeling both sets of eyes on her, Peyton stirred and stretched, then opened her eyes.

"What time is it?" she asked, stifling a yawn. "I didn't mean to fall asleep, but I was so tired..."

Looking toward the bedside table, she let out a little gasp as she saw the time.

"Josie will be up by now," she said, shrugging off the arm he'd wrapped around her and getting to her feet. "We said we'd take things slowly, so she has time to adjust."

Frankie nodded, knowing she was right.

He'd spoken to Beth Hurley about the unusual situation they were in, and the therapist had emphasized the need for

Josie to have a stable environment.

"She's been through so much change already. It may help her heal if she has a chance to settle into a normal routine. If she gets a chance to feel grounded again."

Resisting the urge to pull Peyton back into bed, he swung his feet to the floor and stretched again, still thinking of Josie and her therapy sessions.

"I think the sessions with Dr. Hurley have been helping," he said, more to himself than to Peyton. "And Josie seems to like her. Maybe you would, too."

He glanced back at her with one eyebrow raised.

"What are you saying?" she asked as she pulled on the same clothes she'd been wearing the day before. "You think I need therapy?"

"I think it couldn't hurt after what you've been through this last year," he said, dropping his eyes to the floor.

Coming around the bed, Peyton sat beside him.

"It's not just what *I've* been through," she said. "It's what *we've* been through. In fact, you probably need therapy more than I do after facing off against Bill Brewster. You found your best friend and his wife murdered, and you almost died yourself. Not to mention finding out you had a daughter you never even knew about."

She took his hand.

"I'd say all that justifies a little therapy."

"Okay, so we're both a little messed in the head," he said with a shrug. "Maybe that's why we're so good together."

He bent over to pick up his jeans off the ground,

searching the pockets for the box with the infinity bracelet inside.

Once he had the velvet box in his hand, he opened it and slid off the bed, landing on one knee.

"What are you doing?" Peyton asked.

Her smile faltered when she saw the delicate gold bracelet nestled inside the box.

"It's an infinity bracelet," he said, picking it up and slipping it onto her wrist. "And infinity means forever, right? So, this will always remind you how long we'll be together."

Running a finger over the precious metal, she stared down at the bracelet with a solemn expression Frankie found hard to read. He couldn't be sure what she was thinking.

"It's beautiful," she finally said, her voice as soft as a whisper. "Now, I better get going before Josie wakes up. Finding me here the first morning after I arrive certainly doesn't equal *taking things slowly*."

She smiled and continued getting dressed, leaving Frankie to wonder if she was still having doubts about their future.

"I've been meaning to ask you something," Peyton said as she brushed her fingers through her dark pixie cut.

"Ask me anything," Frankie said, eager to hear what was on her mind. "I'm an open book."

Peyton cocked an eyebrow.

"It's just that yesterday when Kinsey mentioned the name Albert Sharkey, you seemed as if you knew something. You looked almost excited. Then Pagano arrived to ruin the day and we left. So, what were you going to say?"

"I was going to say that I know who Albert Sharkey is. At least, I know someone who knows who he is."

Pulling on his jeans, Frankie began to pace the room with nervous energy as he filled Peyton in on what he'd learned from Anders Nielson.

"The editor-in-chief of the *Memphis Gazette* – a guy called Nielson - told me about a reporter named Albert Sharkey. He called him a stringer, which pretty much means a freelancer, and says he uses him to write up the stories that are too far away or dangerous to assign to his staff writers."

Frankie felt a quiver of anticipation.

"If this Sharkey guy is the same guy who left the fingerprint on the wood, then we've got our killer," he said.

A look of doubt fell over Peyton's face.

"I hate to burst your bubble, but when I was a detective for the Memphis PD, I met most of the reporters in town, and I don't remember running into anyone named Sharkey."

"Maybe he had another source in the MPD," Frankie said. "Nielson said this guy's highly connected with local law enforcement as well as the FBI."

He watched as Peyton slung her purse over her shoulder.

"The FBI, huh? Maybe I can ask Kade about it," she said. "I also want to try to talk to Ralph McEwan. I'm hoping he'll remember me and open up."

"And I'll call Nielson and get Sharkey's address," Frankie said. "I meant to do that yesterday but you distracted me."

Following her downstairs and into the kitchen, he tried to make as little noise as possible.

"Okay, I'd better get out of here before Josie comes down here and sees me. We don't want to confuse her."

Frankie thought he was confused enough for all of them.

Did the fact that Peyton had slept over his house mean that they were back together? Or was she still trying to make up her mind about him? She hadn't exactly been overjoyed with the infinity bracelet, had she?

Was last night just a test drive? Did I pass the test?

Footsteps sounded on the stairs as Peyton's car pulled out of the drive.

"Is she gone?" Josie asked.

"Is who gone?"

His attempt to play dumb didn't work.

"I know Peyton stayed over last night, and I know you guys were trying to hide it, although I'm not sure why."

"We just want you to get used to-"

"Don't make this about me," Josie said.

She sounded upset again.

"What do you mean?"

"I mean, don't drag me into whatever problems you guys are having," she said. "I don't want to be in the middle. I already feel bad enough having to watch as...as..."

She walked to the refrigerator and stared in at the nearly empty shelves.

"As what?" Frankie asked.

But Josie just shook her head.

"Come on," Frankie said, starting to lose his patience with her moodiness. "Don't leave me in suspense. Tell me. What do you feel bad about?"

Josie spun around.

"I just hate watching Peyton make a fool of you with that FBI guy, okay?"

The pained look on her face stopped Frankie's angry reply.

"Hey, what's this about?" he asked, moving forward to put his hands on her shoulders. "There's nothing for you to worry about. No one's making a fool of me."

"But Peyton used to date Kade Mabry," she said. "And I heard them talking about her being single and he said he'd never forgotten what they had together. It made me sick."

Releasing her shoulders, Frankie stepped back.

He resisted the urge to demand she tell him everything she'd overheard. Instead, he smiled.

"Peyton's a beautiful woman," he said. "And I'm sure Agent Mabry isn't a fool. He would be lucky to have a woman like her. But she's my wife and-"

"And she filed for divorce," Josie broke in. "And now you aren't even sleeping in the same house, and Arlene says-"

"My mother doesn't know anything about my marriage," Frankie replied more sharply than he'd intended. "So, if you have any questions, you come to me. You understand?"

Josie nodded, but her eyes were red-rimmed and puffy.

"Are you and Peyton officially back together?" she asked.

Frankie sighed.

"I'm not sure," he admitted. "I sure hope so."

* * *

Frankie drove Josie and Sherlock to Granny Davis' house in Chesterville, hoping a relaxing Saturday with no summer school or homework would cheer the girl up.

"Can't I hang out with you today?" Josie asked as they pulled onto Monarch Avenue. "I can help you do research."

Looking over at her earnest face, Frankie felt a bittersweet pang in his chest. She looked so much like his little sister Franny in that moment, back before their lives had all gone so wrong.

"Maybe you can come back to the office this afternoon," he said. "But I'm not sure where I'll be going this morning. I've got to find a man with some important information."

Josie looked like she was about to say something when Arlene came out on the porch.

"I've got pancakes on the griddle," she called. "And maple syrup. You want to come in, Frankie?"

He shook his head and pointed toward the door.

"You better go," he said. "I'll catch you later."

With a heavy, put-upon sigh, Josie climbed out of the car, waited for Sherlock to jump out after her and then walked up to the porch with slow, dragging steps.

Frankie waved goodbye as he drove away, refusing to let thoughts about Peyton and Kade crash back in.

He needed to focus on the hunt for Albert Sharkey.

Cruising down Arcadia Street, he passed the old

downtown office building where the *Memphis Gazette* had operated for decades before it had been permanently closed.

There was no longer a physical address where he could go to find out information about the newspaper or the reporters who had worked there in the past.

Sometimes it seemed to Frankie that the world around him was all moving online, with virtual workers and everything stored *in the cloud* as the techies like to put it.

If some computer geek kicks the wrong plug or pulls the wrong lever, the whole damn world will go dark. The cloud will go poof.

Parking the Mustang in the tiny parking lot beside his little office on Winchester Way, he hurried inside and sat down at his desk.

He glanced over at Peyton's empty desk, then forced his eyes back to his phone as he scrolled through his contacts in search of Anders Nielson's phone number.

As he tapped on the editor's name, he reminded himself to play it cool. He couldn't just come out and say that Albert Sharkey was wanted for questioning in relation to a series of homicides and abductions.

Nielson might inadvertently tip him off, or even try to pull out the old *I have a right to protect my sources* routine if he thought the *Gazette* could be liable for Sharkey's actions.

Clearing his throat as the phone began to ring, he prepared the story he would give, planning to keep it simple. But the editor didn't answer and the call rolled to voicemail.

"Mr. Nielson, this is Frankie Dawson. I have a few follow-up questions I wanted to ask. Actually, if I could speak to that stringer you mentioned, Al Sharkey, he might be able to help me out directly, so if I could just get his number and address, that would be great."

As he ended the call, the door to the office banged open and Dusty Fontaine stepped inside.

"Just the man I wanted to see," Frankie said, waving for the reporter to take a seat. "I'm trying to find one of your fellow reporters. A stringer called Albert Sharkey."

"Why do want to find Sharkey?"

Frankie quickly decided it was best not to mention the fingerprint inside the barrel, or Sharkey's possible connection. He suspected Dusty might take the information and try to run with it himself.

"I have a few questions about an article he wrote."

Dusty cocked an eyebrow.

"I'm familiar with his work, of course, but I never actually met the guy. To be honest, I always figured he was using a *nom de plume*."

"Nom de *what?*" Frankie asked as he pulled a stick of gum from his pocket and tore off the shiny wrapper.

"It's a pen name," Dusty said. "You know, some writers choose a pen name, sort of like actors choose a stage name."

"Why would they do that?"

"I guess they want something that sounds interesting," Dusty said, sounding exasperated. "Or maybe they don't want anyone to know who they are."

Frankie frowned as he stuck the gum in his mouth.

"So, do you use a pen name?" he asked.

The stiffening of Dusty's shoulders answered his question.

"Of course you do," Frankie said, unable to hold back the laugh that erupted. "What parents in Tennessee would have ever named their son *Dusty Fontaine?*"

The reporter didn't seem amused.

"Okay, sorry, I'm just busting your chops," Frankie said. "But seriously, you think Albert Sharkey is using one of those pen names instead of his real name?"

"Probably," Dusty acknowledged, still sounding peeved. "I can ask around and try to find out. If Nielson assigned Sharkey the article about the body found over at the Starbound construction site, he's bound to be in Buford County questioning the locals."

"I wouldn't risk it," Frankie warned, lifting a finger to his still-tender cheek. "Enrico Sombra's pretty mad. If you go nosing around in Buford County, he's gonna find out about it and sic his men on you the way he did on me."

He looked Dusty up and down, studying the reporter's skinny frame.

"You better leave it to the professionals," he warned. "These guys aren't fooling around."

"Your partner's still not here?"

Dusty gestured to the empty desk.

"I thought you said she'd be here on Saturday."

"She arrived in Memphis yesterday," Frankie admitted. "And she's already out on a case."

Thinking of Peyton, he wondered how her morning had gone. Had she gotten the chance to question McEwan?

Or has she gone to see Kade Mabry? Are they together now?
Josie's words played again in his head.

"I hate watching her make a fool of you with that FBI guy."

Frankie picked up his phone and stared down at Peyton's name in his contact list, then stuffed the phone in his pocket.

When she's talked with McEwan, she'll call. No need to stalk her.

An image of the real estate developer sitting beside Yolanda Alvarez flashed through Frankie's mind.

Why was McEwan risking Sombra's wrath by dating his wife? Weren't the two men already arch enemies?

Maybe that's it. Maybe it's all about revenge.

-

CHAPTER TWENTY-SEVEN

Yolanda Alvarez sat beside Ralph McEwan in his big white Escalade, listening to the conversation he was having with the nameless, faceless voice on the other end of the connection. Normally, she paid little attention to his business calls, which were incredibly boring discussions of building codes, zoning laws, recording fees, and a million and one other topics Yolanda knew little about.

But as they'd left their little love nest on Verona Lane, McEwan had begun talking to the unknown caller about a fingerprint that had been found on a wooden stave.

She waited until he'd ended the call before turning to him.

"Was that about Valentina Rojas?" she asked. "Did they find a fingerprint on the barrel she was in?"

From the beginning, McEwan told her all the details he knew about the barrel's discovery at the building site and the remains found within. He had admitted that he was worried the investigation would delay, and maybe even destroy, his plans to open the Starbound Casino.

So, when he'd started paying a source at the Buford County Sheriff's Department to keep him updated, she hadn't been surprised. It was a business strategy both her father and her husband had used for many years to ensure the smooth operation of their own enterprises.

"The call was about another woman," he said. "A woman named Evelyn Wright in Barrel Creek, Tennessee. You must have heard about it on the news."

"Do you think the two are related?" she asked, instantly intrigued. "And they found a fingerprint? Do they know who it belongs to?"

Merging toward the exit, McEwan nodded.

"Two women found in barrels within an easy driving distance? The police are bound to think they're related."

He glanced over at her

"My source says the print matched a guy named Albert Sharkey. I know I've heard the name before. Isn't one of the regulars at the high-stakes tables called Sharkey?"

When his eyes turned to her, Yolanda managed to meet his gaze with a placid smile.

"It's a common gambling name in casinos, I'm sure."

"So, you aren't worried there may be a killer roaming around the casino?" he asked. "Cause a man with that name was arrested and fingerprinted. His fingerprint was on the barrel found with Evelyn Wright's body."

Lifting a hand from the wheel, he scratched at his beard.

"So, unless Albert Sharkey worked at the factory and made the barrel with his own two hands, he was likely the guy who put her body in it."

Yolanda shifted in her seat, feeling suddenly overheated.

"Turn up the air," she said. "It's so hot outside. The man

on the news said it's going to be the hottest day of the year."

He ignored her attempt to change the subject.

"So, you don't know anything about this Sharkey guy? Cause if he's an associate of your husband, then I may be able to use that connection to my advantage. Imagine the PR nightmare alone?"

His voice had taken on the nasty tone he always used when he spoke about Enrico. It was a tone she'd come to hate.

"As I said, I'm sure it's a common name."

The answer earned a dissatisfied grunt, and then McEwan was again picking up the phone, ready to make another call.

As he began to bark orders into the phone, Yolanda looked out the window at the passing view, catching quick glimpses of the Mississippi River in the distance.

Sliding on her sunglasses, tears prickled her eyes and she had a sudden, painful moment of clarity.

He's just using me to get revenge on Enrico. Just as Enrico used me to gain influence with my father. Neither one ever really cared for me. They only cared about using me for their gain.

As they neared the casino, she looked over at McEwan, seeing him clearly for the first time. Her lips curled in a sad smile as she realized her lover would be in for a surprise.

He doesn't know that my husband doesn't love me – that he doesn't care if I'm with another man. Enrico hasn't really cared about me in decades. Not since Valentina came and went.

As the SUV pulled into the parking garage, Yolanda

thought about what she'd learned and overheard.

If Albert Sharkey's prints had been in the barrel, perhaps she would be the one to use the information to her advantage.

"Should I come over tonight?" she asked as she opened the door and climbed out. "I can drive myself if you want."

"Maybe," McEwan said.

He held a hand over the phone.

"I'll call you."

And then, with a final wave, he sped down the ramp, leaving her behind.

✳ ✳ ✳

Yolanda hadn't gone into the casino after McEwan dropped her off, deciding there was nothing left for her there.

Nothing left for me in Buford County or the whole state of Mississippi for that matter.

Hurrying to her silver Mercedes, she'd taken the highway north until she got to Charrington Road.

She followed the street through an upscale neighborhood full of large houses which were widely spaced and set back from the road behind gracious lawns.

Albert Sharkey's house sat near the end of the street.

It had been purchased with proceeds from some of his luckier runs at Sombra's Casino, of that she was sure, although Yolanda suspected he held down a regular job, if only to provide a respectable cover his snooty neighbors would accept.

She'd only been out to the house once after an epic losing streak had turned into a night of drowning his sorrows. Enrico had insisted Sharkey be taken home in one of the casino's town cars, but they were all in use, so Yolanda had driven him.

She'd always remembered the tree line street in the quiet, normal neighborhood, thinking that if she was a different person, who had lived a different kind of life, Charrington Road was the street she'd want to live on.

Pulling into the driveway, she saw that the blinds were closed and that morning's *Gazette* was still on the porch.

He must have had a late night at the gaming tables. Either that or maybe he's been out putting more women in barrels.

The sudden thought quickened her pulse, and she leaned forward and opened the glove compartment, reaching in to pull out the compact Sig 320 that her husband had given her after several carjackings had been reported in the area.

Sticking the gun in her purse, she slung the designer bag over her shoulder and walked up to the door.

Albert Sharkey responded to her knock with a wary frown.

"Yolanda, what are you doing here?"

"I came to ask if you killed Valentina Rojas," she said, always one to prefer a direct approach. "I can't be mad at you if you did. After all, she was screwing my husband."

The comment was met with silence. Then Sharkey stepped back and gestured for her to come inside.

"I'm assuming this is some sort of joke?" he said,

running a hand through his hair as if trying to rake it into some sort of order. "Am I going to go viral on the internet?"

He gave her a smile, but it fell short of his eyes.

"Another woman was found just a few days ago," Yolanda added. "That time, a fingerprint was found."

She watched his eyes.

"They know you're involved," she said, keeping one hand close to the Sig. "They just don't know who *you* are."

Sharkey's expression didn't change. Years of playing poker had given him complete control over his emotions.

"But I do," she continued. "I know who you are."

Her voice grew cold.

"And don't waste my time trying to bluff me or convince me I'm wrong. I know a lying, cheating man when I see one. In fact, I'm an expert on the subject."

Taking a step further into the room, she looked around at the expensive but tasteful furnishings.

"You've got a nice set-up here," she said. "It'd be a shame to switch all this out for an eight-by-ten jail cell."

"You really have gone mad, haven't you?" he said in a soft voice that made the hair on the back of her neck rise. "Let me take you back to the casino where you can get some rest."

Yolanda shook her head.

"Cut the crap, Sharkey."

She pulled out the Sig and pointed it at him.

"I was raised by a man who ordered hits on people as a normal course of business," she said. "I don't condone that behavior, of course. But I learned to accept it."

Her finger nestled around the trigger as she spoke.

"And, if you felt the need to take out certain people who threatened your livelihood in some way..."

"Are you actually trying to tell me it's okay if I killed two women?" he said. "Do you think I'll confess now? Do you think I'll fall into your trap that easily? Are you wearing a wire or recording this?"

Yolanda's heart was pounding a frightened rhythm in her chest, but she forced herself to smile.

"Wearing a wire? What would I do with that? Turn it into the local cops? Maybe the feds? So they can arrest me and take all the money and assets my family has?"

Keeping the gun leveled at his chest, she shook her head.

"No, I have no reason to turn you in," she said. "That would only cause me trouble. But I do want something from you for my silence. A small payoff."

Sharkey frown.

"You want money? I thought you were loaded."

"My husband is *loaded*," she corrected. "I have nothing in my own name but some designer clothes and some jewelry. Even the car out there is in Enrico's name."

The gun was growing heavy and her arms were starting to ache. She needed to hurry this up.

"Yes, I want money," she said. "But I also want to know why you killed Valentina. What did she have on you? She must have threatened you in some way. Why else would you want to silence her?"

Sharkey stared into the barrel of the gun with hard eyes.

"Valentina was a threat to the whole operation," he finally said. "She was turning informant. Planning to meet with the FBI. I didn't want Enrico to be exposed. I didn't want Sombra's Casino to close down."

Yolanda exhaled at the words.

Now we are finally getting to the truth.

His words made a twisted kind of sense. After all, the man was a compulsive gambler. She knew that much was true.

Thus, he had a vested interest in keeping the place going.

"You killed Valentina to keep the casino open?"

Sharkey nodded slowly, although she knew there must be more to it. She could see it in his eyes.

But perhaps it didn't matter why.

She'd already decided to leave her failing marriage. Could anyone blame her if she used what she knew to extort the soulless shark in front of her for money to start a new life?

Once she was safely settled far away, she could let someone know what he'd done. That he was a vicious animal.

Moving toward the door, she kept her eyes on Sharkey's, knowing she couldn't let her guard down for even a moment.

But as she took a step back, her heel caught in the edge of a braided rug. The distraction was enough to take her eye off her target for the merest second.

It was enough for Sharkey to make his move.

With a vicious lunge, he grabbed her wrist, twisting her arm until she dropped the gun.

"Does anyone know you came here?" he grunted as he looped an arm around her neck. "Maybe your boyfriend Ralph McEwan?"

"Yes, he knows," she lied, managing to gasp out the words in a breathy croak. "He's expecting me...soon."

Sharkey grinned, showing all his teeth.

"Good. Then let's not keep him waiting."

CHAPTER TWENTY-EIGHT

Albert Sharkey pulled Yolanda's Silver Mercedes into his attached garage with little fear of being observed. He'd first been drawn to Charrington Street by the mature trees and gracious homes, but he had remained all these years due to the lack of curiosity and friendliness demonstrated by his stuck-up neighbors who thus far had left him well enough alone.

Dragging Yolanda's limp body through the garage door, he hefted her up and into the trunk, thinking she was heavier than she looked as he slammed the lid shut.

Within minutes he was gloved up and heading toward the little bungalow on Verona Lane that McEwan had purchased as a love nest when he'd started his affair with Yolanda.

Sharkey had seen the record of sale online when he'd been doing research for an article on McEwan's new casino project, and he remembered thinking that the real estate developer had gotten a good deal.

On the drive over, he worked through the perfect plan to kill both Yolanda and McEwan. He would make it look like a murder/suicide. A love affair gone wrong.

But as he pulled up to the house, the big white Escalade

he'd expected to see in the driveway was gone.

McEwan wasn't there.

His plan would need to be adjusted and the first step would be getting into the house. He thought a minute and then popped the trunk and got out of the Mercedes.

Walking back to stare in at Yolanda, who lay just as he'd left her, he dug in her purse for her phone, using one limp finger to unlock the device.

He scrolled through the phone until he found the hidden security system app. Within seconds, the house's alarm had been deactivated and the lock disengaged.

Further options in the app allowed him to turn off the camera and then erase the security video that showed the Mercedes pulling up outside with Sharkey at the wheel.

Hopefully, the video isn't being streamed to a backup server somewhere. If it is, there's nothing I can do about it now.

Sticking the phone back in Yolanda's purse, he looked around to make sure they were alone.

The house was set back among the trees, giving it a sense of privacy that he appreciated. Hefting Yolanda out, he carried her inside, along with her purse, prepared to explain she'd had a bit too much to drink if anyone did happen by.

As he dumped her onto the living room floor, he began mentally outlining the news story he would write about the murder-suicide of the real-estate developer and the casino mogul's wife. It would make a sensational headline.

Looking around the cozy room, he considered taking a few before-and-after photos of the crime scene to add to his personal collection but Yolanda started to stir, so he hurried into McEwan's study.

He took a gun from the well-stocked rack, deciding he'd have to re-stage the planned murder/suicide as a heated lover's quarrel with McEwan in the frame for killing Yolanda in a jealous rage.

As Yolanda opened her eyes and tried to sit up, Sharkey once again took the phone from her purse. This time, he tapped in a message to McEwan.

I'm sorry, I don't want to fight. Let's talk this out.

After chucking the phone under the sofa where it was sure to be found, Sharkey helped Yolanda get to her feet.

Her legs were wobbly and weak, and he sensed they might buckle under her at any minute.

"I'm sorry I have to do this," he said as he lifted the gun. "But this way your husband will never suspect me. He'll think McEwan killed you in a lover's quarrel. Case closed."

When Yolanda lunged forward as he knew she would, he pulled the trigger, putting a bullet in her heart.

Sharkey stood over her body, wanting to make sure the bullet had done the job when he heard something outside.

Is that a car engine?

As he turned toward the sound, a flash of movement outside the front window caught his eye.

He ran and looked through the blinds.

A white Dodge Charger pulled to a stop next to Yolanda's silver Mercedes. At first, he thought it was a cop car, but he could see no markings or logos.

His heart hammered in his chest as a woman in civilian clothes climbed out, walked up to the door, and knocked.

The woman was attractive with short, dark hair and wide, amber eyes that peered through the glass insert.

"Mr. McEwan? I'm Peyton Bell, Frankie Dawson's partner. I was hoping to ask you a few questions."

Holding the gun behind his back, he opened the door.

"Sorry, you've got the wrong man. I'm Albert Sharkey."

CHAPTER TWENTY-NINE

Frankie looked at his phone again, cursing its silence as he paced the office, walking back and forth beside Peyton's empty desk, replaying Josie's words from that morning, trying not to let his mind and his imagination run away with him.

Peyton still hadn't called to check in, and he was losing his willpower in the fight to give her space and let her call him when she had something to report.

His eyes kept returning to her computer, which she'd left on and logged in. He knew he shouldn't go through her private files, but after all, this was a business and maybe there was an email in her inbox from a potential client.

No harm in checking, is there?

As soon as he woke up the computer, he saw she'd managed to find the address of a house McEwan had recently purchased by searching a site that managed deeds and property taxes in Buford County.

Frankie scanned the listing for the quaint yet surprisingly modest home on Verona Lane. It didn't look like the home of a real estate tycoon, but perhaps McEwan was using it as his temporary pad during the casino project.

Checking the time on the computer screen, Frankie decided he'd waited long enough. He would call and ask Peyton if she wanted to meet him for a late lunch after she'd finished talking to McEwan.

Who knows, maybe I'll ask her about Kade while we eat.

But when he finally took out his phone and tapped on her number, Peyton didn't answer, which ratcheted up his worry even further, making it impossible for him to concentrate.

With a frustrated groan, he grabbed up his keys and headed out to the Mustang, ignoring the voice in his head telling him he was overreacting.

Pulling onto the highway, he headed toward Buford County and the little house on Verona Lane.

By the time he got there, he was tempted to turn around, having managed to talk himself off the ledge of panic.

The feeling that he was making a colossal fool out of himself only grew as he pulled up to the house to see that Peyton's white Charger wasn't parked by the curb or in the driveway. McEwan's white Escalade wasn't there either.

In fact, the only car he could see was a silver Mercedes.

Wondering if he'd gotten the address wrong, he stepped out of the Mustang and surveyed the house.

Yep, it's definitely the same house I saw in the listing. But Peyton's not here, so...

As he turned to go, his eyes fell on the front porch.

Did somebody leave the door open?

Walking up the driveway, he was reminded of his recent visit to Evelyn Wright's house, and his prior trauma of finding Dwight and Cheryl Atkins' front door open.

Both times he'd walked in on crime scenes that he still couldn't get out of his head.

Pulling out his gun, he approached the door, bracing himself as he stepped inside.

The dead woman's silky, caramel-colored hair spilled around her head and a pool of blood spread around her body.

It was Yolanda Alvarez.

Frankie froze in the doorway, listening for tell-tale sounds that might mean her killer was still in the house.

But the house was silent.

Moving further into the room, he saw a small handgun discarded on the floor, and a cell phone was peeking out from under a sofa.

He stared around the room with the surreal feeling that he was in the middle of some sort of production, where everything was just where you would expect it to be in a play about a murder.

The scene has been staged. An idiot could see that.

He checked the other rooms, keeping his gun pointed out in front of him, walking quickly and quietly until he was sure that he and the dead woman were alone.

Then he took out his phone and called 911.

* * *

Sheriff Waylon Crockett pulled up to the scene in a dusty white Interceptor with the Buford County Sheriff's logo on the side and a bank of flashing lights on the roof.

He wrestled his wide girth out from behind the wheel and ran a hand over his sweat-shiny head to smooth down the few strands of hair that were still hanging on.

"I'm the one who called 911," Frankie said as a black and white cruiser skidded to a stop behind Crockett's SUV. "I came here looking for Ralph McEwan who owns this place and I found Yolanda Alvarez inside. She's been shot in the chest. I didn't call for an ambulance because-"

"Hold on a minute," the sheriff said as he looked up at the house. "We're gonna need to interview you properly. Now go with my officers and tell them everything that happened. I'll go check out the scene."

Staring after the portly sheriff in frustration, Frankie allowed himself to be led to the cruiser where two uniformed officers took down a detailed statement.

He was still talking to them thirty minutes later when Sheriff Crocket returned.

"This homicide is definitely connected to Evelyn Wright's recent murder in Barrel Creek," Frankie said, worried that evidence inside was being disturbed. "Her murder has already been connected to the remains of Valentina Rojas and a task force has been formed. They can send an evidence response team and-"

The loud roar of an oncoming vehicle drowned out Frankie's words and seconds later a shiny black Range Rover pulled into view.

Cordero Torres was in the driver's seat and Enrico Sombra was riding in the back as if he was a visiting dignitary.

Staring at the new arrivals with wide eyes, Frankie realized that Sheriff Crockett or one of his deputies must have called Sombra and told him about his wife.

The casino owner jumped out of the Range Rover and charged toward the house. He made it halfway through the front door, knocking over a flower pot in the process before two uniformed officers who had been cordoning off the house were able to grab him.

Frankie winced as the man yelled out in anger and wrestled against the officers, who led him back down the porch steps.

"Ralph McEwan killed my wife!" he shouted in Crockett's direction. "Have you arrested him?"

Shrugging off the hands of the officers restraining him, Sombra strode over to the sheriff.

"You know he always blamed me for his father's death, Crockett! He'd been trying to destroy me for years, building his new casino, and trying to ruin my marriage. I suspected Yolanda was seeing someone else and-"

The sheriff held up a hand to stop him.

"Be careful what you say," Crockett warned him. "Right now, it's obvious who's responsible. McEwan did this. It's his house and there's a gun missing from his rack. Maybe he killed Valentina, too."

Frankie couldn't believe what he was hearing. It was as if the sheriff had already made up his mind before a real investigation had even been started.

"If McEwan killed Valentina Rojas, why would he try to

build a casino on the ground where he buried her body?" Frankie asked. "It doesn't make sense."

Cordero Torres stepped forward to glare at Frankie.

"I agree," he said. "The only one who had access to Valentina the night she disappeared was Henry Dawson. He killed her and then ran. He knew if Enrico or I ever got our hands on him...

"Cool it!" Crockett warned as a CSI van pulled up. "In fact, I need you all to leave so we can investigate the scene. I'll keep you updated as possible...now go!"

Moving toward Sombra, Torres put a hand on his boss' arm and tugged him gently toward the Range Rover.

"You, too, Mr. Dawson," Crockett said, his jowls quivering as he spoke. "Get going. We'll let you know when we need to talk to you again. And I guarantee we will."

"Aren't you going to call in the task force?" Frankie asked. "Shouldn't the feds or the Barrel Creek PD be involved?"

Crockett snorted.

"This is a local matter," he said. "The Buford County Sheriff's office will handle this. Now, I can't force you to leave the street, but I can make damn sure you stay behind the crime scene tape."

With a final glare, he turned on his heels and walked away.

Pulling out his phone, Frankie started to type out a message to Kade Mabry, advising the FBI agent to send a response team.

But as he tapped on the screen, Josie's words played

again in his mind, causing his already upset stomach to twist.

He took out a stick of gum and unwrapped it. As he stuck it in his mouth and began to chew, he tried calling Peyton again. Still no answer.

Knowing he had to do something, he paced down the sidewalk and stopped beneath an elm tree, seeking shelter from the blistering sun as he typed out a text to Kinsey, telling her what was going on.

Sweat dripped onto the phone as he waited for her reply.

When it came, he cursed under his breath.

The scene is outside Barrel Creek's jurisdiction. Nothing I can do.

Frankie tapped in another message, along with a photo he'd pulled off social media that showed Yolanda smiling.

McEwan was seen with this woman the night before she was killed, just as he was with Evelyn Wright the night she died.

When Kinsey didn't respond right away, he sent another.

The two murders have to be related. What about the task force?

Her reply gave him a glimmer of hope.

Stay there and stay out of the way. I'll see what I can do.

Frankie paced under the tree for almost an hour as more Buford County cruisers arrived, along with a CSI van.

He was just about to send another text when his phone buzzed and he saw a message come in from Kinsey.

Special Agent Mabry is on the way. Should be there any minute.

Turning toward the corner, Frankie saw a black SUV appear as if on cue. The big vehicle pulled up to the curb and stopped just short of the crime scene tape.

Kade Mabry climbed out and looked around, then ducked under the yellow tape, holding up his credentials as a deputy confronted him, then turned to call Sheriff Crockett.

"The Barrel Creek PD notified me that there was a murder here that may be linked to the open Evelyn Wight murder investigation assigned to our joint task force," Kade said.

His voice carried across the lawn to wear Frankie stood.

"An FBI evidence response team is on the way."

Crockett's face flushed a bright red at the words, and he turned to where Frankie was still standing under the tree.

"Is this your doing?" he asked, glaring over at Frankie, who strode across the lawn toward them. "Did you call the feds on me?"

Before Frankie could respond, Kade put an arm around his shoulders and guided him up toward the house.

"Don't worry about the sheriff right now," the agent said. "Let's just go up there and you can walk me through what you saw when you got here."

Frankie nodded but he still felt uneasy, as if something wasn't right, as he followed Kade up the path.

He pointed to the front door.

"I came here to try to find Peyton and I saw that the door was open," he said. "She was supposed to interview McEwan but then she stopped answering her phone."

His eyes were drawn to a flash of sun reflecting off metal.

Moving closer, he saw a gold bracelet lying next to a flowerpot that had fallen on its side by the door.

Frankie bent to pick it up, knowing instantly what it was.

"This is the infinity bracelet I gave Peyton."

He turned and held it up for Kade to see, his mind spinning with questions.

"Peyton was here after all. But, where is she now?"

CHAPTER THIRTY

Peyton Bell struggled against the thick ropes that cut into the soft flesh of her wrists and ankles as she looked around the dark room with growing panic, not sure where she was or how she was ever going to get out. The walls around her were fortified with some sort of thick stone, and the long, narrow space was illuminated by a single light bulb that hung from the ceiling.

She remembered walking up to Ralph McEwan's house on Charrington Road and knocking on the door.

The man who had answered smiled at her and introduced himself as Albert Sharkey before producing a gun and ordering her into the house.

Her first instinct had been to run, but he'd grabbed her by the arm and pressed the muzzle of the gun to her head.

Despite her fear, she'd had the presence of mind to slide the bracelet off her free hand and let it fall to the ground, hoping to leave some sort of clue behind for Frankie when he came looking for her.

Because I know he will come looking for me.

The only other thing she could remember about the house was the quick glimpse she'd gotten of a dead woman lying in a pool of blood on the floor.

The next thing Peyton could remember, she was waking up in the windowless room with her wrists and ankles bound and her head pounding like a monstrous drum.

Sharkey must have hit me over the head with the gun.

Her mind was still foggy and her eyes felt blurry as she studied the short flight of stairs that ended at the wooden ceiling. Was there a door up there? She thought she could see an outline in the wood.

It's a cellar. He's put you down in a cellar.

Wondering why he hadn't just shot her like the woman she'd seen on Ralph McEwan's floor, Peyton wondered what he planned to do with her.

The possibilities were all unpleasant, prompting her to begin inching across the concrete floor toward the stairs as she told herself there had to be a way to escape.

As she moved slowly across the room, ignoring the throbbing pain in her head, she strained to see into the shadows along the walls and in the corners.

She could just about make out a series of dark, hulking figures that stood outside the light bulb's reach.

Moving closer with excruciating slowness, she finally realized what she was seeing.

A row of large wooden whiskey barrels were lined up against the wall, like a silent army.

One had fallen over and lay on its side.

Ice filled Peyton's veins as she remembered what had happened to Valentina Rojas and Evelyn Wright.

Both women had been killed and dumped into barrels.

No, that's not exactly right. Valentina was put into a barrel first and left to die. She had tried to claw her way out.

The thought caused a surge of panic. There had to be a way to get out of the cellar. Or maybe a weapon to use against Sharkey when he returned.

If he returns. Maybe he won't. Maybe he'll just leave me here to die, then put me in one of those barrels and...

No, she couldn't allow her mind to go down that path.

She couldn't give in to panic and fear while there was still even the slightest chance she could get out of this alive and get back to Frankie and Josie and her new life in Memphis.

But she was already getting thirsty. And she hadn't eaten anything all day. She'd left Frankie's house in a rush and had been too eager to start working their new case to stop for breakfast. Her stomach was already growling.

How long would she last without food and water?

Turning her eyes back to the barrels, she continued to inch along, wondering what could be inside.

Maybe water or wine. Or weapons I can use to fight Sharkey.

Finally, she was close enough to read the words charred into the top of the fallen barrel.

Atkins Barrel Works
Lot number #ABW: B04C24

It was the same name and lot number that had been charred onto the barrel Valentina had been found in.

Just more proof that Sharkey was the killer she'd been looking for. And it made the possibility that there could be guns or other weapons inside the barrels more likely since Atkins Barrel Works had operated as a front for an illegal smuggling enterprise for decades.

Lifting her bound hands, she pried at the metal hoop that held the barrel lid in place, pulling with all the strength she could muster, but it was no use, neither the hoop nor the lid would budge.

She would need a crowbar and hammer, plus the strength to use the tools, in order to get into the barrels.

As she looked down at her wrists, which were being rubbed raw by the rope, she thought of the infinity bracelet she left behind, wondering if Frankie had already found it.

If so, was he looking for her now?

Or had Sharkey picked up the precious gold and thrown it away? Or worse yet, kept it as some sort of sick souvenir?

Tears sprang to her eyes as she remembered how gently Frankie had placed the bracelet on her wrist as she'd tried desperately not to cry.

She hadn't wanted to ruin their first morning together with tears. But it had been all she could do to keep herself together when she'd seen the trust he still had in her after she had failed him so many times before.

And now I've failed him again. I've allowed myself to get caught by a human shark who will kill me without one drop of remorse.

A terrible ache settled into Peyton's chest at the thought of what it would do to Frankie if he never found her. If he never knew what happened to her.

The thought was interrupted by vibrations from above.

Sharkey was home and there was no way of knowing what he planned to do to her.

CHAPTER THIRTY-ONE

Storm clouds were starting to gather in the west as Josie and Sherlock walked down Winchester Way, heading toward the offices of Dawson & Bell Private Investigations. Josie hadn't heard from Frankie all day, and she was starting to worry. He usually called her around lunchtime, and then again right after school.

Maybe since it's Saturday, he forgot. Or maybe he's mad at me for what I said about Peyton and Kade Mabry.

Either way, she had decided to take Sherlock for a walk, not telling Arlene or Granny Davis she planned to go all the way to Frankie's office. But she had to make sure he wasn't sitting there on his own feeling bad.

Maybe I shouldn't have said anything. Not until I knew for sure.

Seeing the new sign for the agency up ahead, she urged Sherlock to hurry, wanting to get inside before it rained.

Frankie will really be mad if I let Sherlock catch a cold.

With one blue eye on the sky, she raced for the door and twisted the knob, surprised when it wouldn't turn.

"He locked us out," Josie said.

Looking down at Sherlock, she saw the Labrador staring

up at her with a confused expression that matched her own.

"Everything okay?"

Josie turned around to see that a baby blue convertible had pulled up to the curb.

A man she recognized as *Memphis Gazette* entertainment reporter Dusty Fontaine was sitting behind the wheel, staring at her through the open window.

Studying the silver emblem on the side of the car with a raised eyebrow, she cocked her head. She'd never heard of a Thunderbird before.

"Yeah, we're okay," she said. "But the door's locked. I guess Frankie already left for the day."

"That's a bummer," Dusty said. "I stopped by to tell him something I heard on the wire. Thought he might be interested, seeing it happened over in Buford County."

Josie frowned.

"Buford County? Isn't that where Sombra's Gambling Hall & Casino is?" she asked. "And where they found Valentina Rojas' remains?"

"How do you know about all that?" the reporter asked. "You're just a kid. You shouldn't know anything about casinos and murders and human remains."

Crossing her arms over her chest, Josie gave him her best *you've-got-to-be-kidding-me* look.

"I can read, can't I," she said. "And all that stuff is in the newspaper. You should know that. You're a reporter."

She frowned.

"So, what is it you heard on the wire?" she asked. "What's happened over in Buford County now?"

Dusty hesitated, then shrugged.

"You'll just look it up online if I don't tell you, won't you?"

"Yep. I'll find out one way or the other. I always do."

She flashed him an impudent smile.

"Okay, well, there's been a shooting over in Buford County. At least one person dead."

Josie's mind immediately turned to Frankie.

What if he'd been over there investigating the casino again? Or looking for Darcy Doyle?

What if he's the one who's dead?

"I knew I shouldn't have told you," Dusty said in a worried voice. "You look like you just saw a ghost."

But Josie wasn't listening. She was taking out her phone and tapping on Frankie's number with a frantic finger.

He answered on the first ring, sounding worried.

"Peyton?"

Relief washed over her at the sound of his voice.

"No, this is Josie. Didn't you see my number?"

"Sorry, it's just that I've been trying to reach Peyton. Have you seen her or heard from her?"

A crack of thunder sounded overhead, causing both Josie and Sherlock to jump.

"No, I haven't," she said as a large drop of rain hit the hot sidewalk with a tiny sizzle. "Is something wrong? Is she-"

"She's fine, I'm sure," Frankie said.

He didn't sound sure.

"Just stay at Granny Davis' house. And stay inside.

There's supposed to be a big storm on the way, and I don't want to have to worry about you, too."

Looking up at the sky, she saw a flash of lightning in the distance. The storm was coming closer.

"Listen, I've gotta go," he said. "Just...stay safe."

She heard a faint siren in the background of the call, and then the connection was broken.

"Is everything okay?"

Dusty was still sitting by the curb in the Thunderbird.

"I think so," she said, biting her lip. "But it sounds as if he's worried about Peyton. He hasn't heard from her and-"

A thought came to her as she stared down at her phone. She scrolled to her smart watch app and clicked on the icon.

There it was. The little dot that showed where her watch was now. If Peyton was with her car, and if Josie's watch was still inside, then the dot was showing where Peyton was, too.

Zooming in on the location, she frowned.

Why would Peyton go there? Is she with Kade while Frankie is going crazy with worry looking for her?

She started to call Frankie back, then hesitated.

No, I can't get him all worked up for nothing.

And she certainly couldn't send him into a situation where he could potentially get his heart broken.

No, she would need to check this out herself, she decided, looking over at Dusty with an innocent smile.

"I've never ridden in a Thunderbird before," she said. "Maybe you could take me and Sherlock for a ride. I know just where we should go."

CHAPTER THIRTY-TWO

Frankie stood outside the crime scene on Verona Lane, listening to Peyton's phone ring again and again before once more rolling to voicemail. Ending the call without leaving another message, he shoved the phone back in his pocket. Now the only thing left in his hand was the infinity bracelet he'd given Peyton that morning.

It seemed as if days had passed since he'd slipped it on her wrist instead of hours.

"Are you sure that's Peyton's bracelet?"

The question came from behind him and he turned to see Kade Mabry pointing at the loop of gold.

"Yeah, I'm sure," Frankie said, trying not to sound as worried as he felt. "But we checked the whole house and she isn't here. And there's no sign of her car."

"Maybe she came here, didn't find McEwan, and left, dropping the bracelet as she went."

It was a best-case scenario. One that Frankie desperately wanted to believe. Only, it just didn't make sense.

From the look on Kade's face, he could see the FBI agent was having a hard time buying the happy-ending story, too.

"Why don't *you* try to call her?" Frankie asked. "Maybe

she thinks I'm checking up on her. Or maybe I pissed her off somehow and she's mad at me."

God, I hope that's all it is.

Kade shrugged and took out his phone. He tapped on a number that, in Frankie's opinion, was way too easy to find.

"Straight to voicemail," Kade said. "It didn't even ring."

Panic fluttered in Frankie's chest.

"We've got to find McEwan. If he has done *this*..."

He pointed back to the house where the Buford County medical examiner was wheeling out Yolanda's body.

"If that's McEwan's doing...maybe he has Peyton. Maybe she saw what happened and he's taken her as a hostage."

"I'm hearing a lot of maybes there," Kade said. "Let's not get ahead of ourselves. Peyton's only been unreachable for a few hours. I know the bracelet isn't a good sign, but-"

"But nothing...look at that!"

Shaking his head, Frankie pointed toward Sheriff Crockett who was standing by the porch laughing at something one of his deputies had said.

"Crockett thinks this is all some big joke. He's not done a damn thing to find McEwan and he hasn't even questioned Sombra. Isn't the husband always the first suspect?"

He started toward the sheriff but Kade reached out a hand to hold him back.

"Don't give him an excuse to take you in," Kade said in a low voice. "If you get yourself arrested that won't help anyone. Especially not Peyton."

Frankie forced himself to take a deep breath.

"So what do you suggest we do?"

"I suggest we take shelter," Kade said.

Pointing at the dark clouds rolling toward them, the agent pulled Frankie toward the Mustang.

They reached the car just as the first raindrops began to splash against the windshield. Frankie jumped into the driver's seat and Kade ran around to the passenger's side, not waiting for an invitation.

"I've got someone working on getting a warrant to track McEwan's phone," Kade said as the rain began to pelt down with a vengeance. "In the meantime, we need to think. Where could he be? Is it possible he's out somewhere and doesn't even know we're looking for him?"

Frankie thought back to the real estate developer's movements over the last few days.

"I guess he might have gone to the casino building site or maybe stopped by the barrel works. Neither place has great reception. And he could be tied up in meetings..."

He wasn't hopeful either suggestion would pan out, but it would keep them busy while they waited for the warrant.

"Okay, let's start with the barrel works," Kade said. "I told Detective Kinsey I'd check in with her today. So why don't I ask her to meet us over there?"

"And you can send McEwan a message asking him to meet you there. He bought the place from you, didn't he? Say you want to buy it back."

Pulling out his phone, he started tapping while he talked.

"If McEwan is there, she can take him over to the Barrel Creek police station for questioning about Evelyn Wright's murder," he explained. "And as a task force member, I can join in and ask about Yolanda."

"What if he doesn't show up?" Frankie asked.

Kade gave an easy shrug.

"Then we'll head on over to the Starbound Casino construction site," he replied in a patient voice. "And maybe by then, we'll have the go-ahead to track his phone."

* * *

McEwan's Escalade wasn't at the barrel works when they pulled up in the Mustang thirty minutes later.

They waited in the car until Kinsey's Interceptor pulled into the lot. Ranger was with her riding shotgun.

"What are we doing out here?" Ranger asked once they'd gathered under the building's overhang.

"There's been another murder in Buford County," Frankie said. "Enrico Sombra's wife was shot dead in Ralph McEwan's house. We're hoping to lure McEwan here to question him."

Both Barrel Creek detectives stared at him in surprise.

"I'm convinced this is related to Evelyn Wright's murder, so we thought you guys might want to join the party," he added. "Oh, and my partner Peyton is missing."

Reaching into his pocket, Frankie felt for the bracelet and gave it a little squeeze, just to remind himself it was still there, even if Peyton wasn't.

"I sent McEwan a message asking to meet him at the barrel works to talk about buying it back," he said. "Who knows, maybe he'll take the bait."

They all stood awkwardly looking at the rain.

"Did you find any more information on Albert Sharkey?" Kinsey asked, looking at Kade.

The agent shook his head, but Ranger cleared his throat.

"I thought the name sounded familiar yesterday," he said. "But I wasn't sure. I haven't heard it in years. But the more I thought about it..."

"You know the guy?" Frankie asked.

Ranger shrugged.

"I guess you could say that," he admitted. "My father used to go on guys-only camping trips with a few of his buddies. A few times he let me tag along.

"He'd hole up in a cabin playing poker with his buddies while I swam in the lake or went hiking. This guy Sharkey always managed to win in the end and my dad would bitch about it the whole way home, saying he must cheat."

"You know where the guy lives?" Frankie asked. "Cause I'm having a hell of a time finding out anything about him."

"I think we did go by and pick him up a few times on the way out to the campsite," Ranger said. "But I have no idea what the address might be. I wasn't old enough to drive at the time. Although I'd probably still recognize the guy if I saw him now."

Ranger crossed thick arms over his chest.

"You said he's a reporter at the *Gazette*, so can't you just go there and ask for him?"

"Actually, Sharkey is what you call a stringer...it's like a freelancer," Frankie clarified. "And the *Gazette*'s physical office shut down a few years back. Everything's handled remotely now, so there's no office to go to."

He glanced down at his phone and scrolled through his long list of recent calls and messages. He'd been ignoring pretty much anything that didn't have to do with Peyton.

"I'm expecting to hear back from the *Gazette*'s editor-in-chief," he said as he scrolled. "I didn't tell him anything. Just asked for Sharkey's address and phone number. Said I had a question about an article."

His heart skipped a beat when he saw the voicemail that had come in from Anders Nielson over an hour earlier.

He listened to the editor's clipped voice reciting a phone number, email address, and several social media accounts for the reporter. The physical address he had on file was a P.O. box in Memphis.

"It's a start," Frankie said. "I'll send Sharkey a message now. Do a little fishing and see if I can get him to bite. He can't hide forever."

Frankie was just starting to type in a message to Sharkey when he heard wheels on gravel.

He turned to see McEwan's big white Escalade.

"Looks as if we've just caught a whale."

CHAPTER THIRTY-THREE

Kade Mabry pulled the hood of his raincoat over his head and slid his Glock out of its holster as Ralph McEwan parked the Escalade beside Frankie's Mustang. The big man stared at the foursome standing by the building with apprehension, then opened the door and stepped out into the rain.

"What's going on here?" he called.

His eyes widened as he saw Kade step forward with the Glock in his hand.

"Mr. McEwan, I'm Special Agent Kade Mabry with the FBI's Memphis field office," he said. "I'm sorry to inform you that there's been an incident at your house on Verona Lane. A woman's been killed."

McEwan looked past Kade to where Frankie stood, his face creased with confusion.

"Mr. Dawson, is this why you wanted to meet me out here in the rain?" he asked indignantly. "To ambush me?"

The rain plastered his hair to his head and ran down his face, dripping from his beard, as he turned back to Kade.

"I haven't been at my house on Verona Lane since this morning," he said. "If there's been an incident there, then someone else is responsible."

"A woman has died, Mr. McEwan," Kade said in a hard voice. "Don't you even want to know who she is?"

A trapped look fell over the real estate developer's face, and for a moment Kade thought he might turn and run.

"Yolanda Alvarez was shot to death in your house. The gun used to kill her was registered in your name," Kade said.

He was growing impatient.

"As we speak, the Buford County Sheriff is at your house gathering evidence, along with an FBI evidence response team. We're here to ask you a few questions about Yolanda Alvarez, as well as Evelyn Wright."

Suddenly, McEwan's face seemed to collapse, and his shoulders sagged.

"This is all...unbelievable," he said.

Swaying on his feet, he reached back and propped a hand on the hood of his Escalade.

"This can't really be happening. First Evelyn and then Yolanda. It's got to be Sombra. He's got to be behind this."

"That's strange," Kade said. "Mr. Sombra is saying that you killed his wife. He said you wanted to ruin his life."

McEwan shook his head in denial.

"I drove down to a business meeting in Biloxi," he said. "Plenty of people saw me and can vouch for me."

He looked around at the faces behind Kade as if imploring them to believe him.

"What about Peyton?" Frankie asked. "She went to your house this morning. She wanted to ask you about Evelyn

Wright. Did you see her? Have you spoken to her?"

"I thought that was her yesterday," McEwan murmured. "I wasn't sure if I was imagining it. It's been so long since I've seen her. But no, I didn't speak to her, although she very well could have called me.

"I was in meetings all day and on a conference call on the way back. I didn't get a chance to listen to the news or check my messages. And I sure didn't have time to kill anyone."

McEwan's clothes were drenched and clung to his stocky figure in a way that made it clear he wasn't carrying a weapon. Satisfied that he presented no immediate danger, Kade slipped his Glock back into his holster

"You should know that Sheriff Crockett is also looking for you," he told the real estate developer as he stepped back to make room for him under the overhang.

"I also know who pays Crockett's mortgage," McEwan said. "And I'm not saying anything to that man without my lawyer in the room. I know that once I check into the Buford County Jail, it's unlikely I'll ever check out."

Holding up her badge, Kinsey stepped forward.

"Mr. McEwan, I think you have some questions to answer in Barrel Creek first," she said. "As soon as Agent Kade is finished with you, we need to question you about Evelyn Wright's murder."

"Let's go inside the building and get out of the rain," McEwan said wearily, trying to shake the water from his hair. "Once we're inside, you all can ask me your questions."

"What I want to know is what Yolanda Alvarez was doing at your house, to begin with," Kade said. "And why did she have access to your security system? Wasn't she the wife of your competitor?"

"I was seeing Yolanda," McEwan admitted. "We'd been together for a while, and she was planning to leave her husband. She knew he hadn't loved her for years. Not since Valentina."

McEwan held up a hand as if to stop the next question.

"And no, I didn't kill Valentina," he said. "She was a lovely girl who'd lived a hard life. I would never have hurt her. What Sombra did to ruin my father didn't happen until after Valentina was gone. Her disappearance changed him. It made him hard and mistrustful. He was merciless after that."

As McEwan continued to talk, Kade took out his notepad.

"My father was a good man, but he had a gambling problem. He'd run up some debts at the casino and when he needed time to come up with the money he owed, Sombra refused to give it to him."

A bitter tone had entered McEwan's voice.

"My father had to sell the business he'd worked his whole life to build. The night he signed the paperwork, he got drunk and drove off the Harahan Bridge."

"I swore then that someday I would be in a position where I could take from Sombra everything he'd taken from my father. I vowed that my casino would be twice as big and that his wife would be on my arm the night it opened."

He glanced over at Kade.

"I guess it's too late for that now," he said. "Everyone will think I'm responsible for Yolanda's death. No one will want to come to my casino now."

"I imagine there will be at least one person who will be there if your casino ever opens," Kade said. "Enrico Sombra will come looking for you, I'm sure. And this time, he'll be the one seeking retribution."

Turning away, Kade saw Frankie walking toward the door and followed after him.

"I'll leave you guys to your questioning," Frankie said. "I've got to go check on Josie. And I want to see if Peyton's come home, yet. I believe McEwan when he says he doesn't know where she is. I don't think he killed Yolanda either."

Frankie opened the door, looking out into the rain-darkened sky with a grim expression.

"Whoever killed Yolanda is still out there," he said. "And so is Peyton."

CHAPTER THIRTY-FOUR

Sherlock rode in the backseat of the old blue car, which smelled like shoe leather and old newspapers. It wasn't a bad smell although he would have preferred to have the windows open so he could enjoy the feel of the rain and the wind blowing outside. Josie sat in the front seat beside Dusty Fontaine, pointing out which turns to take as they made their way through unfamiliar streets.

The soothing automated voice of the GPS system sounded from the car speaker beside Sherlock.

"Turn right onto Charrington Road."

Sherlock stared out the window at the big houses along the street, which was lined with old shade trees that swayed in the rain as the car passed under them.

"I don't see Peyton's car," Josie said as the Thunderbird stopped along the curb. "But this is where the red dot is."

She held up her phone so Dusty could see.

"Yes, I see the dot," the reporter said, sounding irritable. "But I don't see a car. You said she was driving a white Dodge Charger, right?"

"Maybe she took the watch out of the car," Josie said. "Maybe she found it and is wearing it in there. She could be with him, now."

Dusty shook his head in confusion.

"With whom?" he demanded. "Just who exactly are you trying to find?"

Instead of answering, Josie opened the door. Rain spattered in on the old leather seats, eliciting a yelp from Dusty as she climbed out of the car.

Instinctively, Sherlock scurried after her before she could slam the door shut, following her up the empty driveway of a house set back from the road, half-hidden behind two massive oak trees.

Heading straight toward the porch, Josie lifted a small fist and knocked defiantly on the heavy wooden door.

Sherlock heard furtive footsteps inside and then a man was cracking open the door, his face only partially revealed as he peered out at them.

A soft scent of blood drifted out, raising Sherlock's hackles, and the dog let out an unhappy bark.

"Yes? What do you want?"

The man's tone was wary, almost hostile.

He lowered unfriendly eyes in the Labrador's direction as Josie cleared her throat.

"I'm looking for my...stepmother," she said stiffly. "Peyton Bell? Can I speak to her?"

The man's eyes widened in surprise, and he quickly looked past Josie toward the road, scanning the street.

"No one by that name lives here," he said.

But that wasn't true. Sherlock could smell Peyton. Her scent was on the man, if only faintly.

He sniffed at the ground, deciding the smell of blood must be coming from the man's shoes, then looked up to see one of the man's hands snaking out from behind the door, reaching for Josie.

The hand jerked back and the door clicked shut as a voice sounded behind them.

"Josie, you okay?"

Dusty Fontaine was standing on the walkway under a large powder blue umbrella with a *Memphis Gazette* logo.

"Yes, but that man says Peyton's not here."

"Then she's obviously not there," Dusty said. "And we need to go. My boots were not made for this weather."

Reluctantly, Josie followed him back to the Thunderbird.

"But my watch is in there," she complained. "Unless that stupid red dot is broken. Oh well, come on, Sherlock."

The dog watched with worried eyes as Dusty and Josie climbed back into the car. He didn't want to get inside.

Not when Peyton's scent was in the house that smelled like blood. There had been another scent, too.

Suddenly, Sherlock turned and ran back up the driveway, but instead of heading for the front door, he circled the porch and headed around the side of the house.

Within seconds Josie was running up behind him as he sniffed at the door leading into the garage.

She peered through the glass inset and gasped.

"Peyton's car is in there," she hissed down at Sherlock.

Suddenly, the front door banged open, and heavy footsteps sounded on the front porch.

Sherlock tensed, sensing the danger.

He jumped as a hand settled on his collar.

Looking back, he saw Dusty, umbrella gone, standing in the rain with a fearful expression.

The reporter lifted a finger to his lips as Josie looked back at him and pointed to the little window.

"That's Peyton's car," she whispered. "I told you she must be in there. Why did that man lie to me?"

Dusty crept up beside her, his eyes wide and scared as he caught sight of the white Charger in the garage.

"Who's there?"

The man's voice rang out, causing all three of them to jump. Footsteps sounded over wood, and then Dusty was pulling Josie and Sherlock toward the back of the house.

They looked around for somewhere to hide, and Dusty led them toward a big van with a bright red logo that was parked at an angle in the lawn.

As they huddled behind the van, Sherlock sniffed at the back bumper. The scent of dried blood mixed with rubber.

"Who's out there?"

The man had come into the backyard wearing a raincoat.

Sherlock could see his feet on the other side of the van, and as the man turned and made his way back toward the front of the house, he could see that he held a phone in one hand and a gun in the other.

The man had almost reached the corner of the house when he lifted the phone and spoke into the receiver.

"Yeah, this is Albert Sharkey," he said. "I want to book a flight tonight. I need to..."

His words were cut off as he stepped back onto the porch.

Seconds later, the front door slammed shut.

"That's Sharkey!" Josie whispered in a frantic voice as she dug the phone from her pocket. "He's the guy who killed Valentina Rojas. And he has a gun! We've got to let Frankie know that Peyton's in there."

She jabbed at the phone, but the display didn't flash on.

"My battery's dead," she hissed at Dusty.

The reporter reached into his pocket and then groaned.

"My phone's in the car," he said. "We'll call when we get there, come on, let's get out of here."

"But he could be watching," Josie reminded him, pulling Sherlock against her. "He might see us go by. Don't forget he has a gun."

Dusty hesitated, then sighed.

"Okay, you can stay here with Sherlock for now," he said. "I'll go back to the car and call for help. Don't worry, I'll stick to the shadows under those trees."

Before Josie could protest, he was gone.

–

CHAPTER THIRTY-FIVE

Frankie turned onto Monarch Avenue with a sinking sensation in his stomach. Peyton's white Charger wasn't in the driveway as he had allowed himself to hope. The rain was still pouring down as he parked the Mustang and hurried inside, wanting to see Josie and Sherlock, planning to ask Arlene to watch them while he continued the search for his wife.

But Josie wasn't in her room, and Sherlock wasn't lying in his usual spot in the kitchen. Even his mother's favorite spot on the sofa in front of the television was vacant.

Granny Davis sat in an armchair with an embroidery hoop in her lap and a tall glass of iced tea in easy reach.

"Where's Josie?" Frankie asked.

His grandmother looked up with a confused smile.

"No one here but me," she said, looking around the room as if to reassure herself of the fact. "I took a little nap and when I woke up, everyone was gone."

She turned her eyes back to her embroidery.

"Franny said she was going to the library earlier," she added. "That girl does love to read."

Frankie stopped and looked down at his grandmother's

bent head. He had stopped trying to tell her that Franny was gone and that the girl in the house was Josie.

"If you're going out, don't forget your raincoat," she added softly. "You'll catch your death of cold."

He stooped to kiss her softly wrinkled cheek, then headed toward the door, grabbing his old rain jacket off the coat rack as he checked his watch.

Is the library even still open? It's almost dark.

The dim interior of the Chesterville Public Library was an answer to his question as he drove past in his Mustang a few minutes later. It had closed over an hour before.

Could Josie have gone home to Barrel Creek?

Taking out his phone, he tapped on her number but the call went straight to voicemail, which usually meant her battery had gone dead.

As he headed north, it seemed to Frankie as if everyone around him was vanishing and that soon he would be left on his own in a lonely, empty world.

The idea was unsettling, and he jumped as his phone began to buzz on the dashboard and Dusty Fontaine's number appeared on the display.

"Sorry, Dusty, but I'm looking for Peyton and now Josie's gone, too, and–"

"I'm with Josie," the reporter said, sounding flustered. "She and Sherlock are with me. Well, they're not exactly with me right now, but...I think we've found Peyton. At least, we've found her car."

Frankie's heart jumped.

"But we've also found Albert Sharkey," Dusty added. "He

seems like a very angry man. You should have told me he was the one who...anyway, he has a gun."

The words sent a tremor of fear up Frankie's spine.

"Where's Josie? Is she okay?"

"Yes. Well, I think so. I've just sent you my location. Get here fast. Sharkey's making plans to leave tonight."

* * *

Frankie made a sharp turn onto Charrington Road, sending the Mustang skidding toward a line of thick oak trees that stood guard over the slick street.

Managing to straighten the wheels with only inches to spare, he brought the car to a stop behind Dusty's baby-blue car, dropped his Glock into the pocket of the jacket, and jumped out into the rain, which was still pelting down with relentless fury.

He ran to the Thunderbird's window, pushing back soggy strands of hair to look inside, and saw that it was empty.

His eyes flicked up to the house, studying the front porch where lights had blinked on to combat the falling darkness.

Was Josie inside? And Peyton?

And what about Albert Sharkey? Was he in there waiting for him with a gun?

Sucking in a deep breath, Frankie ran toward the house, keeping to the shadows and the cover of the big tree branches which sagged over him, heavy with rain.

He crept around the side, skirting the garage until he came to a door with a little window inset. Peering in, he saw the Charger, lit up by a small light on a workbench.

The car trunk was open, and it appeared as if someone had been interrupted in the process of loading or unloading several suitcases, which had been left unattended on the concrete floor.

Pulling the thick, nylon sleeve of his raincoat over his fist, he smashed the glass inset with one hard rap, then carefully reached past the remaining shards of glass to turn the bolt.

The door creaked as he eased it open and stepped inside, leaving a trail of water on the floor as he crossed to the door leading into the house.

He held his ear to the wood and listened for a long beat, then slowly pushed the door open and stuck his head inside.

The house was silent and appeared to be empty, other than a glow of light under the door at the end of the hall, which he assumed must be the kitchen.

Taking his Glock from his pocket, Frankie stepped into the hall and walked quietly forward, reminding himself that if he wasn't careful, he could end up shooting Peyton or Josie.

His hand had just settled onto the doorknob when he felt the muzzle of a gun come to rest against the base of his skull.

"Drop the gun or I'll put a hole in your head."

A grisly image of Yolanda Alvarez lying on the floor with a hole in her chest flashed through his mind. It was safe to bet that the man behind him wasn't bluffing.

Frankie dropped his gun.

"I knew it would be *you* who would ruin everything," the man said with a bitter laugh. "Your father almost had me, but he was on the booze. Now you almost had me. But in the end, I'm still one step ahead."

His voice sounded familiar, although Frankie couldn't quite place it. He had to keep him talking and stall for time.

"Is that you, Sharkey?" he asked, not daring to turn his head. "I can understand you coming after me, but why Peyton? She never did anything to you."

He held his breath, expecting to hear a final blast of the gun behind him at any moment.

But Sharkey only shoved him forward through the kitchen door, prodding him across the room, and then pushing him out into the backyard.

"I think it's time for a little family reunion," he said, as the rain once again began to beat down on Frankie's head. "Come on, hurry up. Your partner's downstairs. You don't want to keep her waiting."

As Frankie moved toward the cellar doors, he glanced over, catching sight of a bulky van parked on the lawn. He frowned as he recognized the familiar logo on the side.

"Open the cellar door," Sharkey commanded, keeping the gun pressed tightly to the back of Frankie's head.

Reaching forward, Frankie grabbed the metal handle on one of the double doors and wrenched it open.

He looked down into the dimly lit space and took a tentative step forward. A rough shove to his back sent him tumbling down the short flight of stairs.

As he landed at the bottom, all the breath left his lungs,

and his head hit the floor with a reverberating *thunk*.

Frankie lay still for a long moment, his head spinning, then slowly opened his eyes to see Peyton lying motionless against the far wall. Her wrists and ankles had been bound with heavy rope and her eyes were closed.

Struggling to catch his breath, he watched his captor walk down the stairs, his face starkly lit by the overhead bulb.

Frankie managed to gasp out one breathless word.

"Nielson?"

CHAPTER THIRTY-SIX

Anders Nielson stared down at Frankie with cold gray eyes, keeping the little Ruger pointed at the P.I.'s dripping head, tempted to just go ahead and shoot him. It was about time to get the wretched week over with. He could activate his escape plan and leave the area.

Hell, I may even leave the country.

But something held him back. It wasn't like him to fold on a hand that could still win him the whole jackpot.

And there was still a sliver of a chance that he could get away with what he'd done. He might escape prosecution and prison, and if he got really lucky, he may even be able to keep his fortune and save his reputation.

But to make any of that possible, he had to play it smart.

He couldn't afford to have blood or other trace evidence found in his own home. There could be nothing that would conclusively link him to any of the murders, or to Frankie and Peyton's impending disappearance.

Thus far, the task force only knew they were looking for a man named Albert Sharkey. A high roller with connections in all the casinos along the Mississippi.

And few people in Sharkey's orbit knew that in the real

world, he operated as Anders Nielson, the mild-mannered editor-in-chief of the *Memphis Gazette*.

His secret life, carefully constructed on fabrications and lies, might never have to be exposed.

Not if I play my cards right.

His musing was interrupted by movement at his feet.

"What did...you do...to Peyton?" Frankie managed to say.

The P.I. was starting to get his wind back. He would need to be sedated and restrained until Sharkey could figure out how to dispose of him without too much mess.

"Don't worry, she's only sleeping. I had to give her something to make her quiet down," Nielson said, pointing to an empty water bottle on the floor. "She was very angry and very thirsty."

He kicked the bottle away in frustration.

"It would have been easier to keep her quiet if I'd had another barrel. That would have allowed me to silence her without so much fuss. Like I did with Maisie and...the others," he said with a wistful sigh. "And I couldn't very well risk a repeat of what happened with Evelyn Wright, could I?"

The thought of all the blood he had to clean up prompted a grimace of disgust.

"I'd hoped to make Evelyn just disappear without a trace, as I'd done with Maisie. I didn't anticipate she would fight back. I didn't count on all that blood."

"And of course, I couldn't kill Peyton as I did Yolanda. At least, not in my own home. The blood spatter would have been impossible to completely erase."

He gestured to the barrels.

"But the barrels are almost all gone. And they're getting old, as well,' he said. "You know, I got these from Atkins Barrel Works around the time I killed Valentina."

He pointed to one of the barrels.

"That one was full, but most of the whiskey's gone now."

Cocking his head, he pointed to another.

"That one had bags of white powder in it, which I emptied into the lake," he said, adopting a self-righteous tone. "I don't approve of drugs, you know. It ruins lives."

"Why kill Valentina?" Frankie croaked. "And my father?"

Nielson smiled at the memory.

"Yes, Valentina was special. I took a certain satisfaction in that one that I didn't feel with the others. After all, she'd rejected my advances and then turned to your father, who in my estimation, was a much lesser man."

"I have to admit there was no real need to kill her. Oh, I had some worries she might share my secrets with the feds, but a little intimidation would probably have shut her up."

"It wasn't until I saw her with your father that I decided she had to die. I knew Henry Dawson wouldn't be so easily stopped. Not if he set his mind to something. You see, drink had dulled his senses and his logic. And Maisie had already talked him into becoming an informant with the FBI."

He shook his head in regret.

"I guess pushing her aunt off the top of the parking garage wasn't my best idea," he acknowledged. "But she was on to me. She'd recognized me as Maisie's news editor at the *Gazette*. And she'd seen me gambling at the high-stakes table with Enrico using my gambling name, Albert Sharkey. She suspected I was involved with some of his activities. I couldn't let her make that call..."

He could still picture the night he'd faced Lottie Doyle in the parking garage. The woman had been triumphant as she'd shrieked at him.

"You're Maisie's boss. I've seen you at the office. You're the man she's always talking about. The prick who will never put her stories on the front page."

"I couldn't very well let her tell Maisie that I was Albert Sharkey. After all, I'd been acting as a stringer to write articles for the *Gazette*, and as the news editor, I'd been buying and paying myself for those articles.

"You can imagine it presented a conflict of interest that the owners of the paper would certainly have frowned upon. So, I had to shut Lottie up. That's the only reason why I pushed her. It was all very quick and painless."

"And my father?" Frankie asked as he pushed himself up on one elbow.

"Oh, his death wasn't painless," Nielson assured him. "You see, after I followed your father and Valentina back to her house, I waited for your father to leave, and I killed Valentina. Then I went after your father and killed him, too."

"I dumped Valentina's body into an empty barrel and I took it to a field a few miles away. I didn't realize how much time and energy it would take to bury that barrel."

"Well, by the time I was done with that, I was exhausted.

I decided to try something a little less labor-intensive to conceal what I'd done to Henry."

He pointed to the concrete floor.

"I dragged his body down here, to the cellar. He was lying just about where you are now, although there were more whiskey bottles in here at the time."

"Some were full and some empty, and luckily your father was as skinny as you, so I was able to fit him in a barrel that was still half full of whiskey."

A nasty laugh escaped his throat.

"I figured the alcohol would mask the smell, and for the most part, it did. But then, I wasn't sure where to dump Henry's bloodstained truck.

"I cleaned it out the best I could and then left it at the airport. I took a taxi home. I figured eventually, the car would be towed, or a ticket would be sent to him. But he wouldn't be there to receive it, would he?

"The thing was, in all my plans, I'd almost forgotten about Maisie. Then later that week, she stopped by my house to apologize for yelling at me and storming out of the *Gazette* the week before when I'd told her she couldn't work on the Sombra story.

"She told me that Henry had bailed on her. She said there was a rumor going around that he'd run off with Sombra's young girlfriend."

"But then while she was there, someone called. Back then I had an answering machine. When it picked up, the caller was a poker buddy. He used my gambling name. He called me Sharkey and asked if I wanted to join a game that night."

Nielson's tone was now amused and light-hearted as if all the stories of murder were making him nostalgic.

"Well, Maisie was a smart woman and something clicked in her mind. She suddenly realized that I was Sharkey. I could see the questions turning and knew she wasn't the type to let a question go until she had the whole story."

He shook his head as if in regret.

"I knew I had to act fast, so I strangled her. And then I shoved her body in a barrel, too. When people started asking questions, I typed up Maisie's resignation letter and sent it to myself at the *Gazette*. It was all very official."

Nielson grew silent, remembering how things had returned to business as usual. He'd continued gambling at the casino and he'd managed to hush up any rumors.

He'd even managed to derail the FBI's investigation into Sombra, making sure his revenue stream wouldn't be interrupted. Henry's FBI handler, Trent Boone, had been furious. The whole mess had ruined his career.

Cordero Torres had been suspicious of him but hadn't been able to prove anything.

"Everything was fine for years after that," Nielson said. "Even decades. And then Dusty Fontaine and Evelyn Wright started asking questions again and hired you."

"And now you've almost ruined everything. But I'm not ready to fold and go home yet."

Aiming the gun at Frankie, he grimaced.

"I'm going to kill you, Dawson, just like I killed your father," he gritted out. "And once I'm done with you, I'm going to kill your wife."

CHAPTER THIRTY-SEVEN

Nell Kinsey felt the wheels of the Interceptor start to slide on the rain-slick highway as they headed west. Lightning cracked overhead as she fought to control the wheel, feeling Ranger's nervous eyes on her as he sat beside her in the passenger seat.

"I can drive if you want," he offered.

Rolling her eyes, she stared ahead. Looking for the exit.

"Are you sure Albert Sharkey lived on Charrington Road?" she asked. "I thought you said you couldn't remember."

Ranger held out an old Polaroid photo.

"That's my father," he said. "We stopped to pick up Albert Sharkey for one of our camping trips and I'd just gotten a camera for my birthday. For a while there I thought I wanted to be a wildlife photographer."

Kinsey glanced at the photo.

Like his son, Ike Ranger had been a handsome man, although the arrogant smirk on his face sent a shiver of distaste down Kinsey's spine.

Ranger tapped on the photo.

"See the street sign behind him?"

Keeping one eye on the slippery highway, Kinsey risked another look at the photo.

"Yes, I see that. It says Charrington Road," she agreed. "But what makes you think he still lives there?"

"I checked the online property records before we left the station," Ranger assured her. "The place has been owned by the same man since the late nineties."

Kinsey nodded, impressed with his initiative.

"You saw Albert Sharkey's name listed on the deed?"

Shaking his head, Ranger frowned.

"Actually, no. That confused me at first," he said. "The place is owned by a man named Anders Nielson. According to his online profile, he's the editor-in-chief for the *Memphis Gazette*."

He tapped on his phone.

"But when I looked at Nielson's photo, I recognized him."

Again, he held the phone up.

"He's older, of course. And his hair was different, but I'm positive Anders Nielson is the same guy who used to go camping with us. He's the guy my dad played poker with and called Sharkey because he always won."

As they pulled onto Charrington Road, Ranger checked the GPS again, then pointed to a big house set back from the road.

"Should be that one right there," he said.

Kinsey pulled the SUV up to the curb behind a baby blue Thunderbird.

"You think he has visitors?" she asked.

"I'll call in the plates," Ranger said.

He was already reaching for his phone when a man's face appeared next to Kinsey's window.

She jumped back in surprise, then released a relieved breath when she recognized Dusty Fontaine's thin face.

The reporter was drenched. Wet strings of hair had been plastered to his forehead by the downpour.

Kinsey pulled up the hood of her rain jacket as she rolled down her window.

"Thank God you're here!" he blurted out before she could ask what he was doing standing out in the storm. "Albert Sharkey is in that house. And he's got a gun."

Kinsey climbed out of the Interceptor with Ranger close behind her. As her partner circled the vehicle, she saw movement in the shadows by the house.

Stepping in front of Dusty, she lifted her weapon.

"Barrel Creek PD!" she called out. "Come out with your hands up."

Josie Atkins stepped out onto the lawn, followed by a black dog. Kinsey recognized Frankie Dawson's Labrador retriever.

Both the girl and the dog were shivering.

"No, no, no!" Dusty shouted. "They're with me. We came looking for Peyton and saw her car in the garage. We figured he must be holding her hostage, so we called Frankie."

"Where's Frankie now?" Ranger asked.

Lifting a weary arm, Dusty pointed to the front door.

"He went inside a while back and hasn't come out."

"Okay, we'll take it from here," Kinsey said, waving over Josie and Sherlock. "You guys can wait in the Interceptor with the doors locked until we come get you."

Josie shook her head in protest.

"But Frankie and Peyton are in there and-"

"And we won't be able to help them until we know you're safe," Ranger said, opening the back door. "Now, get in quickly so we can go see what's going on."

"Okay, but please hurry!" Josie urged. "I think he's the man who killed the others."

As Ranger called on the radio for backup, Dusty climbed into the backseat, scooting over to make room for Josie and Sherlock. But the Labrador didn't want to get in and the girl had to tug hard on his collar to get the dog to comply.

"It's like he thinks he's being arrested," Dusty joked as Kinsey closed the door and made sure it was locked, before heading toward the house behind Ranger.

Looking back at the Interceptor, she saw all three faces staring after them with worried eyes.

"Maybe we should wait for backup," Ranger said as they approached the dark house. "If this guy's as dangerous as-"

"We don't have time for that," Kinsey said, stepping onto the front porch. "It might already be too late."

She lifted her hand and knocked as Ranger covered her with his Glock. Butt there was only silence inside, so they hurried around to the side, stopping to look into the garage.

A white Charger sat with its trunk open, but the room appeared to be empty.

"You think he took them out the back?" Kinsey asked as she followed Ranger into the backyard.

Ranger motioned for her to be quiet as he pointed to a series of boot prints on the ground.

Standing beside the cellar doors, he held up a hand.

"On the count of three...one, two, three!"

CHAPTER THIRTY-EIGHT

Frankie stared up at Anders Nielson between slitted lids, trying not to let the murderous man see that he had gotten the wind back in his lungs and that his head had stopped spinning with quite so much force. If he could catch the man off guard, he might still have a chance to get Peyton out of the cellar alive.

"Let's handle this like men," Frankie said, keeping his voice weak and slightly winded. "Let's make a bet."

"I don't need to make a bet," Nielson scoffed. "I've already won the game. That's why I'm holding this gun and you're lying there broken at my feet."

Frankie nodded as if he understood.

"I get it. You're not really a high-risk player after all. That was just you pretending to be Albert Sharkey. In reality, you're still just scared little Mr. Nielson."

"Don't make me use this," Nielson muttered, glaring down at Frankie with contempt. "It'd make a big mess. And I don't have another empty barrel. I used the last one for Darcy Doyle. She's in that one."

As he gestured to the fallen barrel, Frankie's size thirteen boot shot out, connecting sharply with Nielson's hand, sending the gun spinning end over end.

Nielson yelled out as the Ruger sank behind a barrel, then turned, his face twisted with rage to find Frankie on his feet.

Stepping back, Nielson pulled a switchblade from his belt.

"To hell with the mess," he yelled. "Once I'm done slitting your throat, I'll gut your wife from-"

Frankie lunged at the man's knees, hoping to take him to the ground, but Nielson was too fast.

He slashed at Frankie, slicing a long gash in the back of his rain jacket before dodging out of reach.

As Frankie prepared to make another lunge, Peyton moaned. Looking over, he saw her eyes blink open.

With a smile of triumph, Nielson backed toward her, waving the switchblade from side to side.

"Make another stupid move like that and-"

A gust of wind and rain drowned out the rest of his words, sucking Nielson's voice up and spinning it away as the cellar doors burst open and a bullet whizzed past Frankie's head.

With a terrible scream of pain, Nielson jerked back, then staggered to the side, slamming hard into the fallen barrel, before collapsing to the floor.

Frankie looked up to see Kinsey and Ranger descending the stairs with their guns drawn.

They crossed to Nielson, who lay on the ground, a stream of blood seeping from beneath him, worming its way toward the barrel, which had cracked open from the impact.

"Do you see the knife?" Kinsey asked, looking frantically for the weapon Nielson had been wielding.

"It's there," Ranger said, pointing to the handle, which was protruding from Nielson's ribcage. "He fell on it."

Checking Nielson's pulse, Kinsey shook her head.

"He's dead."

Rushing over to Peyton, Frankie gathered her into his arms, relieved to see her eyes were open and alert.

"Call an ambulance," he yelled back at Ranger.

"There's one on the way," the detective assured him. "Should be here any minute."

Frankie nodded in relief and brushed Peyton's dark hair back from her forehead, then turned as he heard a soft moan.

It was coming from the cracked barrel.

Circling to the head, Frankie pushed aside the broken lid and stared in at a young woman.

The woman stared back at him with tortured eyes.

"It's Darcy Doyle," he said, unable to believe his eyes. "It's really Darcy Doyle, and she's alive!"

Kinsey gaped down at him in shock as sirens sounded somewhere nearby.

"Get the paramedics down here fast!" she yelled at Ranger. "And we need tools to open up this barrel."

Moments later two paramedics were jogging down the cellar stairs. They made quick work of the old oak barrel, wrenching off the metal hoops and prying open the staves to reveal Darcy curled up in a fetal position.

"She's been without food or water for up to three days,"

Frankie said as the paramedics loaded her onto a stretcher and hefted her up and out of the cellar. After assuring Frankie they'd send a second ambulance for Peyton, they were gone.

Crossing to the row of remaining barrels, Frankie dropped to his knees in front of one and leaned his forehead against the rough wood.

"My father's in one of these," he said, turning to meet Peyton's eyes. "All this time I thought he'd given up on me. But I'm the one who gave up on *him*."

"That's not true," Peyton said, shaking her head as he moved back to her and pulled her into his arms. "You found him, didn't you? Just like you found me. You didn't give up on us, Frankie. And I'm never going to give up on you."

Blinking back tears, Frankie took the infinity bracelet out of his pocket and slid it back where it belonged.

He looked up to see that the promised paramedics had arrived. As they made their way down the stairs, Frankie watched them load Peyton onto a stretcher and lift her up and out of the cellar, before transferring her onto a gurney.

He walked beside Peyton as they wheeled her toward the ambulance, passing the big van with the red *Memphis Gazette* logo on the side. His heart squeezed when he saw Josie and Sherlock waiting for him beside Dusty's car.

"Are you okay?" Josie asked, running up to give him a hug, her blue eyes swimming with tears. "I'm sorry I left without telling you. Is Peyton going to be okay?"

"She'll be fine," he said. "They're taking her to the hospital for some tests. She may have to stay overnight."

"You go with Peyton to the hospital," Josie said. "Dusty can give me a ride home."

"No, we're a family now," Frankie insisted, taking her hand. "And from here on out, we're sticking together."

CHAPTER THIRTY-NINE

Peyton and Frankie held hands as they followed Josie into Beth Hurley's office. The last few weekly sessions had gone well, and the teenager seemed less moody lately, even going so far as to suggest they all go out to dinner and to see a movie that evening after Peyton and Frankie got home from the office.

Before Peyton could settle into a chair in the waiting room, Dr. Hurley appeared in the doorway.

"Josie has made a request. She wants you both to join her session today," the therapist said. "And I think it's a good idea. I believe therapy could be cathartic for your family."

Frankie hesitated but Peyton was nodding.

"Just hearing you call us a family makes me feel better already," she said.

Turning to Frankie, she took his hand.

"It'll be a little like AA was at first," she told him. "We just go into a room and talk about how damaged we are."

"And I already know you're both damaged," Josie said with a mischievous smile. "So, what do you have to lose?"

Frankie looked back and forth between Peyton and Josie, then lifted his shoulder in a resigned shrug.

"Looks like I'm outnumbered," he said, then turned to Dr. Hurley. "Okay, let's do this."

* * *

After the therapy session was over, Peyton and Frankie dropped Josie off for her last day of summer school.

Peyton was pleased to see the teen greeted by a group of other girls and disappear inside the school amongst a chorus of happy giggles.

"I think she's going to be okay," Frankie said as they pulled onto the highway. "I think we all might be okay."

The smile on his face dimmed a little when they pulled into the tiny parking lot beside the office on Winchester Way and saw Kade Mabry's SUV taking up one of the spaces.

"You aren't still jealous of him are you?" Peyton asked as they climbed out of the car. "I've explained all that and-"

"I was never jealous," Frankie protested indignantly. "I was just concerned. More like sad, really."

Peyton laughed and raised an eyebrow as they walked toward the door.

"Okay, if that's what you say."

She lowered her voice as he moved past her into the room.

"But I say you were jealous."

Turning to greet Kade, who had made himself comfortable in a chair, Peyton offered him a cup of coffee.

"No, I can't stay," he said, running a hand through his dark wave of hair. "I just wanted to let you both know that

Anders Nielson has just been indicted posthumously on five charges of first-degree murder, four counts of attempted murder, and three counts of kidnapping, among other charges.

"The indictment closes the case, so the task force will be disbanded, although a federal investigation into the Buford County Sheriff's department has been opened."

Peyton was relieved to hear that someone might be held accountable for enabling Sharkey's murder spree.

As Kade stood to leave, Frankie offered him a hand.

"I want to thank you for helping me find Peyton," he said. "I don't know if I could have held it together on my own."

"It's all part of the job," Kade said. "Just make sure you take care of her. You've got a good one there."

After he left, Frankie glanced over at Peyton.

"He's got it bad for you, doesn't he?"

Peyton shrugged.

"Oh, I don't know about that," she said, taking his hand in hers. "But I've definitely got it bad for *you*."

The door opened and Peyton looked up, thinking Kade must have forgotten something. She was startled to see Cordero Torres standing at the door.

"It's like Grand Central Station around here today," Frankie murmured as the big man stepped forward to drop a thick, padded envelope on Frankie's desk.

"A delivery from Mr. Sombra."

"What is it?" Frankie asked, grinning up into Torres' stone-cold face. "An invitation to a duel?"

The casino owner's second-in-command didn't crack a smile at the attempted humor.

"I don't read Mr. Sombra's personal correspondence," he said. "I just deliver it."

With a final glare, he turned and left the building.

Frankie carefully opened the envelope and pulled out a note wrapped around a thick stack of hundred-dollar bills.

He read the note aloud to Peyton.

"Mr. Dawson, payment is enclosed for services rendered in finding the man responsible for killing the only woman I ever loved. Consider my debt to you as paid. Enrico Sombra."

Turning to Peyton, he held up the stack of cash.

"You think we should keep this?" he asked. "I mean, we certainly earned it. And I'd say that note serves as a receipt."

Peyton frowned as Frankie began to count the cash.

"Who do you think he means when he writes *the only woman I ever loved*? Yolanda or Valentina?"

"I don't know," Frankie said. "I never pictured Sombra as the type to fall in love. Maybe I underestimated him."

Looking down at her bracelet, Peyton nodded.

"I guess even the most damaged hearts can be broken," she said softly. "But I've found that they can also be healed."

CHAPTER FORTY

Frankie made his way through the neatly manicured lawn of the Old Dominion Cemetery, following the small procession of mourners who were heading down the winding stone path that led to the grave site. Twenty years too late, Henry Dawson was finally being laid to rest next to his daughter.

Looking back, Frankie saw his mother holding one of Granny Davis' arms, while Josie held the other. Uncle Rowdy and Cousin Colton trailed behind them, looking hot and uncomfortable in their Sunday best suits.

Peyton brought up the rear, leading Sherlock on a leash as they all passed row after row of white gravestones baking in the summer sun.

Coming to a stop at Franny's grave, Frankie silently read the epitaph on his sister's gravestone.

Our Sweet Girl
Francis Susan Dawson
Beloved Daughter and Sister

He then turned to the freshly dug plot next to it, which

was open and waiting to receive the pitifully small bundle that constituted his father's remains.

Staring down into the open grave, Frankie was determined to bury all the pain and grief of the last twenty years along with his father. Hopefully he, like Henry, would finally find some peace after all this time.

He motioned over to Josie, who came forward carrying two bouquets of yellow roses. She carefully placed one bouquet in the vase over Franny's grave, and the other at the head of Henry's new resting place.

After the pastor from Granny Davis' church had said a few words, Frankie went to stand with his mother under the shade of an ancient oak tree.

"It's good to know your father was already there to greet Franny when she arrived on the other side," Arlene said, wiping her eyes. "And it helps to know he didn't choose to leave us. Despite his drinking, he was a good man. He wanted to do right by you kids."

Digging in her bag for a tissue, she dabbed at her eyes.

"It hurt when I thought he'd left us just like that," she said. "But maybe if my pride hadn't gotten in the way..."

"Don't start blaming yourself for what Anders Nielson did," Frankie said. "That shark ruined enough of our lives already. I for one am done suffering for another man's sins."

As he led his mother back to Granny Davis, he saw Darcy Doyle standing a few yards away. She looked pale but stood steady on her feet.

"I know I've already thanked you for saving my life, but I wanted to come and show my respects to your family," she said. "Thanks to you, I got to bury my Aunt Maisie yesterday. It was a real nice service. She's resting next to my mother now in the Buford County Cemetery."

Once the rest of the mourners had gone, and Arlene had led Granny Davis back to the car, Frankie stood beside Peyton and Josie watching Sherlock chase the squirrels who lived in the oak tree.

As a warm breeze lifted Josie's hair, Peyton turned to her.

"If you hadn't come to find me at Nielson's house, you might have been laying me to rest, too," Peyton said. "I've been meaning to thank you, Josie. Without you, I wouldn't be here right now."

"Well, I'm really glad you are," Josie said. "I'm glad we're all here together. I think my parents would like that."

Frankie thought it sounded as if she meant it.

"You know, you're a pretty good investigator," he said, wrapping an arm around Josie's shoulders and blinking away the sting of tears behind his sunglasses as they began walking toward the car.

"Maybe someday you'll take over the family business. It'll be Dawson, Bell, and Atkins Private Investigations."

He held his breath, hoping he hadn't said the wrong thing again as Josie stopped and cocked her head.

"I think Atkins, Bell, and Dawson Investigations sounds better," she said with a sly smile. "After all, we really should list the names alphabetically, just for fairness' sake."

Peyton laughed along with Josie, and then Frankie joined in.

"Okay, you've got a deal," he said.

Picking up Sherlock's leash, he motioned toward the car, lifting his face toward the sun.

"Now come on, everybody. Let's go home."

The End

If you enjoyed *His Heart of Darkness*,
you won't want to miss Melinda Woodhall's
Lessons in Evil: A Bridget Bishop FBI Mystery Thriller.

In the first book of the series, criminal psychologist and FBI Profiler Bridget Bishop tackles a chilling string of homicides which bear a startling resemblance to a series of murders committed by a man since convicted and executed for the crimes.

Read on for an excerpt from Lessons in Evil!

LESSONS IN EVIL

A Bridget Bishop Thriller: Book One

CHAPTER ONE

The needle on the gas gauge hovered on empty as Libby Palmer steered her mother's old Buick down the Wisteria Falls exit ramp. The heavy traffic on the interstate had added an extra hour to her drive back from D.C., and Libby had just decided she was going to run out of gas when the Gas & Go sign came into view.

Eyeing the gas station with relief, Libby turned into the parking lot, brought the car to a jerking halt beside an available pump, and shut off the engine with a resigned sigh.

Her trip into D.C. certainly hadn't turned out the way she'd hoped when she'd left home that morning. Despite her new clothes and valiant efforts to impress the hiring manager at the Smithsonian, she was still woefully unemployed.

So much for showing Mom once and for all that majoring in art history wasn't a colossal mistake.

A fat drop of rain plunked onto the windshield and slid down the glass as Libby opened the door and stepped out into the dusky twilight, credit card in hand.

A hand-written note had been taped over the card reader. *Machine broken. Pay inside.*

Looking up at the darkening sky in irritation, Libby pulled the hood of her jacket over her dark curls and hurried toward the store. She hesitated as she saw the missing person flyer taped to the glass door.

It was the third time that day she'd seen one of the flyers with a picture of the pretty blonde girl who'd gone missing from her apartment near Dupont Circle the week before.

Brooke Nelson hadn't been seen since; foul play was suspected. The FBI had been asking anyone with information to call a dedicated tip line, and a slew of the flyers had been posted around Washington D.C. and the surrounding area.

"You going in or not?"

A man in a black jacket and faded jeans held the door open, waiting for Libby to pass through.

"Uh...yeah, sorry about that," she said, ducking her head as she stepped into the brightly lit building.

Wrinkling her nose against the pungent scent of stale coffee which hung in the air, Libby made her way to the counter and presented her credit card to the clerk.

"Twenty dollars on pump one," she said, hoping her card wasn't maxed out. "And can I get the key to the restroom?"

The clerk looked her up and down, taking in her disheveled curls and rain-spattered jacket as he handed her a receipt and a silver key on a red plastic keyring.

His eyes held a suspicious gleam.

"Restrooms are outside to the left." He held up her credit card. "You'll get this back when you return the key."

Libby nodded and stepped back, bumping into the solid figure of a man in line behind her.

"Sorry," she murmured, avoiding eye contact as she turned and headed outside.

Keeping her head down against the spitting rain, she hurried around the little building to the restroom, stuck the metal key in the lock, and found the tiny, tiled room surprisingly clean.

She stopped in front of the chipped mirror over the sink, wiping at the mascara smudged under her disappointed brown eyes.

"You didn't want to work at that stupid museum anyway, did you?" she asked her reflection. "I mean, who'd want to live in boring old Washington D.C. when they could live in exciting Wisteria Falls?"

Rain was falling in a steady downpour by the time Libby had returned the key to the clerk, retrieved her credit card, and pumped twenty dollars' worth of gas into the Buick's big tank.

Dropping back into the driver's seat, she started the engine and pulled back onto the highway, lowering the volume on the radio as she picked up speed, uninterested in the local weather and traffic report.

As she drove over Landsend Bridge, she glanced down toward the Shenandoah River but could see nothing of the dark water churning below the metal and concrete structure.

Always fearful the ancient truss bridge might suddenly give way beneath her, Libby drove cautiously, holding her breath until the Buick's wheels were back on solid ground before pressing her foot toward the floor, eager to get home.

She didn't see the girl standing on the side of the road until she rounded the sharp curve just past Beaufort Hollow.

Stomping on the brakes as the Buick's headlights lit up a pale face framed by sodden blonde hair, Libby brought the car to a sudden stop in the middle of the empty road.

Worried another car may round the curve behind her and plow into her rear bumper, she steered the Buick onto the shoulder and shut off the engine.

With a quick glance in the rearview mirror, she climbed out into the rain and ran toward the girl, who stood beside a black sedan. The car's trunk was wide open, and the emergency lights were blinking.

"Are you okay?" Libby called as she approached the car.

The girl's face was hidden in shadow, no longer illuminated by the Buick's headlights, but the jarring blink, blink, blink of the sedan's emergency lights revealed the outline of her bowed head and thin shoulders.

"Did your car break down?"

Libby's question was met with silence. She wondered if the girl had been in an accident. Perhaps a tire had blown.

Maybe she hit her head on the dashboard. Or maybe she...

The thought was interrupted by the girl's raspy whisper, but Libby couldn't make out what she was saying.

Stepping close enough to put her hand on the girl's thin

shoulder, she inhaled sharply.

"You're trembling," Libby said, impulsively pulling off her jacket and draping it over the girl's shoulders. "You must be hurt. Come with me to my car and..."

"Help...me."

As the girl lifted her head, the emergency blinkers lit up a heart-shaped face, which looked strangely familiar.

Libby stared into the girl's tormented blue eyes, her pulse quickening as she pictured the missing person flyer on the door at Gas & Go.

"You're that girl, aren't you? You're Brooke Nelson."

"I'm...sorry," the girl croaked and swayed on her feet as if she no longer had the strength to stand. "I'm so sorry."

The crack of a branch behind Libby sent her spinning around just as a dark figure loomed up in front of her.

A scream froze in her throat as she stared up, gaping in terror. The man's face was half-hidden by the hood of his jacket, but she recognized his cold stare.

Adrenaline shot through her as she saw the knife in his hand. Lunging toward the road in a desperate bid to get back to the safety of the old Buick, she slipped and fell to her knees.

An iron fist reached out and grabbed a handful of her hair.

Snapping her head back, the man pulled her to her feet and wrapped his free arm around her neck.

He tightened his hold until Libby could no longer breathe.

"Brooke and I were...waiting for you," he hissed, his breath coming in excited gasps. "The time...of reckoning is...here."

Waves of dizziness washed over Libby as she scratched and pried at the unyielding arm around her throat, and hot tears blurred the flashing lights around her.

"Stay still...or I'll break your neck."

His breath was hot in her ear as he dragged her toward the open trunk of the sedan, then forced her inside.

She opened her mouth to scream as she looked back and met Brook Nelson's anguished eyes but could only manage a raspy cry before the trunk slammed shut, throwing her into darkness.

* * *

Water trickled somewhere nearby as Libby struggled to open her eyes. Her throat burned, and it was hard to swallow as she blinked around the dimly lit room.

Where am I? What is this place?

Rough walls and a cracked wooden floor held a small metal-framed bed and a straight-backed chair. Rickety stairs led up to a small landing and a narrow door.

"You awake?"

She jumped at the man's voice.

"I thought maybe I'd squeezed too hard."

A dark figure stepped into view. The man who'd forced her into the trunk of his car stared down at her.

"It'd be a shame to go through all that trouble to snatch you only to kill you off so soon."

Studying her face, he reached out a hand to tuck a still soggy curl behind her ear.

Libby cringed in terror but found she couldn't pull away. Her hands were bound to the chair with bright blue duct tape, as were her ankles.

"Where am I?" she croaked, wincing at the pain in her throat. "Why are you doing this?"

He appeared not to have heard her questions as he moved toward the stairs. Propping a booted foot on the bottom step, he stopped and cocked his head as if listening.

"I know what to do," he finally said, giving a resolute nod. "I've read the handbook. I won't take any chances."

Libby looked around the room, confused.

Who's he talking to?

She suddenly remembered Brook Nelson's terrified eyes. The poor girl must have been abducted, too. Was she being held in the same place?

"Where's Brooke?" Libby wheezed out, ignoring the stabbing pain in her throat. "What have you done to her?"

Turning to face her, the man frowned.

"You're not gonna try anything stupid, are you?" he asked, shifting his weight on the creaking wooden floor. "My mentor warned me you'd cause trouble. He told me not to be fooled."

"Who warned you?" she asked, looking up the stairs toward the door. "Is someone else here?"

The man cocked his head.

"I guess you could say that. Now stop asking so many questions. I've got important work to do."

"Please," Libby called out as he turned away. "Tell me what you did to Brooke. Tell me where she is."

Looking over his shoulder, the man shrugged.

"She's served her purpose," he said softly. "As will you."

Continue Reading *Lessons in Evil* from The Bridget Bishop FBI Mystery Thriller Series

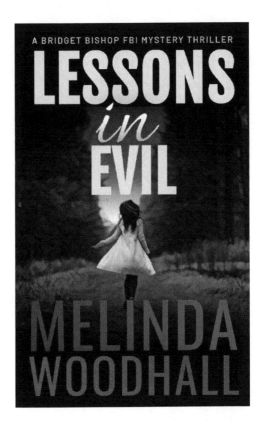

Want More Thrills?

Sign up for the Melinda Woodhall Thrillers Newsletter to receive upcoming bonus scenes and exclusive insider details at www.melindawoodhall.com/newsletter

ACKNOWLEDGEMENTS

IT WAS SO MUCH FUN TO RETURN TO FRANKIE DAWSON'S world for Book Two in his very own series. As always, during the writing of this book I relied on the constant support and love from my wonderful husband, Giles, and five fabulous children, Michael, Joey, Linda, Owen, and Juliet.

Thanks are also due to my extended family, including Melissa Romero, Leopoldo Romero, David Woodhall, and Tessa Woodhall, for their unfailing support and encouragement.

This book is dedicated to the memory of my mother, who taught me to read and to love books, as well as to my late sister, Melanie, who supported my writing career from the very start.

ABOUT THE AUTHOR

Melinda Woodhall is the author of heart-pounding, emotional thrillers with a twist, including the *Mercy Harbor Thriller Series*, the *Veronica Lee Thriller Series*, the *Detective Nessa Ainsley Novella Series*, and the new *Bridget Bishop FBI Mystery Thriller Series*.

When she's not writing, Melinda can be found reading, gardening, and playing in the back garden with her tortoise. Melinda is a native Floridian and the proud mother of five children. She lives with her family in Orlando.

Visit Melinda's website at www.melindawoodhall.com

Other Books by Melinda Woodhall

Her Last Summer	*Steal Her Breath*
Her Final Fall	*Take Her Life*
Her Winter of Darkness	*Make Her Pay*
Her Silent Spring	*Break Her Heart*
Her Day to Die	*Lessons in Evil*
Her Darkest Night	*Taken By Evil*
Her Fatal Hour	*Where Evil Hides*
Her Bitter End	*Road to Evil*
The River Girls	*When Evil Calls*
Girl Eight	*Save Her from Evil*
Catch the Girl	*Betrayed by Evil*
Girls Who Lie	*His Soul to Keep*

Made in the USA
Middletown, DE
10 August 2024

58893474R00189